RAWHIDE ROBINSON
RIDES A DROMEDARY

RAWHIDE ROBINSON RIDES A DROMEDARY

THE TRUE TALE OF A WILD WEST CAMEL CABALLERO

ROD MILLER

WHEELER PUBLISHING
A part of Gale, a Cengage Company

Farmington Hills, Mich • San Francisco • New York • Waterville, Maine
Meriden, Conn • Mason, Ohio • Chicago

LIBRARY OF CONGRESS CIP DATA ON FILE.
CATALOGUING IN PUBLICATION FOR THIS BOOK
IS AVAILABLE FROM THE LIBRARY OF CONGRESS

ISBN-13: 978-1-4328-6779-9 (softcover alk. paper)

Published in 2019 by arrangement with Rod Miller

Printed in Mexico
1 2 3 4 5 6 7 23 22 21 20 19

Rawhide Robinson Rides a Dromedary

CHAPTER ONE

Rawhide Robinson heard raindrops pattering the crown and brim of his thirteen-gallon hat. He found that odd, locked as he was in a fierce battle with a salty bronc set on tossing him from the saddle. But instead of hearing the accustomed clamor of the horse bawling and bellering, saddle leather screaming, stirrup leathers slapping, hoofs pounding, bones cracking, grunts and groans, there was only the soft plop of raindrops up top.

He felt the horse's front feet land to stop a drop that compressed his entire frame, which instantly stretched to its very seams as the bronc again took to the air, propelled by a violent thrust of its hind legs. As the leap reached its apex, the animal's spine bent at an untenable angle, launching Rawhide Robinson straight into the air. He felt his high-top Texas-star boots slide out of the stirrups and the bridle reins slip through his fingers as he lifted out of the now-empty saddle, rising and rising into the air as raindrops plinked his hat brim.

Soon, the noon sky darkened as he rose and rose, and stars became visible. But, before dark enveloped him, the cowboy's ascent slowed, stopped, and switched directions to become a descent. Still, the raindrops tapped their soft rhythm on his hat.

Rawhide Robinson — although an altogether ordinary cowboy — was brave and adventurous and no stranger to danger, so he felt no fear. Still, there was relief when his ankle-length India-rubber slicker ballooned, slowing his fall. The eternal night at the edge of outer space faded and the gray sky brightened as he descended, floating aimlessly with the raindrops through the atmosphere.

Broad swatches of color below gained focus and definition as he drifted ever lower. But it was not the faded dun colors of south Texas rising to meet him; rather, brilliant forests spread to the horizons — splashes of emerald, chartreuse, olive, jade, lime, laurel, moss, myrtle, mint, shamrock, sage, and countless other shades of green.

Tree branches and limbs and leaves parted with his passing and the cowboy settled gently onto the deep duff of a forest floor.

He might have noticed a change in the rhythm of raindrops hitting his hat brim, now interrupted as they were by the thick forest canopy. His attention, however, was riveted on the person — creature — thing — standing before him.

Colored to match the surrounding forest, the otherwise ordinary-looking skin of the creature was a variegated pattern of green and greenish blotches and splotches, rendering its outline indistinct. Rawhide Robinson blinked repeatedly and scoured his eye sockets with his fists, attempting to keep the critter — or person — in focus.

The green thing looked almost human. More like two humans, the cowboy thought, as it towered over him, nearly twice his size. A skirt, or wrap, fashioned from braided and plaited strands of grass, covered the creature's legs from waist to knees, maintaining the color scheme and contributing to the camouflage. And it was definitely of the female species, evident owing to the lack of clothing above. Flowing waves of lime and olive locks of luxuriant hair fell from the head, loosely gathered and bound with thin lengths of vine to hang in twin hanks over each shoulder, offering some — but not much — semblance of what humans would call modesty.

9

A sharp intake of breath marked Rawhide Robinson's arrival at the face of the creature. It was green. And altogether beautiful. The perfectly formed physiognomy reminded the astonished cowboy of a photographic likeness he had once seen of the lovely Lillie Langtry. Only, if such a thing were possible, lovelier still than the celebrated actress.

But Rawhide Robinson's rapt attention was soon distracted by the spear in the woman's — creature's — hand, and his heart, swelling with infatuation, deflated when she — it — aimed the lance in a threatening manner at the fluttering organ.

He felt the bite of the spear's point against his ribs, repeatedly, as the critter — person — poked and prodded. To his relief, the thrusts seemed prompted by curiosity rather than violence. Still, the persistent jabbing and stabbing grew tiresome. The cowboy brushed the spear aside time and again, only to again feel its sting soon after.

Poke and prod. Push away.

Bite and sting. Slap aside.

And again.

Rawhide Robinson thought he heard a voice.

"Hey, cowboy!"

The sound wrinkled his brow, as it did

10

not fit the picture.

He felt another poke and again heard the voice.

"Wake up!"

Again, the sound furrowed his forehead.

And another prod to the ribs.

In the brief silence, Rawhide Robinson heard once more the now familiar pitter and patter of raindrops hitting the crown and brim of his hat, which was, he realized, propped over his face in the ordinary cowboy fashion when napping.

He batted aside another bite of the spear at his ribs and lifted the thirteen-gallon lid. Rather than being greeted by the extraordinarily beautiful (albeit green) jungle girl, his eyes filled with the extraordinarily ugly image of a red-headed, red-bearded, red-mustachioed, red-faced United States Army sergeant dressed in dusty blue. Rather than a spear, the annoyance at his ribs was the bayonet at the end of the soldier's military-issue carbine.

The soldier gave the cowboy another poke. "Wake up, you eejit," he said. "Ain't you got the sense to get out of the rain?"

Rawhide Robinson looked around to renew his familiarity with his campsite on the outskirts of Brownsville, not far from Fort Brown.

Another prod.

"Your name Rawhide Robinson?"

"Quit pokin' me with that thing, or you'll get to know who I am a heap better than you want. I'll rise from my recumbent pose and be all over you like ugly on an ape if you don't leave off."

"Answer me, you insubordinate fool!"

"Who wants to know?"

"I be Sergeant Donald O'Donnell of the United States Army. But that is neither here nor there. It is the commander back at the post as wants to see you. Sent me to fetch you — if you be Rawhide Robinson, that is."

"He is me," the cowboy said as he rose to a sitting position then stood, flexing his back and arms and shoulders to work out the kinks caused by the erstwhile bronc ride in his dream. "Or is it 'me is he'?"

"Let's go," O'Donnell said, waving the bayonet in the direction of Fort Brown.

Rawhide Robinson lifted his hat, resettled it, and tugged it down tight by the brim as if readying himself for action.

"You see any blue on me?" he snarled.

"No."

"Any other trace of a uniform?"

"No."

"Then it ought to be clear that I ain't in

12

your army. Right?"

"Right."

"Then it ought to be clear I don't take orders from you nor any other fool with stripes on his sleeves and a nasty attitude stuck in his craw. Right?"

"Right," the sergeant said, his complexion more rubicund than before.

"Good. Now that we got that cleared up, what is it you want?"

"Are your ears painted on, boyo? Like I said, you're wanted at the Fort."

"Why?"

"Can't say. Don't know. Only that the major sent me to fetch you."

Rawhide Robinson mulled it over for a moment then hitched up his britches. "Give me a minute to saddle my horse."

"Horse? #$%&* man, the Fort is right there!" O'Donnell said, emphasizing his point with a thrust of the bayonet in the direction of the military post. "Can't be more than forty rods away!"

"I ain't blind, you know. But I ain't walking, neither. Ain't no cowboy in the whole of the West would walk when he can ride."

Within minutes, the cowboy swung into the saddle, with feet in the stirrups and reins in hand.

"You ready yet?" the soldier said.

"Quit jackin' your jaws and rattle your hocks," Rawhide Robinson said. "Let's go see this colonel of yours and find out what he wants."

CHAPTER TWO

The polished wood surface of the desk spread before Rawhide Robinson was as clean as a billiard table. Not a single sheet of paper, or even a writing instrument, interrupted its expanse.

The rest of the office was likewise severe. The books in their case were carefully arranged, with not a volume out of alignment. Items on shelves along the walls stood at attention as if soldiers lined up for review. A credenza displayed a saber in its glistening sheath, a row of glittering medals in velvet-lined boxes, and a framed tintype of an army officer in dress uniform standing before a painted backdrop of Corinthian columns entwined with ivy.

The full-length portrait of the man revealed gleaming boots into which were tucked rigid trousers with a sharp crease, layered beneath a starched tunic with a double row of glowing brass buttons, shoulders topped with boards and epaulets. The officer, bareheaded and boasting a well-trimmed set of Burnside whiskers, stood as straight as if stiffened by an iron rod, with a gloved and gauntleted hand propped atop the grip of a saber — likely, Rawhide Robinson thought, the very weapon lying next to the framed likeness.

The cowboy sat alone in the room in a spindle-back chair placed precisely before the desk as if a team of surveyors had located it with transit, chain, and plumb bob. A spit-and-polished young officer had ushered Rawhide Robinson into the room with word that the major would be along soon.

"Soon" had long since passed, by the cowboy's reckoning. Waiting in the wooden chair, elbows propped on knees, hands slowly rotating his thirteen-gallon hat by the brim, had lost its charm. A split second before he decided to write the visit off as a loss and leave, the door opened and the man in the portrait — who by now seemed a long-time acquaintance, for the cowboy had studied his image for so long — walked through the door.

"Rawhide Robinson, I presume," the officer said as he stopped at near attention beside the padded, wheeled chair behind the desk.

"Yessir," the cowboy said, standing and offering his hand across the desk.

Without acknowledging the proffered handshake, the major seated himself and, with a dismissive wave of his hand, indicated his guest do the same.

"I am told you are something of cowboy. A good hand with livestock, they say."

"Oh, I ain't nothin' extra. An ordinary cowpuncher is all. I get by, but that's about it."

The major looked askance at the cowboy. "Have I been misinformed as to your capabilities, Mister Robinson?"

"Can't rightly say, sir. Don't know what you've been told."

The officer propped his elbows on the arms of his chair, steepled his fingers, and studied the cowboy. "I have been told you are a cowboy of long experience. Veteran of many a trail drive. Well versed in the ways of cattle. Experienced breaker of horses. And an inveterate liar."

Rawhide Robinson propped a boot atop the opposite knee and idly jingled the spur rowel as he contemplated a response.

Then, "I reckon all that's so. Except the part about lying, if that's what you were accusing me of with that fifty-cent word, whatever it means. I tell only the truth."

The officer laughed.

"Does that include, Mister Robinson, the story you are said to tell about riding horseback to the Sandwich Islands?"

A slight grin twisted the corners of the cowboy's mouth. "Well, I might be prone to a touch of exaggeration from time to time," he said. "But spinnin' a campfire tale can't be counted as telling a lie."

A pause. A smile. Then, "Besides, every one of them stories is true."

A pause. A frown. Then, "Be that as it may, Mister Robinson, the United States Army has a job for you. Your experience at sea — assuming there is even a kernel of truth in said story — will serve you well."

Rawhide Robinson wrinkled his brow. "I don't recollect enlisting or joining up or any other such thing as would put me in the employ of the army."

"Your service will be strictly voluntary — albeit under terms of a well-compensated contract — I assure you. But, should you refuse, Mister Robinson, things will not go well for you. I needn't tell you that the tentacles of the army are expansive, the reach of the government extensive, and the arm of the law long. All of which can be brought to bear to encourage your cooperation."

Rawhide Robinson rose to his feet, pulled his thirteen-gallon hat firmly onto his head, and said, "Can't say it has been a pleasure meetin' you, Major. I'll be taking my leave now. Unless of course, you intend to call out your troops to prevent my going."

The major snorted. "Sit down, cowboy. Hear me out. It may well be that what the army has in mind will be of interest to a man like you."

As the cowboy lowered himself slowly back to his seat, the major opened a desk drawer and pulled out a folded sheet of paper. He unfolded the page and looked it over, shaking his head in disgust and disbelief at its contents.

After a time he said, "I cannot fill you in on the details, Mister Robinson, as much of what is in the document before me is classified by order of the War Department. But I can tell you this. The Army is embarking on a new initiative related to locomotion of troo—"

"— Loco what? You mean like Mexican for crazy?"

The major laughed. "You are more correct than you realize concerning this cockamamie scheme, but, no. Locomotion. It means movement. As, in the present instance, troops and supplies throughout the Southwest. As you are aware from your travels, roads and trails here are rough, the terrain rugged, and wheeled vehicles restricted in their ability to reach remote areas."

"So it's pack trains you're talking about."

"In a word, yes."

Again, Rawhide Robinson rose to his feet. "Sorry, but I am a cowboy. And while I know a thing or two about packing camp equipment and trail supplies and draggin' a packhorse along at the end of a lead rope, I will have no truck with mules."

"Mules?" the major said. "Who said anything about mules? Sit down, please, and let me finish."

Again, Rawhide Robinson took his seat.

"I assure you, Mister Robinson, this document does not mention mules. But you discern correctly that it has to do with pack animals. Again, we are not referring to mules — which, by the way, to my mind, have served this man's army well and honorably and will continue to do so far into the future despite this . . ." he rattled the paper in Rawhide Robinson's direction, ". . . this hare-brained, half-baked . . ." The major trailed off, his face scarlet and the paper still shaking — albeit now involuntarily — in his hand.

He collected himself, then continued.

"What the War Department proposes is importing animals for the purpose of forming experimental pack trains to determine their suitability to our Western climates and landscapes. Given your purported experience and expertise with livestock, you have been selected to take a hand in acquiring and training the necessary animals to implement the trial."

"And where are these critters to come from?" Rawhide Robinson asked, his curiosity now piqued.

"The Levant. The arid deserts bordering the eastern Mediterranean."

"What, you mean Egypt and Arabia and such like?"

"Precisely. And, of course, the larger region."

The cowboy's mind filled with visions of fleet-footed Arabian horses skittering like the desert wind across shifting sands. He saw stallions, mares, fillies, and geldings milling about a verdant oasis, tended by young men in flowing robes, who, in turn, were tended by bejeweled beauties in skimpy, exotic costumes. He could almost taste the figs and dates and sweet wine (although, truth be told, he had no experi-

21

ence with such fare) fed him from the tender hands of these sultry princesses of the mysterious Middle East.

But, mostly, he saw horses. And while he imagined them too fine to act as mere beasts of burden, the temptation to be among such storied equine excellence was irresistible.

Again, he rose from his seat and screwed his thirteen-gallon hat down on his head.

"Major," he said, "I'm your man."

This time, the officer accepted his extended hand.

Chapter Three

The rowels on Rawhide Robinson's spurs jingled as he clomped up the ship's gangplank. Slung over his shoulder hung his bedroll and the strap of a canvas bag in which he carried most of the rest of his earthly belongings.

He lowered it all to the planks when challenged by a uniformed junior officer — the cowboy figured him to be a junior officer as he looked young enough to still be a stranger to a straight razor and shaving soap. Rawhide Robinson doffed his thirteen-gallon hat and removed the official paperwork he had secreted there. The navy man studied the documents with a wrinkled brow, shifting his gaze from time to time from the paper to the cowboy and back again.

"Looks like everything is in order, sir," the young man said. "Welcome aboard the USS *Cordwood.*"

"Who's the captain on this here boat?"

Rawhide Robinson asked as he stepped onto the deck.

"Begging your pardon, sir, the USS *Cordwood* is not a boat. You are now aboard a ship — a full-rigged naval supply ship displacing five-hundred-forty-seven tons. She's one-hundred-forty-one feet stem to stern, and twenty-nine feet in the beam. While not a fighting ship, she does carry a complement of four twenty-four-pounder cannons. Forty officers and men make up the crew of the *Cordwood,* commanded by Lieutenant Howard Clemmons."

"Sorry about that, young feller. Now, where would I find this Lieutenant Howard Clemmons?"

"His quarters are aft, sir, below the poop deck. You will likely find him there."

"Aft?"

"Uhh . . . rear end of the ship, sir."

"Rear end. I see. That have anything to do with — what did you call it? Poop deck?"

The young officer stuttered and stammered as his neck, face, then forehead turned crimson. "No, sir. Nautical term. Completely unrelated. From the Romans, sir, who carried *pupi* — little gods — there for luck and protection."

"You are a wealth of information, ain't you, young feller."

The officer snapped to even sharper attention than he already was. "I do my best, sir."

"What's your name?"

"Ensign Scott, sir. Ian Scott."

"Well, I thank you for your help, Ensign Ian Scott. I'll wander on back thataway and see what I can find," the cowboy said as he hefted his bedroll and war bag. "Don't suppose I can get too far lost, seein's as how I'm on a boat."

"Ship, sir. I'm sure Lieutenant Clemmons will have someone show you to your quarters and help you stow your gear."

Rawhide Robinson moseyed along the *Cordwood*'s deck, taking note of sailors at their work and admiring the miles of rope stretched, hanging, and coiled almost everywhere he looked. While no stranger to a sailing ship, his prior experience was short-lived, so his curiosity was as wide as a Great Basin alkali playa. He queried the men at work from time to time, but was rewarded only with terse replies, irritated grunts, and dirty looks. But he realized they were busy and knew there would be plenty of opportunities for conversation when on the high seas.

The cowboy eventually located the proper hatch and passageway to take him to the captain's quarters. He knocked and a gruff voice invited him to enter. He opened the door and ducked under the low doorframe to avoid bumping his thirteen-gallon hat. Another guest already occupied the cramped quarters.

"You must be Rawhide Robinson," said the man sitting next to a small desk attached to the wall, his raspy voice made even more gravelly as it wound its way around the stem of a pipe.

"Yes sir. And you must be Lieutenant Clemmons. Or is it Captain Clemmons?"

The man squinted through the tobacco smoke as he puffed on the pipe, then pulled it from his mouth. "Both. Lieutenant being my rank, ship's captain being my job."

"And who might you be?" the cowboy asked the other man. He, too, was in uniform.

"Major Benjamin Wayne, United States Army," he said with a smile. Unlike the captain, Wayne stood and shook hands. "The War Department has entrusted me with the command of our mission, and kindly placed Lieutenant Clemmons and the *Cordwood* at our disposal in order to carry out our orders."

The major resumed his seat in a wooden

chair beside a small work table. "Have a seat."

Rawhide Robinson hooked the toe of a boot under the rail on the other chair, dragged it away from the table and sat.

"What do you know of your assignment?" Wayne asked.

The cowboy studied the army officer. Unlike the major at Fort Brown, this one's uniform was rumpled and showed evidence of wear, and the front of the tunic carried hints of a recent meal. "Not a whole lot," he said. "That there bigwig at Fort Brown didn't tell me much. Only that we was a-goin' to someplace called the Levant to acquire for the US Army some fine Arabian horses for mounts and pack animals."

"He said that?"

"Well, not in so many words. But that's what I made of it."

Wayne pursed his lips and thought for a moment. "There's more to it than that, Mister Robinson. But we'll leave it there for now."

"Fine by me. But let's get one thing straight between us right now. You're not to call me 'Mister Robinson.' If ever there was such a person, that would be my old daddy. Me, I'm just Rawhide."

"As you wish, sir."

"And none of that 'sir' stuff, either."

Wayne laughed. "Fine, then, Rawhide. For the sake of military discipline I will ask you to address me more formally, if you don't mind. 'Major' or 'Major Wayne' would be most appropriate, particularly when junior officers or sailors are present."

Rawhide Robinson nodded in agreement and Wayne turned his attention to the ship's captain.

"Lieutenant Clemmons, I trust you will see to Rawhide's accommodations."

The captain gnawed on the stem of his pipe and growled, "He'll bunk with the sailors in the crew's quarters. His gear he can stow in a footlocker." Then, to the cowboy, "I will assign a junior officer to see to your needs, Robinson."

"Why, that's right kind of you, Captain — I suppose I should call you Captain?"

Clemmons nodded through the curtain of pipe smoke.

"Say," Rawhide Robinson said. "How's about that young Ensign Ian Scott? He available to look after me?"

The captain gnawed on his pipe stem for a moment. "I suppose so. Any particular reason?"

"Not really. I met him first thing when I got on the boat — ship — and he seems a

28

sharp young feller. It appears as he knows his stuff."

"He is an eager one, if still a bit green. Consider it done. Now, if you'll excuse me, Major Wayne and 'Rawhide,' I must see to final arrangements before sailing. We'll be underway within the hour."

CHAPTER FOUR

Rawhide Robinson craned his neck until he
grew dizzy. There was no end to the fascination he felt watching the sailors scramble
and clamber and climb through the ship's
masts and yards and sails and rigging like
so many squirrels in a Black Hills pine forest. On deck and below decks, the sailors
and officers were likewise efficient, going
about their business with little wasted motion.

It called to the cowboy's mind a branding
crew, where each hand knew his job and
how it affected the work of others. How the
ropers and flankers and knife men and those
who handle the hot irons and even the tally
man orchestrate a fluid, rhythmic symphony
of efficiency and grace.

Then, Rawhide Robinson, with a violent
shake of his head, rattled himself back to
reality and the realization that branding was
dusty, dirty, dangerous work where the days

ended with grit and grime in every crevice and crease of man's parts and pieces, smoke-saturated clothes covered with mud and blood and other effluents, ears overwhelmed with bovine bawling and bellowing, bones stretched and twisted until tired, hands red and raw, and even teeth feeling the pain.

He imagined the work of the ship workers likewise challenging. Still and all, he thought with a smile, a job of work that had to be done might as well be done well.

It was, after all, The Cowboy Way.

A few days out, with nothing to fill the eye but an endless expanse of sea and sky, life and work aboard ship became less hectic and fell into a routine. A routine, by the way, the footloose cowboy found confining in more ways than one. Rather than unrolling his assigned hammock at night, he preferred unfurling his bedroll on the quarter deck under the stars. The rank and fetid atmosphere of the crew's quarters was the match, he thought, of any ranch bunkhouse he had ever occupied.

Not being the solitary sort, however, Rawhide Robinson enjoyed evenings in the cramped accommodations before bedtime. He found the sailors much like his cowboy compadres — ever ready to shuffle the pasteboards and deal a friendly game, share a song, recite a verse, or spin a story. And when it came to the telling of tales, no man on land or sea was a match for Rawhide Robinson.

"You ever been on a ship before, cowboy?" one sailor asked one quiet evening.

"Not to speak of," Rawhide Robinson said. "I was at sea one other time, but I was a-horseback at the time."

"^&@($*!" said a sailor.

"%+^=!" said another.

"Now, hold on there a minute, boys. It's true — and mayhap I'll tell that story sometime. I brung it up only to say that when my horse pooped out, we was fished out of the sea and finished our journey on a ship sort of like this one. But I was so worn out that I slept most all the time, so I don't rightly recall much about it."

The cowboy squirmed his backside into a new position on the deck floor and leaned back against the bulkhead. "But, boys, I am no stranger to salt water."

"What do you mean?" asked a sailor.

"You're a landlubber sure as you're born," said another.

And yet another: "What do you know about salt water?"

"Well, if one of you-all will freshen up this

cup with what passes for coffee around here, I'll tell you-all about it."

Someone did.

And Rawhide Robinson did.

"You see, fellers, it was a few years back that I found myself kicking around Utah Territory with no particular place to go and in no hurry to get there. One afternoon I was ambling around the streets of the city when a stranger buttonholed me and offered a thirst-quenching libation at a local grog shop and suds palace."

"He what?" said a voice from somewhere among the assembled sailors.

"He wanted to buy me a beer."

"Why don't you just say so?"

"I did. Now, hush up and let me get on with it before my train of thought jumps the tracks, or the thread of my story unravels, or —"

"— C'mon, cowboy, tell the story."

"Certainly. Now, where was I?"

"About to have a libation with someone."

"Ah, yes. Here's what happened. See, he was an agent of some kind for this here cattle ranch that was on an island in this enormous lake outside the city. I tell you, boys, you ain't never seen the like of that lake. Miles and miles of clear, cool water as sweet as a mountain spring. And fish — you

33

wouldn't believe neither the size nor the number of finned critters swimming around in that body of water. And there weren't no mistaking they was there, either, because that water was so clear as to be invisible — there didn't appear to be anything at all between you and the bottom, no matter how far down it might be.

"And beaches — lovely little alcoves at every turn, with sand so smooth and soft it was like walking through clouds. If the sandy shore didn't suit your fancy, why you could walk inland a few steps and find your repose on a carpet of grass so green it would turn Ireland the same color out of envy. Trees, of course, to spread cooling shade over you when you wanted respite from the warmth of the sun, and to offer shelter to songbirds that could stir your soul with their melodious ditties. I swear, fellers, there ain't no place on this entire earth more fitting than that lake for courtin' women — which I did my share of, mind you, but that's another story.

"Anyway, back at the ranch. Or, I should say, to the ranch. As I was saying, this man who bought me that drink that day was the agent for a cow outfit on an island in that big lake. With roundup and fall works in the offing, he was a-lookin' for an extra hand or two. With me being dressed like a cowboy and all, he figured I must be the man for the job, which of course I was.

"He told me to shake my shanks out to this place by the lake where boats came and went, and in two hours' time I was to hitch a ride on this supply boat that was delivering a load of foodstuffs and such to the ranch. I got there in plenty of time, of course, what with 'Reliable' bein' my middle name, and I found the boat.

"Now, I don't rightly know the name for a boat like that. It wasn't near as big as this cork we're a-floatin' on, but it was of a good size. There weren't any sails, but it had a little steam engine. That there boat had a flat bottom, and it didn't stick out of the water more than a foot or two. There weren't no downstairs like on this ship, just that one floor that spread out from side to side and end to end."

A sailor offered, "Sounds like a barge to me."

Another, "Could be a big bateau."

And another, "Or a punt."

"Naw," said yet another. "If it was somewhat large and had a flat deck like he said, I believe a barge is what it was. Them other watercraft you mention is puny."

"I'm with you," said still another. "Especially if it was outfitted to haul supplies, which he said."

"And a steam engine — that's the give-away. Barge for sure," yet another opined.

The discussion carried on for a time until, finally, a growing segment of the audience agitated for the continuation of Rawhide Robinson's story until their demands proved overwhelming.

"One question before you continue," a sailor said. "You said this story was about you and salt water. And here you are telling us about a fresh-water lake. And a barge. It don't make no sense."

"Hang with me for a minute and quit chompin' at the bit. Your patience will be rewarded, I promise. Like as I said, I found that boat or barge or whatever you want to call it. It was tied up there by a little boardwalk that floated right on the water. (Rawhide Robinson's unfamiliarity with maritime nomenclature drew laughs and snickers from the sailors at this point, but he kept on with his tale.) That boat was stacked wide and deep with crates and boxes and barrels and bags of supplies of all kinds, mostly destined for the cook shack. And quite the cook shack it must be, I remember thinking, to need that much grub. Turned out it was, as that island ranch was bigger than ever I imagined, and took a right bunch of cowhands to keep it running, and a right bunch of grub to keep them running.

"But that is neither here nor there. What matters now is that I could not find another soul anywhere around. I shinnied all around the edges of that boat looking for someone but it appeared I was as alone as Adam in the Garden of Eden before he came up missin' a rib. Then I heard some sound, like maybe a hog rootin' for acorns in the Arkansas woods, only real faint-like. I squinted my ears to get a better listen and determined it came from atop that load of goods somewhere.

"I climbed up the edges of some boxes and crates until I could see over the top, and there, halfway sunk into a stack of sacks of rolled oats was a man near as round as he was tall. Snoring to beat the band, he was, and even from a distance I could smell alcohol so strong that if you was to light a match over his blowhole it would shoot flames high enough to singe the feathers off a seagull — of which there was plenty around, by the way.

"A bundle of pitchfork and shovel handles was at hand, so I pulled one out of the wrappings and reached out and rapped that feller on the foot with it.

"Didn't do no good. He snored right along. As he kept on doing when I adjusted my aim to tap a kneecap, pound his pulchritudinous paunch, and slap his shoulder. It wasn't till I bounced that stick of wood off the end of his nose that I was able to get his attention. He labored out of his rest with a flapping of his eyelids and fluttering of his lips, and elbowed his way upright — leastways, the top part of him, the rest being sunk in among them sacks of cereal.

"After a while he managed to stagger and stumble out of there and made his way to the back of the boat to where the steam engine that made the boat go was, and the little spoked wheel he drove with. With nary a word to yours truly, he set out towards that island. Me, there I was a-sittin' on the edge admiring the view into the depths of that lovely lake when all of a sudden he shut that engine down faster than slammin' a door. 'Mermaid!' he let out with a yell. I scurried around to where he was and he hollered, 'Look! Off the starboard bow!' "

Rawhide Robinson paused in his story, enjoying the sight of the assembled sailors as taut with anticipation as a fiddle string awaiting the bow. So the cowboy stood, he stretched, he moseyed a moment to loosen his legs, and he topped off his coffee.

Soon, the sailors set up a racket fit to wake the dead, demanding he continue. So Rawhide Robinson squatted amongst them, as if by a campfire, and continued.

"Well, I hesitate to say it, boys. But despite that man bein' as drunk as a magpie peckin' sour mash under a moonshine still, he was right.

"There, standin' upright in the water not ten feet from the boat was as beautiful a young woman as ever walked the earth. Only this one couldn't walk the earth, you see, on account of her being a mermaid. That water being crystal clear and all, you could see her bottom parts was like those on a fish.

"The boatman, he hustled his way up to the front of that boat and, despite his being round as a ball, and with a bellyful of alcohol, he pranced over and around that load of goods swift as a rat with a cat on his trail. He pulled the lid off a bulky barrel and set into tossing double handfuls of white stuff at that nautical nymph.

"I asked what it was he was throwing into the water and he said, 'Salt!' Me being the curious sort, I inquired as to why and I don't hardly believe to this day what he said. Seems where he come from, it was common knowledge that you could catch a bird if you shook salt on its tail. Him being three sheets to the wind — note the sailor palaver there, boys — he believed you could do the same with a mermaid — if you could shake salt on her tailfins, you could catch her.

"He would not be dissuaded, boys. He kept tossing salt at her as fast as he could, first by hand then with a scoop and then with a shovel. When she would swim away, he would fire up the engine and follow, flinging salt every inch of the way. Now, it might not seem it would make much of a difference to throw salt in a big lake like that. But there was a bunch of barrels of salt on that boat, and when they was all empty and heaved over the side, he took to throwing salt blocks meant for the cattle at that mermaid. Fortunately, he was so sloshed and his aim was so bad, he never got near that fine-looking fish-woman.

"The lake, however, did not fare so well," Rawhide Robinson said as tears made tracks down his cheeks.

"It's a sad, sad thing to see a lake like that die, but that's what I witnessed that day. It didn't happen all at once, of course, but whilst I worked on that ranch I watched that salt spread through those waters, killing everything in sight as it went and turning that sweet, clear water into a turbid, briny, smelly mess that would choke you to death should you partake of it. Not only that, all that salt shriveled the trees and grass along the shore and rendered the sand slimy and stinky. Turned that lovely lake into a dead sea."

"Nonsense!" some anonymous sailor said with a measure of vehemence. Others agreed, and the disbelief spread like salt in water.

Rawhide Robinson allowed his audience to vent for a time, then hollered, "Hold on a minute, boys!" he said. "Hasn't any one of you-all ever been out to that Utah Territory?"

The men exchanged blank looks and traded shakes of the head in the accustomed nonverbal signal for a negative response.

"Well, then, is there a map on this here boat?"

"Boats ain't got maps. We got charts. And this ain't no boat, besides. It's a ship," said a sailor.

Another seaman said, "Wait! That army lubber, he's got an atlas. Saw him studying it the other day. Looked to have enough pages to hold the whole world, it did."

The crowd dispatched a sailor to find the army officer and ask the borrow of his book of maps. Which request was answered in the form of Major Benjamin Wayne himself showing up, atlas in hand. He looked around the cramped crew quarters, unsure how to proceed.

Eventually, after letting the uncomfortable silence grow for effect, Rawhide Robinson said, "Is there a map of North America in that there book?"

Wayne nodded in the affirmative. "Several of them."

"Let's take a look at the western part of the country — Utah Territory to be exact."

The major spread the oversized book open on the deck and leafed through the pages until locating a map of the interior Intermountain West. "Will this do you?"

Rawhide Robinson tipped back his thirteen-gallon hat and studied the lines and squiggles on the page. "Sure thing," he said. "Now, Major, help me out here. What's this here splotch of blue?"

"Why, that's the Great Salt Lake. Says so right here," he said, pointing out the words printed over the body of water.

Sailors pushed and pressed for position, each hoping to get a glimpse.

"Say that again, if you would, Major."

"It's the Great Salt Lake. Plain as day."

The murmuring among the sailors grew

louder, expressions of disbelief breaking through.

"You ever seen it?" the cowboy asked.

"As a matter of fact, I have. Led a mapping excursion through the deserts west of there years ago."

"So what's that there lake like?" Rawhide Robinson said as he tapped the map with an extended index finger.

"Foul. Stinks to high heaven all summer long. Nothing lives in it, so far as we could discover, except pesky little flies that hatch and die and wash up on the shore in fetid waves."

Rawhide Robinson's smile spread from ear to ear. Then, the ultimate question: "Is it salty?"

"Absolutely," the major said. "According to our measurements, the salt concentration was around ten percent. More than twice the salinity of the oceans we are sailing."

The major wondered at the sailors' dumbfounded expressions. And at the mischievous grin plastered across Rawhide Robinson's physiognomy.

He didn't ask.

CHAPTER FIVE

Day after day, Rawhide Robinson wandered the decks of the USS *Cordwood.* Sailors scrambling through the rigging, oblivious to the law of gravity. Men swabbing already clean decks, then starting again. Endless shifting of cargo below decks, as officers ordered sailors to seek a more economical arrangement of crates and barrels, boxes and bins, bales and bags, containers and cartons. Others acted as carpenters, modifying and altering the hold to accommodate livestock in anticipation of a cargo of critters with hair and four legs.

Oh, there were days when the winds were stiff and the seas were rough when the bowlegged cowboy couldn't find his sea legs, and spent long hours and days and nights miserable in his hammock, upchucking into a bucket until he thought he would turn inside out. Seasickness was an unfamiliar malady to the landlubber, not to mention unpleasant. But as storms came and went, his acquaintance with and tolerance of the roll and pitch and yaw and heave and sway and surge of the ship improved.

When feeling chipper and on the prowl and observing shipboard activity, Rawhide Robinson was incessantly intrigued with all the ropes on board and their many uses. Having been recognized for years as a cowboy so adept with a lariat it was said he could write poetry with his rope, he appreciated skilled handling of twine in any circumstance. And there were plenty of circumstances aboard ship, as there were ropes everywhere, doing everything.

"Them boys sure know how to handle them ropes," he observed one afternoon to Ensign Ian Scott, who ofttimes served as tour guide and author of all information related to the ship and the sea.

"Lines."

"Lines?"

"Lines. Once a length of rope is put to work aboard ship it is no longer referred to as a rope, but as a line," the ensign explained.

"Hmmm," Rawhide Robinson muttered as he mulled that idea over. "You only got but the one name? They're all lines, from them up there holding them sails, to that one over there lashing down that box?"

"That's right, Mister Robinson. Lines, one and all."

"It's Rawhide, I done told you. But, lines. Cowboys, now, they wouldn't never be satisfied with but one or two names for ropes. Why, we're as apt to call it a reata as rope. And there's cable and catgut, clothesline and coil. Or gutline and fling line and twine. Lariat, lasso, lass rope. Ketch rope and hemp. Maguey, manila, mecate. It might be a string, a skin string, or a seago. And, naturally, a line. But no matter what you call it, I don't reckon I've ever seen a cowboy any handier with a rope than these sailor boys," Rawhide Robinson said. " 'Specially when it comes to tyin' knots."

The officer laughed.

"What's so funny, Ensign Ian?"

"Well, Mister Robinson, there are knots, as you presume. You'll find them at the end of a line. But, other than that, it's not a knot."

"A knot's not a knot?"

"No, it's not, sir. When we tie two lines together, we don't call it a knot, but a 'bend.' Which means, I have been told, to 'join.' If we are securing, or tying off a line we use not a knot, but a hitch."

"Well I'll be hornswoggled. You got all

them names for knots, but only one name for a rope. Don't make no sense at all, to my way of thinking."

"Give it time, Mister Robinson, you will —"

"I told you enough times already not to call me that. No more of this 'Mister Robinson' nonsense. It's Rawhide."

"Yes, sir, Mister Rawhide. As I was saying, you will grow accustomed to nautical nomenclature in the course of time."

"I suppose so. Come to that, tyin' a hitch in a line ain't a whole lot different than takin' a dally with a reata."

They strolled some more over the deck as the young navy man pointed out this and that to the curious cowboy.

"Everybody seems to keep plenty busy around here."

"True enough. Shipboard life can become mundane without work."

"That why you keep havin' men do jobs that don't need doin'?"

Ensign Scott laughed. "I can assure you, sir, every task needs doing. Perhaps not as often as they are done, but even routine work is better than idleness. Keeping men at sea occupied maintains morale and allows less time for mischief."

"I reckon that's so," the cowboy said as

the pair descended a ladder down a hatch so the officer could keep tabs on the retrofitting of the ship's hold.

"The work is coming along fine," Ensign Ian Scott observed as they watched sailors measuring and marking, sawing and shimming, fitting and hammering as they worked their way around crates and barrels, containers and kegs, boxes and hogsheads. "Of course there will be much to do once the military supplies are offloaded, freeing up the remainder of the hold. But we are off to a good start with the construction of stalls."

"They're roomy, that's for sure," Rawhide Robinson said, tipping back his thirteen-gallon hat and squatting in the sawdust to lean against a bulkhead. "Them horses will have plenty of room to move around. Too much, maybe."

"Horses? What horses?"

The question prompted a perplexed look from the cowboy.

"Why, them horses we're going after in Arabia and where all. Arabian horses bred for desert life, for use by the army in Texas and the Southwest."

The answer prompted a perplexed look from Ensign Ian.

"But Mister Robinson —"

"— Rawhide —"

"— Mister Rawhide. It's not horses these stalls are meant to hold. Nor is it horses we shall be acquiring at eastern Mediterranean ports of call."

The pronouncement prompted a perplexed look from the cowboy.

"Whatever can you mean? Of course we're goin' after horses."

"Oh, no, sir. You are misinformed."

"Then what in blazes am I doing on this here boat?"

"Ship, sir."

"Ship, then. If we ain't goin' after horses what are we goin' after?"

The question prompted a pained look on the young officer's face. An expression, in fact, bordering on panic.

One by one, sailors let their tools fall idle. Hammering stopped. Sawing ceased. Augers stilled. Conversation came to a halt. It became so quiet in the hold you could hear motes of sawdust fall to the floor. Had not every man present been holding his breath, it is likely inhalation and exhalation would have roared like hurricane-force winds in the silence.

Unable to endure the pain, the agony, the anguish any longer, Ensign Ian Scott uttered a sound. A single word. Two simple syllables that squeaked out of his larynx, up his throat, and through his lips with a softness so soft the sound was lost in the pent-up breath that accompanied it.

"What?" Rawhide Robinson asked.

"Camels," came the reply, but still so soft as to be unintelligible.

"What?"

The officer cleared his throat. "Camels," he said, barely above a whisper.

"Camels?"

"Camels."

"Camels!"

"Camels."

"Camels," Rawhide Robinson uttered under his breath as realization arrived. Slowly, ever so slowly, his boot heels scraped across the deck as the pointed toes plowed furrows through the sawdust. Slowly, ever so slowly, his back slid down the bulkhead until his backside landed and his legs splayed outward.

"Camels," he said again.

CHAPTER SIX

"Shiver me timbers!" is a well-worn phrase in seafaring lore. In sum, it expresses fear, awe, astonishment, surprise, shock, bewilderment, wonder. But it is an expression born of the actual trembling and quaking of the frame of a wooden sailing ship in angry seas as waves pound the timbers and threaten the very breakup of the vessel.

It is a vociferation ill-suited, owing to its weakness, to describing the ruction, the ruckus, the hubbub, the turmoil, the perturbation emanating from the captain's quarters on the USS *Cordwood* once Rawhide Robinson came to himself and regained his senses following the disclosure of the nature of the cargo to come, with which he would have association.

"Camels!"

The word was heard to echo in the holds and bilges, ricochet off the masts and rigging, reflect off the sheets and sails, bounce off the bulkheads and hull, and, as it were, shiver the very timbers of the ship.

It was uncomfortably close in the captain's quarters as Rawhide Robinson filled the air with a torrent of language, a flood of words, an inundation of vituperation. Captain Clemmons withered before the storm, sitting in shocked silence as he watched his army counterpart, Major Benjamin Wayne, wilt in the onslaught.

Rawhide Robinson said, "I'm mad, I tell you! I'm on the prod! I'm ringey and riled and ornery enough to eat the devil with his horns on! Why, I'm just in the mood to toss my own horns and paw up the sod!"

Major Wayne attempted to wedge his way into the conversation with, "Calm down and let's discuss this like reasonable men —"

"Men! You ain't no man! You ain't nothin' but a dirty rotten lowdown skunk!

"You ain't worth a barrel of shucks!

"You're lower than a snake's belly in a wagon track!

"You're so low you'd have to climb a ladder to kick a gnat on the ankle!

"You've got no more conscience than a cow in a stampede!

"Why, I wouldn't trust you as far as I could throw a post hole!

"A man might as well try to find hair on a

frog as an honest bone in your body!

"You're soft as butter on a summer day and weak as water in a whiskey glass!

"If I was of a violent nature, why, I'd knock you plumb into next week! I'd kick your britches up around your neck so high you could wear them for a collar! I'd stomp a mud puddle in your middle then walk it dry!"

And so it continued until Rawhide Robinson had overdrawn his account of exclamation points. He rounded the final turn with, "Major Benjamin Wayne, you ain't no better than a sodbuster!" and topped off his tirade with the ultimate insult:

"You! — you! — you! — ! You ain't fit to herd sheep!"

Once the smoke cleared and the stink of sulfur dissipated, Captain Clemmons made a meek attempt at moderation.

"Robinson," he said to the cowboy, "there is no doubt you are upset. Am I to understand you have embarked on this expedition and spent these many days at sea unaware that our mission is to secure camels for use by the Army?"

"Durn right. That's the story."

"Major Wayne, how did this happen?"

"I cannot say."

"Sure you can say," Rawhide Robinson

53

said. "That's the whole trouble. You didn't say. Nary a word. The word 'camel' never once passed your lips. Not yours, nor the officer at that fort I got dragged into, nor that florid-faced sergeant who prodded me out of my dreams to drag me there. Camels! No one ever said camels was what we was after until Ensign Ian let it slip!"

"That so, Wayne?" the captain asked.

The major hemmed and hawed, stuttered and stammered, whiffled and waffled, and suffered through fits and starts before spitting out, "I was just following orders."

"Hmmph!" said Clemmons.

"Hmmph!" said Rawhide Robinson. "You knowed, then, that if I knowed it was camels we was after, that instead of bein' here I would be horseback on the plains, punching cows and living the good life and lounging 'round a campfire instead of puking up my guts into a bucket and swinging in that infernal sling I'm supposed to sleep in, and slipping and sliding all over floors that won't never stand still."

"That was the fear, yes. Those up the chain of command overseeing this project believed you would not consent to accompany the expedition if fully informed of its nature. So, I was ordered to dispense information only on a need-to-know basis.

It was the intention of the army that before you were fully briefed that you be beyond the point of no return, as it were."

"So you, and all them others, decided to lie to me."

Major Wayne's face colored like port wine, his jaw tightened, and sparks shot from between squinted eyelids.

"I resent that implication, you two-bit saddle tramp! Not once, not ever, did anyone in the uniform of the United States Army utter one untrue word concerning this expedition!"

"Bull pucky. You never said nothing about no camels."

"That is true."

"I was led the whole time to believe it was fine and fleet Arab horses we was after."

Major Wayne laughed without humor. "That is not so. While we never mentioned camels, we certainly did not mention horses. Not once. Not ever. Not a word. If you chose to believe we were going after horses, that is purely your own invention, a product of your own imagination, a fantasy formed all on your own."

After listening patiently the whole time, Captain Clemmons pitched in. "Did you do anything to disabuse Mister Robinson of that notion, Major?"

The sheepish expression on Wayne's face was concealed as he dipped his head like a child caught in a fib. "No, sir. I did not. I saw no reason to interfere with Robinson's fictional construct of our expedition. In fact, his misguided and imaginary ideas supported our purposes."

The major, confidence restored, stared intently into the captain's eyes, then shifted his gaze to Rawhide Robinson. "Besides, as I said, I was only following orders."

There seemed nothing more to say. But, for a man as loquacious as Rawhide Robinson, saying nothing was not on the menu. Still, it took some minutes of uncomfortable silence before he spoke.

"I don't suppose it ever occurred to any of you army types that the only camels I ever saw was in a picture book. I ain't never seen one in real life."

Wayne said, "As a matter of fact, it did occur to us."

"Then what on earth led you to believe I'd be any help?"

"Your reputation, Robinson. We were told, and you did not deny, that you were handy at handling livestock — a student of long experience breaking and training horses and handling cattle. There were even reports of your successfully herding cats, as I recall.

56

The army figures that animals are animals, and your affinity for managing them would extend to dromedaries."

"Animals is animals, for certain," the cowboy said. "But horses ain't hogs and cows ain't crocodiles. And, sure as heck, camels ain't kitty cats."

"Surely a man of your talents can tame camels," Captain Clemmons wondered.

"Maybe so. Maybe no. I've heard tell a camel is a fractious critter that stinks and spits and is so stubborn a mule would pay it homage."

Major Wayne said, "And I have heard tell a camel can carry a significantly heavier burden than a mule or a horse, can endure heat more successfully, travel greater distances without water, thrive on less forage, and outpace the pack animals currently in service to our armed forces. Seems to me — and to certain of my superiors — to be an ideal candidate for supplying our outposts in the desert Southwest."

"Hmmph," said Rawhide Robinson.

"Be that as it may, our objective lies before us. It is our job to do and you, Mister Robinson, signed on to do it — albeit, I will admit, under circumstances some may deem dubious. But I fully expect you will, nevertheless, fulfill the obligation of your contract. For that is, I am given to under-stand," the major said with a sly smile, "The Cowboy Way."

And with that, Rawhide Robinson rose, grasped the front and rear of the wide brim of his thirteen-gallon hat, cinched it down firmly till it ever-so-slightly tipped the tops of his ears, and stomped out of the captain's quarters. As he departed, he left behind a single word, spit out with a mixture of disdain, denial, dismissal, and despair:

"Camels."

CHAPTER SEVEN

Rawhide Robinson was depressed. Demoralized and despondent. For days, he barely stirred from his hammock, content to sway slowly with the roll of the ship on the ocean waves. Unlike his previous bouts in bed, he was not suffering from seasickness.

But he was suffering.

In a way, he bemoaned his fate all the more.

Camels.

The prospect of wrangling camels subdued his spirit and quelled his enthusiasm. Try as he might, he could not imagine himself — a tried and true, through and through, true blue cowboy — casting aside horse and saddle for a humped ship of the desert. It was wrong. Just plain wrong.

Without a doubt, without fear of contradiction, with absolutely no question about it, Rawhide Robinson was in the doldrums.

Then, one morning as he awoke in his

hammock, he noticed something strange. Or, to be more precise, he noticed nothing. No swinging. No swaying. No rocking. No rolling. No tipping. No listing.

Nothing but stillness.

The cowboy eased himself out of his hammock and stood carefully on the deck. It was as smooth and steady as the *Llano Estacado,* with no hint of motion in any direction. A yelp escaped his lips when he pinched himself sharply to make sure he wasn't dreaming. He took a step. Hesitated. Then took another. And yet another until he reached the ladder, which he climbed through the hatch and onto the main deck.

No hint of a breeze greeted him. No swells or troughs troubled the sea. Sails hung slack in the still air. Like Rawhide Robinson, the ship was in the doldrums.

He made his way along the deck, his steps surprisingly unsteady, as his developing sea legs were unaccustomed to navigating a steady surface.

"What's going on?" he asked his source of all knowledge of seas and ships, Ensign Ian Scott.

"The doldrums. The calms of Cancer. It happens now and again in the horse latitudes."

With wrinkled brow, the cowboy said,

60

"Horse latitudes? What's a horse got to do with it?"

"It's a sad story," Ensign Scott said. "And especially so for a cowboy such as yourself whose very living depends on the horse. But, the story goes, when Spanish sailing ships en route to the New World became becalmed in these regions of subtropical high pressure, extending the length of the voyage and, subsequently, reducing the ship's stores, sometimes the horses and other livestock in transit had to be jettisoned to conserve water for the officers and crew. Hence, the horse latitudes."

"Too bad they wasn't haulin' camels," Rawhide Robinson said.

Throughout the day, the sailors performed their usual tasks, although it seemed to Rawhide Robinson they worked as if slogging through waist-deep molasses. Every motion was slow, every movement restrained.

And so it was the next day, following a fitful, unrestful night of little sleep.

When the day ended and only the services of the few sailors on night watch were required, the crew gathered in small bunches on the stifling deck to sweat and stagnate and swear about the state of things.

"This cannot last forever," one said.

"&*@#$!" said another.

"That's right," offered a third. "Besides, it don't have to last forever. Just long enough for the water to run out."

"Then, we shall surely dry up and blow away."

"Nonsense," said another. "That would require a wind. Of which there isn't any, in case you haven't noticed."

Thinking to lighten things up before the entire crew became as dejected as he was, Rawhide Robinson built a metaphorical loop and tossed it into the conversation.

"You fellas really think we'll run out of water?" he said.

"It could happen," a sailor said.

"Has happened," said another.

"There's ghost ships floating becalmed all over these horse latitudes, manned by the skeletons of sailors who perished for want of water."

"But," the cowboy contradicted, "we're surrounded by water. Don't seem it can ever get all that dry, bein's as we're on an ocean and all."

"Aye, but it's salt water, matey. It ain't fit to drink as well you know. Although many a man has tried it, only to hasten his own demise."

"Right he is," a sailor said. "You don't

know dry until you've been at sea with nothing in the water barrels but a memory."

"Oh, I don't know," Rawhide Robinson said. "I've been plenty dry before. Why, there was this one time when my horse pulled up lame out in the Mojave Desert. When I set out across that country, you see, I wasn't too concerned on account of an old sourdough prospector told me they get twelve to fourteen inches of rain on a fairly regular basis.

"What I didn't know was, when them desert rats say twelve to fourteen inches of rain, what they mean is twelve raindrops that land fourteen inches apart. Then that desert soaks them up so fast they don't leave any trace.

"So, anyway, there I was afoot with a hobbling horse, two miles as the crow flies from the middle of nowhere."

The telling of the story brought a thirst to the cowboy raconteur, so he treated himself to a dipper full from a handy water bucket. He sipped slowly, savoring the fluid as it flowed down his throat. He squatted again amongst the sailors, using the bib of his wild rag to mop the dribbles from lips and chin.

"Well?" said a sailor.

"What happened?" asked another.

"Finish your story," demanded a third.

"Hold your horses," Rawhide Robinson said. "Which is exactly what I had to do — as much as I was leading that lame horse, he was leading me. And now and again, we'd lean ag'in' one another to keep from tipping over when we rested. But once we caught our breath, we'd try to outmaneuver one another for shade. Soon as I'd find a place to stand where that horse shaded me from the sun, he'd rotate right around me to reverse our positions, so I was shading him some. But no matter what, there wasn't much shade to speak of and so we'd walk on.

"After a while of that hot sun and dry air — days and days after — I got to noticing I couldn't tell where that horse's hide ended and the leather of my saddle started. One was as dry and stiff as the other and there weren't no telling them apart. I reckon I looked much the same, for I felt some stiff and brittle myself.

"Dry? You want to talk dry, boys? Why me and that horse both would have donated an arm and a leg — or, in the horse's case, a leg and a leg — for the slightest sniff of water, even if it was an ocean. But it wasn't to be and we maintained ownership of our limbs, even as they wrinkled and shrunk and dried out and turned to leather."

Rawhide Robinson once again halted the tale in its tracks. He unknotted his silk kerchief and dabbed at his forehead, removed his thirteen-gallon hat and mopped the sweatband where brim met crown. He unfurled and refolded the wild rag then reknotted it loosely around his throat.

All the while, anticipation among members of his audience built until boiling over in a string of demands to finish the story.

And so he did.

"Sometime later — can't say how long, and can't say how it happened, as I had long since succumbed to the blind staggers and let fate take me where it may — that horse and me stumbled into a small town that all but sprung up around us on account of a silver strike. For a long time we was nothing but a curiosity, what with folks wandering by to watch us stand there in the sand as they offered comments and observations on what we were and where we come from. I looked like a stick of buffalo jerky wearin' boots and spurs and a hat, is what they mostly said.

"Anyway, a couple of kids — you know the kind, them as is always up to something — decided to play a prank and for reasons of their own or none at all hauled me down Main Street a piece and plopped me into a horse trough.

"I'll tell you, boys, heaven holds no pleasure to compare to the relief I felt when I hit that water. Relief don't begin to explain it. I was refreshed, rejuvenated, restored, reinvigorated, revived, and revitalized.

"And, as the local sawbones was to explain later, rehydrated. Which, he said, was a scientific term meaning replenished with the fluids a body needs to function. Swelled right up, I did, and filled out to look like my normal self again. Which, I'm sure you'll agree, ain't that much to look at. But it sure beats eyeballin' a man who resembles a hunk of buffalo jerky dressed in cowboy attire."

"What about the horse?" a chorus of wondering voices inquired.

"Sad to say, boys, he would have been better off cast off a ship in the horse latitudes, where a chance at rehydration might have been his. As it was, there wasn't enough water in that desert town to immerse the critter so he stayed dry. Got even drier, for a fact. Then, when I fetched my saddle and outfit off his back, he met his demise. Seems my cinches and latigos was all that was holding him together, and when I unloosed them that horse crumbled into nothin' but a puddle of dust at my feet. Too bad, too, for he had been a fine horse in his day.

"Anyway, boys, don't get to thinkin' you know what dry is, sittin' as you are on a ship in the middle of an ocean with nothing but water as far as they eye can see in any and every direction."

And with that, Rawhide Robinson descended the ladder to the crew quarters, unfurled his hammock and felt, for the first time in a long time, that rest awaited him in its web.

CHAPTER EIGHT

The ship was still in the doldrums when Rawhide Robinson next rolled out of then rolled up his hammock.

But he was not.

Being generally sanguine in temperament, little of what life threw his way could keep the cowboy down for long.

Even the prospect of babysitting a bunch — herd? horde? flock? drove? troop? bevy? mob? muster? gang? pack? string? caravan? — of camels, outlandish and outrageous though the very thought of it may be, was set aside, at least for now. Rawhide Robinson determined to deal with declining the distasteful duty at some future, indeterminate date.

He strolled the stifling and stagnant decks of the becalmed ship, noting a marked lack of enthusiasm among the officers and sailors. Most simply sat, squatted, sprawled, and slouched in neglect of their usual duties. Some engaged in listless card and dice contests. Others played sluggish games of mumblety-peg. Still others apathetically pitched pennies. One singularly dejected deckhand, settled somewhere out of sight, made mournful music with a mouth harp, whose woeful refrain wafted about the decks, further dampening the mood.

The USS *Cordwood* itself languished limp and lifeless like its cohort. Lank lines lolled. Slack sails sagged. The masts, yardarms, and spars themselves seemed to slump.

For as far as Rawhide Robinson's sharp eyes could see, the sea in every direction looked as still and smooth as the surface of a shaving mirror on a shelf. Rays from the recently risen sun reflected off the water, intensifying the orb's glare and escalating the temperature of the air — close, confining air; repressive, oppressive air reluctant to release its oxygen to the respiring, perspiring sailors.

It all changed in an instant.

At first, the ship's company believed themselves under attack, unlikely though the possibility may be. But the whack, the thwack, the bang and boom, the rap and report that blasted them out of their lethargy resembled the concussion of an incoming cannon ball.

Officers sprung to their stations. Sailors scrambled to the rails to assess danger and damage. The lookout high above in the crow's nest turned in circles seeking the source of the startling sound.

Then came a second strike, more explosive than the first.

"Whales!" a sailor shouted from the foredeck.

"Thar she blows!" yelled another from the quarterdeck.

"Cetaceans off the starboard bow!" came a call from the poop deck.

Soon, sailors were sighting whales and more whales, surrounding the ship. The mystified men watched as this leviathan then that one slapped the sea's surface soundly with its flukes. This lobtailing, they realized, was the source of the original whack that awakened them — rudely — from their lethargy.

While some whales lobtailed, others breached, flinging themselves out of the water and crashing back into the sea. Still others rolled in the now roiled water, slapping the surface with sizeable pectoral fins. The more relaxed among them spyhopped — standing on their tails with heads out of the water, returning the stares of the goggle-eyed sailors.

Ever in search of enlightenment and new knowledge, Rawhide Robinson sought out the well-read Ensign Ian Scott, source of information all and sundry concerning the sea.

"Ensign Ian, what in tarnation is going on?"

"It's a wonder. These are humpback whales. They seldom school like this. Sometimes, in summer, when feeding. But this is strange."

"How's that?"

"This time of year, their feeding time, they should be well north of here — way up in the low latitudes where it's nice and cool. This is their winter range, you might say. They come to warmer waters in winter to mate and calve," the wide-eyed young officer reported.

The curious cowboy mulled all that over for a moment. "You reckon they'll be leaving soon?"

"I shouldn't be surprised, given the fact that they shouldn't be here in the first place."

"How far they likely to go when they do?"

"Who's to say? Humpbacks are migratory, covering ten thousand miles and more in a year's time."

Rawhide Robinson tipped back his

71

thirteen-gallon hat, pursed his lips, and furrowed his forehead. The ensign imagined he could hear whirring and clanking inside the cowboy's cogitating cranium.

"Ian, follow me," Rawhide Robinson said with a smile, then turned and hurried toward the ship's bow. The ensign followed obediently.

"Hey, sailor, hand me that there coil of rope," the cowboy said to a seaman.

The sailor hefted the coil from the deck and passed it to the cowboy as he hurried past. Rawhide stuck an arm through the coils and went to work on one end.

"See this here knot, Ian? It's not likely one you use on a boat. We call it a honda, and it's what turns a rope into lariat — a catch rope, in cowboy parlance."

"So?"

"So what I'm gonna do is build me a loop and shinny out on that beam pokin' out front of the boat and make me a heel catch on one of them humpbacks." The cowboy grinned. "I'm gonna catch a whale by the tail!"

"And?" the shocked young officer said.

"I'll need your help, or the help of one of these sailors that's handy with a rope. When I jerk my slack, I'll be needin' one of you-all to take a dally on one of them little posts there on the rail." Ensign Scott considered how the cowboy's request would sound in nautical talk and issued orders to a nearby sailor he knew to be quick and capable.

"See here, sailor. Rawhide Robinson will station himself on the bowsprit and cast a line around a whale's flukes. You are to stand by here on the fo'c'sle and once the loop in the line is drawn taut, take a double hitch around a belaying pin and hold fast."

"Aye-aye, sir!" the sailor said with a snappy salute.

Rawhide Robinson peeled off several coils of his lengthy lariat for his own use and handed the remaining rounds to his dally man.

"Ensign Ian, soon as this sailor takes his dallies, have someone else tie off so we don't lose our fish when he runs."

"You there," the officer said to a nearby sailor. "As soon as practical after the catch, find a sturdy cleat and secure the line with a cleat hitch. The load will be heavy, so be mindful and make it proper."

Excitement built among the officers and crew and they crowded into every available space before the mast, even climbing into the rigging and perching on yards to witness a thing the like of which they could not have even imagined.

Fortunately for Rawhide Robinson, the sea was still relatively calm despite the turbulence caused by the pod of whales. He had little trouble maintaining his balance on the bowsprit, and soon found himself perched perilously above the open ocean. But rather than contemplate the tenuous nature of the situation, he focused his concentration on shaking out a loop of appropriate size and determining which of the many shots — the roper's term for the several types of loops and throws, varying by size, rotation, spin, angle, flight, position, and such — in his repertoire he should employ to provide the best opportunity of catching his whale by the tail. A small, tight dog loop, or a wide open Mother Hubbard? Should it be a simple toss, as in a horse corral? The single overhead whirl of the California twist? A Blocker loop, or perhaps a hooleyann? Rollout or *magnana*? Overhead loop? Underhand pitch? Backhand?

All this and more mulled around in Rawhide Robinson's mind as he watched the whales swimming about, waiting for one to lobtail nearby. But all that thought came to naught when a pair of flukes presented themselves — the cowboy reacted instantly and instinctively, and cast his twine with the perfect loop. It was a long throw, farther than he would have wished. But not knowing if a better opportunity would present itself he took his shot.

The ship's crew and officers watched with restrained breath as the loop sailed out, with the uncoiling rope trailing as it soared. It flew. It floated. It seemed to hang suspended in the air, then suddenly drop, surrounding the dripping flukes as they reached the apex of their path to a resounding slap on the water.

Even before the report, Rawhide Robinson jerked the slack out of the loop, tightening it around the tail. As ordered, the sailor behind him stretched taut the line between himself and the cowboy and took not one, but a safe two, wraps around a belaying pin. As soon as his twists were taken, the sailor behind him executed as handsome a cleat hitch as ever witnessed.

And so the humpback was caught. Never before, and perhaps never again, would any cowboy in the history of the craft dab a loop on such a trophy. Later, Ensign Ian Scott estimated the length of the leviathan at fifty feet, and calculated its weight as near forty tons.

For a humpback whale of such proportions, a tight loop around the tail was a mere irritant. No doubt the giant felt a significant tug when he hit the end of the rope, but any reaction was indiscernible. That tug arrived even before the raucous cheer from the crew for the success of the cowboy's capture had dissipated, and when the ship's bow started carving a wake in the water with the propulsion of whale power, the celebration erupted anew.

As anticipated by the resourceful Rawhide Robinson, the whale swiftly towed the USS *Cordwood* out of the doldrums and into favorable seas. A timely yank with a gaff hook released the loop and freed the humpback rescuer, who waved goodbye with a pectoral slap and dove for the deep, never to be seen again. His (her?) departure was accompanied by heartfelt huzzahs and hoorahs from the officers and crew, and the ship continued its voyage utilizing more accustomed motive power — wind and currents — to carry it toward the Straits of Gibraltar, the Mediterranean Sea, and Levantine ports of call.

And, toward Rawhide Robinson's expected showdown with Major Benjamin Wayne over the completion of this cockamamie quest to acquire camels.

CHAPTER NINE

The USS *Cordwood*'s prow sliced through the sea with a hiss as it ran before the westerlies, northward and eastward toward its destination. Rawhide Robinson and Major Benjamin Wayne stood together as far forward (or fo'ard, in sailor parlance) in the bow as possible, cooled by the refreshing mist stirred up as the ship's stem slapped the crests of passing waves.

The cool went unnoticed, however, for a chill of another kind hung in the air between the men.

"You could have told me the truth," the cowboy said. "There weren't no need to lie."

"As I've said before, Robinson, no one lied to you."

"Then how is it I find myself in the middle of the ocean before knowing I am on a fool's errand to fetch camels?"

"Because you chose — chose — to believe in a fantasy of your own fabrication con-

77

cerning Arabian horses. No one, at any time, ever mentioned horses."

"No one ever mentioned camels, neither!"

The major stalled, shifted, shuffled, and sheepishly acknowledged the fact. "But," he said, "would you have signed on if we had?"

"No! Not just no, but @#%% no!"

"That's the gist of it right there, Robinson. The army required your services and skills, and my orders were to acquire them. I took the steps necessary to fulfill my orders. When you latched onto the idea of horses, I felt it best to let you hold to that notion. We needed a man with a demonstrated ability to handle livestock and we've got one. You. The army — at least I — am confident your expertise with animals will translate to camels."

"Maybe so, maybe no," Rawhide Robinson said. "And maybe I'll hang back and let them critters mind their own business and I'll tend to mine."

Crimson crept up the major's neck as the chill between the two dissipated to be replaced by heat. "Need I remind you, Robinson, that handling and training the camels we acquire *is* your business! I have a contract that says as much, with your signature affixed."

Rawhide Robinson found himself speechless — a condition as rare as teeth in a hen's beak. Still not content, the major piled on.

"Besides that, Robinson, you are an American! This mission we share is in service to our country, and I say it is your patriotic duty to carry it out to the best of your ability!" Now it was the cowboy's turn to stall, shift, shuffle, and sheepishly reply.

"I reckon you've got a point, Major Wayne," Rawhide Robinson said. "I suppose you can count on me. Maybe. We'll have to see. Now, what is it about them camels that's got you-all fired up?"

The major explained that, despite opinions to the contrary, the idea to employ camels was carefully considered. It had been reviewed, evaluated, assessed, appraised, weighed, and measured for years. Support had waxed and waned depending on who led the War Department, who controlled Congress, and on shifting circumstances within the armed forces. But, despite the disapproval of many in the War Department and Congress, when all was said and done an agreement was reached, funds were allocated, and the mission in which the men were now entwined was mounted.

"Camels are marvelous beasts," Major Wayne said. "Given the conditions in the Southwest, there is no creature on earth better equipped to carry freight and supplies over the rugged terrain there to outfit our remote outposts in the region."

Rawhide Robinson lifted his lid to scratch his head. "I confess not knowing much about camels. I've picked up a bit here and there from reading and from picture books and such. I am of the opinion they are ugly, unruly, and stink to high heaven. And, as likely to spit on a man as look at him. Ain't that so?"

"Ugly is a matter of opinion. I would venture that rather than ugly, camels are simply unfamiliar in our society. If an everyday presence, it is unlikely anyone would give them a second look. I admit they appear ungainly, but that is appearance only. Their locomotion can just as easily be seen as graceful, and they are surefooted.

"Like any domesticated animal, the camel's disposition varies. As with horses, mules, donkeys, oxen, water buffalo, reindeer, yaks, elephants, llamas, dogs, or other beasts of burden, most are docile while some can be uncooperative. Some so by nature, certainly, but more likely owing to insufficient or incompetent training and handling. Their odor, again, is a matter of opinion and familiarity. Hogs are smelly to the uninitiated. As are cattle, sheep, goats

— well, I need not continue, Robinson. You take my point."

The cowboy nodded. "What about that spitting business?"

Major Benjamin Wayne laughed. "I have heard that myself. According to our investigations — which are not firsthand, mind you — that is true. Then again, it is false."

"Huh?"

"You see, the camel, like a cow, is a ruminant and chews a cud. When agitated, they say a camel might regurgitate a cud. Then, when shaking its head in anger or anxiety, will scatter the partially digested fodder hither and yon, indiscriminately spraying all within the vicinity with malodorous moisture."

"Sounds like fun," Rawhide Robinson said. "There must be something more about them camels that convinced you-all to want them in your pack strings."

The army officer eagerly launched into a lengthy discourse on the advantages of camels as beasts of burden over the army's accustomed horses and mules. He told how camels can easily carry twice, even three times, as much weight as a horse or mule. How dromedaries can cover half again as much country in a day. How they are less affected by temperature. How their hoofs, with hard nails and webbed toes and soft soles, are surefooted in all kinds of terrain. His enthusiasm overwhelmed the cowboy; the eager onslaught fairly tipping him back on his boot heels.

Then, the major reached the acme of his argument.

"As a sometimes inhabitant of the Southwest, Robinson, you are aware of its most serious lack — water."

The cowboy nodded. "I have experienced a mighty thirst many a time in that country," he confessed.

"Therein lies the camel's greatest advantage," Major Wayne said with a smile and so much enthusiasm the cowboy feared the man might burst on the spot, with a resultant shower similar to what might originate from an agitated camel.

Rawhide Robinson said, "That's because they carry water in that there hump on their back, ain't it."

Major Wayne smiled. "That is a common misconception. One I, myself, held until my studies of the camel informed me otherwise. The hump is simply fat and flesh. But imagining it as water storage is a natural misreading given the camel's unique metabolism — one that allows it to absorb much of the moisture it requires from plants and feed. In cool weather, a camel may not imbibe for weeks, even months, at a time. When the dromedary does drink, it can suction up twenty-five gallons of water in a matter of minutes," the major said. "Unlike with horses, such gluttony does not cause sickness. And the camel is acclimated to desert conditions, so even in hot weather it requires less water and does not suffer from thirst as horses and mules do."

"Well, don't that salt your *frijoles*!" Rawhide Robinson stood tall, tugged at the tails of his vest, lifted his thirteen-gallon hat, reset it with a firm tug and said, "Well, Major Wayne, I ain't sayin' I'm fond of the idea. But it looks like I'm stuck with being a camel caballero, a dromedary wrangler, so you can count on me to ride for the brand — or whatever they call it when herdin' them humpback critters."

CHAPTER TEN

The sea biscuit, thrice-baked and six months and more in the bin, approached in hardness and tensile strength a Ninja throwing star. Which is what it resembled as it spun and sailed across the table, grazed the cheek of a young sailor named Norman, then embedded itself in the bulkhead a good three-quarters of an inch.

Norman returned the favor of flung food, bouncing a bowl of dried peas boiled to mush off the bib of a man named Micah, he who had heaved the hard tack.

Rawhide Robinson looked on in dismay, as the altercation and the ensuing mess in the mess resulted from a conversation, a debate, an argument of his making. It seemed a simple question when he asked it — the opinions of the several and sundry sailors sharing mess, concerning the superiority — or inferiority — of various breeds and kinds of horses.

The cowboy was transfixed — and surprised — by the heated conversation aroused by his inquiry. He had not imagined these seafarers held such strong opinions about steeds nor, in fact, did he expect the equine expertise they displayed. But, as he mulled it over, he realized these men, while sailors in service of their country, were not born on a boat (ship), or raised on a boat (ship), nor did they live on a boat (ship) continuously. And while on solid ground, they, like everyone else, relied primarily on horsepower to get around. Whether ridden or driven, horses moved most people most places they needed to go, town and country. Sure, railroads handled long trips to and from cities large and small, but beyond that, it was horseback, buckboard, buggy, omnibus, or some other equine-operated perambulator.

And so the sailors held forth with vim, vigor, and vehemence on the subject of which breed of horse was best for an assigned task. Given the dispersion of their natal places and their raising in widespread areas, sectional differences entered the argument, as did individual experience and plain old personal preference.

A sailor raised on the Texas plains, familiar with cowboys and cattle and no stranger to the work himself, swore no horse could match the tenacity of the Spanish mustang.

Another, raised on a Texas dirt farm, held forth for the Shire. "Them scrawny mustangs can't hardly tow a steer, let alone pull a plow!" he said.

Another sailor, of unknown origin, argued for crossing mustangs with American horses or Morgans or even oversized European stock like Clydesdales and Percherons. "Gives them bunch-quittin' bangtails some size and strength and serenity," he claimed.

"That don't do nothin' but ruin a cow horse," a kid from the Northwest averred. "Where I come from, they call them crossbreeds Percheron Puddin' Foots or Oregon Bigfoots, on account of they got hoofs the size of a dinner plate and about half as agile." The shavetail puffed out his chest and said, "You want a horse — a good horse — there ain't none better than a Cayuse or an Appaloosa. Them Indian ponies is as good as they come."

"That may be true if you don't mind a horse whose spotted hide might be mistaken for a milk cow's," someone countered. "You uncouth Westerners don't know a thing about horseflesh! Kentucky and Tennessee — that's where they know how to breed horses. Thoroughbreds. American Saddlers.

Standardbreds. Those are horses!"

An old salt, who had heretofore held his peace, entered the fray with a travelogue of sorts, populated with favorable reports of the horses he had observed in places far and wide. He reminisced about Brumbies in Australia, the Paso Fino of Puerto Rico, the Welsh Cobb of Great Britain, the leaping Lippizans he saw in Vienna, the Batak Pony of Asia, and many, many others. His vivid descriptions of fleet-footed Arabian horses prancing and pawing on desert dunes near brought a tear to Rawhide Robinson's eye.

The discussion went on. And on. And on, until devolving into hearty disagreements, harsh arguments, wholehearted quarrels, serious squabbles, and, in the end, the aforementioned eruption of victual violence. Which, in turn, invited the presence of angry officers, threats of incarceration, a week-long withdrawal of the daily ration of spirits, and a plea, offered in no uncertain terms, for civility.

Once the argument abated and the near-riot was quelled, Rawhide Robinson, in an attempt to lighten the mood, offered his views on the subject.

"Boys," he said, "I never dreamed I was settin' a match to such kindling when I asked the question. Cowboys such as myself, well, we augur over horses at some length at most any opportunity. But with us, it's all in good fun. I ain't never seen no cowpunchers come to blows over horses.

"Wait — I take that back. I do recall a cowboy from Colorado one time flailin' a feller with his hat, on account of him questioning his cowhand credentials 'cause he had a mare in his saddle string. But that ain't here nor there, neither one.

"I've heard your boys' ideas about the ideal horse, and as one who has made his living forking them critters for more years than I care to remember, I say you're all wrong — every one of you."

That, as you might imagine, launched a sortie of angry ripostes and threatened the fragile peace.

"Boys! Boys!" Rawhide Robinson said, rising and waving his hat overhead to waft the irritation out the room. "Calm down! When you hear what I am about to tell you, I guarantee that every last man of you will agree that this one particular equine I am aware of is better adapted to its occupation than any other four-footed creature of any kind, let alone horse."

While waiting for the murmuring and mumbling to subside, Rawhide Robinson scared up a coffee urn and refilled his mug.

Then he sauntered over to the far side of the mess and hunkered down against the bulkhead — checking carefully so as not to lean against and impale himself on the sailed slab of sea biscuit still protruding from the plank. He blew the hot off the top of his coffee and waited until, like so many ocean swells, the recently subsided anger rose in a wave of eager anticipation, sweeping irresistibly over the cowboy until he tipped back his thirteen-gallon hat and launched his tale.

"Out there in California there's a range of mountains they call the Sierra. I reckon you've all heard of it."

Affirmation rippled through the room as sailors sounded their agreement.

"Well, them mountains cover so much country — sideways, longways, and up and down — there's places in them where nobody hardly ever goes. Even some places, I reckon, where nobody's ever been. It's a wild country. Rough and rugged and rocky. And steep. I'll tell you boys, there's places on them mountains where, if a man was to fall, he wouldn't stop rollin' downhill till next Tuesday."

Rawhide Robinson stopped to sip his coffee and contemplate the continuation of his anecdote. Soon enough, anxious sailors spurred him on, with a range of encouragements, exhortations, and downright threats.

"Calm down, boys," the cowboy said after another sip of steaming joe. "I'll get to it." He studied the bubbles floating atop the coffee mug until tension in the mess was as taut as the latigo on a roping horse, then he talked on.

"I was in that country one time, punchin' cows for an outfit in Nevada Territory. The ranch lay right against the east face of the Sierras, and in summer we pushed the herds up onto the slopes to graze in the high country.

"The cattle that ranch ran was a mixed bunch — some havin' been driven up from Texas, others down from the Oregon country, and still others from old Spanish and Mexican herds over in Californ —"

"Enough!" some anxious sailor shouted.

"What about horses?" someone said. "You said you were going to tell us about horses!"

"Who cares about cows?" another asked.

"Nobody!" came the answer.

"Get on with it!" came a chorus of restless voices.

Rawhide Robinson again assessed his coffee, then said, "Take it easy, boys. No need to boil over like foam on a warm beer. Sit back and relax and I'll get to it."

"Get to it then!"

"All right, all right. Here's the deal. I was up in them Sierras hunting lost cows after fall roundup. All on my lonesome, which ain't all that unusual in them circumstances. But I have since wished I'd had a saddle pal along. Not that I couldn't handle the work, understand. Just that it would have been nice to have a witness to what I seen. Nobody believed it then, and nobody's believed it since."

Again the cowboy paused to check the level in his coffee cup.

And, again, sailor voices rose in unison to urge him on.

"Thing is — and I ain't ashamed to say it — I got lost. I was following this one cow track up a canyon, you see. It got steeper and narrower to the point I could reach out on either side and grab hold of bushes and rocks and tree limbs. Which was a good thing, for it was so steep I was liftin' that horse and me up the hill as much as he was — when I wasn't keepin' us from slippin' and slidin' back down the slope, that is.

"After wearin' ourselves to a frazzle, we broke out into this little valley. I'd never seen it before, and as difficult as it was to get there, I doubt many others had, either. It was your typical high-country valley — a

91

pretty little lake out in the middle, grassy meadows painted with wildflowers, clumps of trees here and there. And all around, mountainsides as steep as the canyon my horse and I climbed out of to get there. It was as pretty a place as you could imagine.

"Well, we wandered across that little valley and around that little lake till we found the creek that drained it. I let that horse drink his fill then piled off and buried my own nose in that clear, cold wate —"

"*&%#!" some sailor said. "Get on with it! What about the horses?"

"I'm gettin' to it. Just calm yourself," Rawhide Robinson said. "Now, where was I? Anyways, I loosened the cinch and pulled the bridle off that horse so he could graze on that tender grass that was brushing his belly — I weren't afeared of him goin' anywhere as there wasn't anywhere to go — and propped myself against the trunk of a tree to take in the scenery and maybe inspect the insides of my eyelids for leaks.

"As I studied the mountainsides around that valley, I got to noticing my horse wasn't the only one of his kind thereabouts. I counted twenty, maybe twenty-five head of equines on them slopes. There might have been more, but they wasn't all that easy to see on account of their hides were of a mousy blue-gray grulla color that blended right in with them granite mountains.

"Being an aficionado of horseflesh, I thought I'd catch me up one of them animals to add to my string. So, I pulled my rope off the saddle and set out to sneak up on and snare one. They was a bit skittish, but I managed to work my way close to one. But, soon as I got a lariat's length away, that horse took off, mane and tail unfurled like a flag. Same with the next one, and the next one. I parked my carcass on a rock and watched them for a while, determined to determine where I might set a trap for one.

"As I got to studyin' them steeds I saw the darndest thing I ever did see when it comes to horseflesh."

Again the cowboy paused, much to the chagrin of the spectators, and moseyed — taking his own sweet time about it — to the coffee urn for a refill. Prodded by the protestations of his audience, he eventually settled into his accustomed squat against the bulkhead, relaxed into the rocking of the ship on the sea, and continued.

"Them horses, see, was so accustomed to living on them steep slopes that the legs on one side of them — the uphill side — was shorter than the legs on the other side — the downhill side."

93

"Oh, pshaw!" came a protest.

"Twaddle!" came another.

And, "Nonsense!"

And again, "Baloney!"

"Balderdash!"

"Bosh!"

The cowboy waited for the many and varied expressions of disbelief to subside.

"It's the truth, boys, as sure as I'm sittin' here. Them horses was so accustomed to them slopes and sidehills they adapted themselves to the terrain. And, watching them, I can tell you there ain't never been no horse nowhere as well adjusted to their occupation as them Sierra sidehill horses. They could scurry around the slopes so fast you couldn't keep up on three regular horses. They was surefooted as a spider on a ceiling — never a misstep, never a slip, never a slide. Now and then I'd spook a bunch of them with no thought but to admire their locomotion.

"They could angle up, they could angle down, they could circumnavigate the mountain so fast they was back before you even knew they were gone. Around and around and around they'd go, up and down and around.

"But then I got to noticing that while there were horses going both directions, each horse could only go one way, depending on which way his legs was built. If he wanted to get somewheres behind where he was, he'd have to go clear around the mountain to get there — which didn't amount to much difficulty for them, on account of they was so quick about it.

"Watching them like that, I figured out how to go about gettin' a loop on one of them — I set me a trap. What I did was, I spooked a bunch of them around the mountain on a downhill course and whilst they was goin' 'round the other side I hid out in a cluster of rocks above where I figured they'd pass by when they came back. I shook out a loop and waited about two beats of a bat's wing and lo and behold, here they come.

"I backhanded as fine a hooleyann as ever you did see and that loop settled around the neck of the horse I was aiming for. I pulled up the slack and scrambled out of that rockpile, wrapped that rope around my backside, dug in my heels and sat on it. That horse dragged me a rod or two before givin' it up and I drove him on down the slope to the meadow — took us two trips around the mountain to do it, but by the time we did it I had him broke to lead.

" 'Tweren't no trouble at all, till we got to

the bottom."

Yet again, Rawhide Robinson paused in his peroration. And again, the assembled sailors protested until he resumed.

"Boys, you can imagine what the problem was. Surefooted as that Sierra sidehill horse was on the slopes, he was as useless as a whistle on a plow when on flat ground. Couldn't stay upright at all. Soon as he'd take a step, why, he'd tip right over!"

"So what did you do?" came a query.

"Well, there weren't nothin' I could do, except slide that steed over against a slope where he could stay upright. Then I swatted him on the rump with my thirteen-gallon hat and, with a tear in my eye, watched him tear across that sidehill slick as a trout in a water trough."

"So what you're saying, cowboy," one of the sailors said, "is that these Sierra sidehill horses you bragged on so much is basically useless."

"Oh, you'd think so. But I've thought about it and think not," Rawhide Robinson said.

"Well, what are they good for, then?"

Rawhide Robinson tipped his hat back and adopted a more serious demeanor.

"I aim to go back there. I aim to catch me up another one of them Sierra sidehill horses — one that goes around the mountain to the left. Then, I'll catch me one that travels right. Then, I'll hitch them together nice and tight. That way, they'll prop each other up on the short side, you see.

"Between the two of them, they'll be as good as three ordinary horses."

Silence permeated the mess as the sailors cogitated on the thought. Then, as if on cue, a chorus of perfectly synchronized voices erupted with a voluble and vociferous "@*#&$%!"

CHAPTER ELEVEN

After a month at sea — more or less, as he had given up any attempt to differentiate the stultifying sameness of days — Rawhide Robinson was hungry. Oh, not that there wasn't plenty to eat aboard the USS *Cordwood.* The stores were well stocked, the galley always busy, and tables in the mess laden with food.

Accustomed as he was to the monotony of chuckwagon and bunkhouse food — beef and bacon, biscuits and beans, with the occasional addition of raisins in huckydummy or with rice in spotted pup, and the rare dried apple pie — he had to admit seafaring fare offered more variety.

There were salt pork and salt beef by the barrel. Peas, pickles, and potatoes. Rice. Cheese. The occasional onion or turnip. Sauerkraut. And, an offering not available — even banned — on a cattle drive or at the ranch, a daily dose of stimulating spirits in the form of a rum ration.

Still, shipboard sustenance, all boiled to mush, was — and Rawhide Robinson mined the hollows of his mind for the right word — bland. Or was it banal? Humdrum, perhaps? Or insipid? In the end, he opted for plain dull.

For despite the monotony of the cowboy menu, the cook — call him cookie, coosie, cocinero, sourdough, dough belly, dough roller, dough wrangler, biscuit shooter, belly cheater, bean master, sop n' taters, hash slinger, pot rustler, or kitchen mechanic — knew, without fail, his way around a chili pepper. Ranch and chuckwagon fare, having originated in Texas and the Southwest where Mexican cuisine was common, involved piquant peppers and assorted south-of-the-border seasonings that added vim and vigor. The resultant cowboy palate — those parts of it not perpetually scorched by repeated applications of hot peppers — appreciated flavorsome fare.

And so Rawhide Robinson, sitting and stirring a bland bowl of boiled something or other whilst fantasizing about chili stew, welcomed the interruption when Ensign Ian Scott stormed into the mess.

"Come along, Mister Rawhide! There's something you must see!"

The cowboy put the quirt to shank's mare and hastened after the excited officer, wondering what unlikely image interrupted the endless sea. As he followed young Ian forward (or fo'ard, in sailor speak), he saw a smudge on the horizon. Two of them, in fact, rising from the water.

"What is it?"

"The Strait of Gibraltar!"

"I see," Rawhide Robinson said. He had read of the place somewhere, sometime, but his knowledge of it would not fill half a page in the tiny tally book in his vest pocket. "What about it?"

"It's the entrance to the Mediterranean Sea!"

Rawhide Robinson attempted to muster some excitement at the announcement, but his blank look informed the ensign that a modicum of education was in order.

"You see that pinnacle starboard off the bow? That's the Rock of Gibraltar. Europe! The other eminence, to port, is a mountain called Jebel Musa. That's in Africa!"

"I see," the cowboy said, his interest piqued. He tipped back his thirteen-gallon hat and said, "I'm sure there's a story about that."

"Many, many tales," Ensign Ian gushed. "The Strait has a long and storied history in seafaring lore. The Greeks, who knew the Strait from the opposite side, said the god Hercules pried the Atlas Mountains apart there. They called the Rock and Jebel Musa the Pillars of Hercules."

"Must have been something, this fellow Hercules."

"Indeed. There are books written about his escapades — not so different from yours, I may say. They say Hercules posted a notice at the pillars warning off ships: 'Nothing lies beyond,' he said. You see, the Greeks believed the Strait marked the end of the earth. The Romans thought so, too, designating the Strait on their charts as the entrance to Hades."

"I can see that, given the nature of the scenery I've seen these past weeks," the cowboy said. "Seemed like Hades in more ways than one."

"Well, we'll soon be in different waters. I had better get busy. Preparations are already underway."

"Preparations? What preparations? Why not just sail right through?"

"With luck, that's what we will do. But it can be treacherous. The Strait is narrow — barely eight nautical miles in places. And the steep sides of Europe and Africa funnel the winds through there at high speed. The current, too. We'll hold to the center, where the water tends to flow eastward, as much as we can. But, unless I miss my guess, there will be winds to deal with."

Ensign Ian Scott's prediction proved prescient. While the USS *Cordwood* was able to find favorable current flowing eastward, a stiff wind from the Mediterranean roared through the Strait. Once the sails and course were set and the sailors well situated to carry out their assignments, Ensign Ian rejoined the spectating cowboy in the wind-whipped fo'c'sle (which Rawhide Robinson, prior to his shipboard schooling in sailor lingo, read in books as "forecastle" and incorrectly iterated each and every syllable).

From his station, the cowboy and his companion could observe the action on the ship and enjoy an unobstructed view of the approaching Strait.

"As you have no doubt observed over the passing weeks, Mister Robinson, a sailing ship usually moves forward by sailing somewhat side to side; crossing at an angle, repeatedly, the desired direction."

"Well, I did wonder about all the wandering, but I never could make no sense of it. 'Course one direction seemed as good as another on all this water. Worse than trying

102

to trail cattle across the empty plains in Indian Territory, where everything looks alike. So, if weren't for the sun you could go 'round and around in circles and not even know it. I guess I figured it was the same with you-all — you were trying to keep the ship on the trail, but kept losing it."

As the winds picked up, the ship angled into it, then later came about to take on the opposite angle. "Not quite, sir," the ensign said. "It's the wind, not the sea. Seldom does it blow steady in the direction you wish to sail, allowing you to 'run with the wind' as we say. So it is necessary to 'tack' — set the sails and rudder so the wind pushes the ship in the general direction of travel. You sail at that angle for a time, then use the rudder and set the sails to turn the ship; still in the general direction of travel, but angling across it in the opposite direction from before."

Rawhide Robinson lifted his lid and scratched his head and contemplated the notion of tacking. "I reckon I can see how it works. You could trail a beef herd the same way, but it would take a whole lot longer to get where you was goin'."

"True enough. But with a sailing ship, there's no alternative to tacking. Often the only way to get where you're going is to go what seems the wrong way, as the alternative is going nowhere."

Again, the cowboy contemplated the finer points of seamanship as the ship once again changed its tack. "How do you know when to turn?"

"Experience. Seamanship. It's what makes a man a sailor. Captain Clemmons excels at the art. Sailing into the wind, as we are, requires a master's hand. The idea is to close haul as much as possible —"

"Haul?"

Scott kneaded his chin as he considered a translation. "Heading up into the wind is most difficult. As the ship changes tack, it reaches a point where the wind is straight on and the sails are useless. 'In irons,' we call it, or in the 'no-go zone.' If the ship isn't moving fast enough to maintain momentum through the zone, you're dead in the water. So, the angle of your tack is critical. 'Close hauling' means sailing into the wind at the sharpest angle possible while maintaining enough speed to tack through the no-go zone."

Rawhide Robinson screwed his hat down tight in the ever-increasing wind and spread his legs to maintain balance in ever-rougher seas. Boiled mush sloshed around inside like the waves outside. "Don't sound none too easy," he said, swallowing hard in an attempt to counterattack the rising contents of an uneasy stomach.

"It isn't. But Captain Clemmons will get us through."

And indeed he did.

Later, in the calmer waters of the Mediterranean, weary sailors relaxed on deck. Rawhide Robinson sat with them, as still as possible, as his stomach had yet to recover from the high winds and rough water of the recent passage. Impressed though the rest of him was with the majesty of the Strait of Gibraltar, his digestive system was less than enthralled.

One sailor, still mopping sweat from a sparkling brow, said, "Mighty high seas for these waters. Last time I sailed the Strait, the waves weren't so rough."

"Tossed us about a mite, they did," said another.

Still another said, "The wind — that &*#$ wind — liked to blow me right out of the rigging!"

The conversation turned, as such conversations often do, to recollections of past challenges equal to or greater than the recent difficulties. Rawhide Robinson heard stories of gales that shredded sails, winds that shattered masts, a wind so stiff a ship sailed backward for two days and a night, and even a questionable account of a gust that plucked the feathers from seabirds.

"Aw, shucks, boys," Rawhide Robinson said to fill a lull in the discussion. "You ain't never seen wind. I mean a *real* wind."

The cowboy's pronouncement prompted clamorous protests, culminating a collective challenge: "So tell us about a *real* wind!"

As was his custom, Rawhide Robinson, the raconteur took his time, allowing anticipation to accumulate until it turned to tension. "Here's how it happened," he said when he got around to speaking.

"I was between jobs at the time, ridin' the grub line and looking for any work that could be done horseback. Seeing no prospects in the country I was in, I set off across this empty ol' desert hopin' for a shortcut to other ranges.

"Well, it clouded over and I lost all sense of direction as you can do in empty country — or at sea, I might add. Somehow, I wandered into a part of that desert that was solid rock. Nothing but stone underfoot, and more of the same no matter where you looked. I'm telling you, boys, that place was so barren there was no sign of trees or bushes or brush or even a blade of grass. As

106

dry and barren as Lot's wife once she turned into a pillar of salt, it was."

The cowboy paused to locate a water barrel and sip a dipper full until it was empty.

"C'mon!" the sailors chorused. "Tell the story!"

"Sorry, boys. Just thinking about that place parches my gullet." He squatted against the rail and carried on. "I wandered around out there for a few days, hardly knowing up from down, let alone compass directions. Ran out of water and soon my horse and me was sufferin' from the lack. I don't know about that horse, but my tongue swelled up and felt as dry and hard as an ax handle. Hot as an oven full of biscuits, it was, even though the sun didn't show at all through them thick clouds that kept on building up and boiling around.

"About the time we was on our last legs, both me and the horse, a little breeze kicked up. Felt mighty fine, I'll tell you. But the novelty soon wore off and the breeze turned into a wind. A hot wind, that felt like it would scorch the skin right off a feller. Somehow that horse I was ridin' had sense enough to turn his head into the tempest and back up ag'in' one of the few boulders thereabouts that hadn't blowed away already.

"I'll tell you, boys, it ain't The Cowboy Way to pull leather when in fear of losin' your seat in the saddle. But I ain't ashamed to say that on that particular occasion I was grabbin' the apple, squeezin' the biscuit, chokin' the nubbin, and whatever other name you care to apply to hangin' onto the saddle horn for all I was worth. Even at that, my feet lost the stirrups and my thighs lost the swells and my backside lost the seat. So there I was, both hands wrapped around that saddle horn and holding on tight while the rest of me whipped in the wind like a flag on a mast."

Again, Rawhide Robinson paused in the telling, squatting against the rail and examining his hands — front, back, and fingernails — as if they were strangers. Or, perhaps, he was marveling at them for saving his very life that day in the wind.

Patience soon ran thin among members of the audience.

"Get on with it!"

"Say it!"

"Tell the story!"

"What happened?"

Eventually, the cowboy raised his eyes to the crowd, cocked his thirteen-gallon hat, and re-commenced the telling of the tale.

"At first, it weren't nothin' but wind. Then

dust kicked up. And dirt. And rocks. I was pelted and pummeled and pounded and thumped and thrashed till there wasn't a stitch on me. The only thing in the way of clothes I was still wearing was my hat, and that was on account of that wind kept driving it farther and farther down on my noggin till the brim was wedged ag'in' my shoulders and couldn't go no farther.

"Then, it set into raining. Leastways I guess it was rain 'cause it was wet. But it fell sideways instead of down, so not much of it ever hit the ground. Good thing, too, or it would have made a river and washed me and that horse downstream to who knows where.

"When that wind decided to let up some, my seat found the saddle again and my feet the stirrups. After that tempest died down to being but a breeze again, I ventured to work my hat back up to its accustomed place, on my head instead of my shoulders. Once I did, and the gift of sight was once again mine, what I saw was an amazement."

Again, the cowboy paused. And again, the sailors protested.

"Take it easy, boys," Rawhide Robinson said. "All in good time."

"Ain't no time like the present," a sailor said. "So get to it."

So he did.

"Well, boys — and this is the honest truth — every inch of that rock was gone. See, that wind had filled that whole valley with dirt. Soil. Must have been feet, maybe rods, thick of it."

The sailors protested (in alphabetical order):

"Balderdash!"

"Baloney!"

"Bull!"

"Bunkum!"

"Claptrap!"

"Folderol!"

"Hogwash!"

"Horsefeathers!"

"Malarkey!"

"Nonsense!"

"Rubbish!"

"Poppycock!"

"Pshaw!"

"Tommyrot!"

"Twaddle!"

The cowboy allowed the sequential dissent to run its course. Then, "I'm here to tell you, boys, it's the truth. Happened just like I said. But that ain't the best of it. Not only had that wind filled that valley right up with soil, it was already carpeted with grass!"

Again, the sailors expressed dismay.

And again, Rawhide Robinson held firm. "Absolute truth. Now, I can't say what happened. I don't know if that wind scattered seeds and that rain watered them enough to sprout, or if it blew in sod and unrolled it like a rug. Whatever happened, there I was, sittin' horseback atop a hill in the middle of what looked to be the finest cow country ever invented. Grass belly-high to my horse as far as I could see, only interrupted now and then by a lake or stream of water that wind and rain must have dumped. Truth is, boys, I had to pinch myself to be sure I hadn't died and gone to heaven."

"An unlikely place for a liar like yourself," some skeptical sailor said.

Rawhide Robinson grinned. "Be that as it may, there I was. I can see it as clear as if it was yesterday. And that, boys, is proof in the pudding that none of you knows what a *real* wind is like."

"That's it? That's all? That's the end of the story?"

"More or less. Oh, there's a little more. With the sun out and the world back on its axis, I found my way out of that valley. Rode on back to Texas and worked a deal with a cowman I knew to pasture his herd on shares. Drove a bunch up there to that valley and started us up a ranch. I'll tell you, the livin' was so good for them cows in that country they all had had twin calves come spring. And them calves put on pounds like none you ever seen and was at market weight before they was even weaned. Like I said, that place was paradise.

"But after a time, livin' easy got to be a bit dull, so I settled up with my partner, saddled up and rode off into the sunset one day, never to return."

"What did ya do next?"

"That, boys, is a story for another time," Rawhide Robinson said as he leaned against the rail, spraddled his legs before him, tipped his thirteen-gallon hat over his eyes and set into a serious bout of snoring.

CHAPTER TWELVE

Rawhide Robinson stood in the center of the busy street turning in circles and side-stepping to avoid traffic. Coaches and carts and wagons and buggies of all kinds, hauled by ponies and burros and horses and oxen and men maneuvered for position and passage. People of all sizes stepped lively, some toting burdens bigger than themselves, others with baggage and rucksacks and satchels of every shape. Velocipedes added to the traffic, their riders contributing to the babel and bedlam of hundreds, thousands, of yawping, yelling, yammering voices.

An occasional word reminiscent of the border Spanish familiar to the cowboy winged by now and then, but the language — languages — he heard were alien and exotic in his overworked ears. And what he noticed most about all the talking was that flapping hands were as much a part of it as flapping lips. Given all the gestures and gesticulations, Rawhide Robinson was of the opinion that if he bound the hands of these people they would be rendered mute.

Palermo.

That's where Ensign Ian Scott had informed him they were. And where they would be for a few days, offloading supplies from the USS *Cordwood* to help provision other naval ships that called at the busy port. According to the well-informed young officer, Palermo, on the island of Sicily, part of the Kingdom of Italy, had been an important seaport for more than 2,000 years — all of which was news to the Texas cowpuncher.

Despite the confusion and commotion, Rawhide Robinson enjoyed exploring the cosmopolitan city. Topping his list was the chuck. While its spices and seasonings were unfamiliar to his Southwestern palate, he found the food toothsome — and a welcome break from the flavorless fare he had been fed aboard ship these many weeks. Accompanying every Palermo meal were wines of sundry flavors and shades — more kinds of wine, the cowboy calculated, than there were hairs in a horse's tail.

Accompanying the city's appeal were perils. More than once, the thirteen-gallon hat atop his head came in handy as a flail to fend off pickpockets attempting to pilfer the pelf from his pants' pouches. Desperados lurking in dark alleys with their eyes on robbery hightailed it in the opposite direction upon encountering the cowboy's unholstered Samuel Colt six-shooter.

But the greatest danger, Rawhide Robinson learned, was an organized gang of criminals whose very name struck fear into the heart of every innocent on the island — *Cosa Nostra.* Members of the malicious mob, the *Mafiosi,* controlled all crime and much commerce in the city, extorting businesses, smuggling, pandering, gambling, moneylending, and — as the cowboy was to learn — kidnapping.

Warned by their officers to be ever alert, the allure of dimly lit bars in the wee hours and the influence of ever-present wine sometimes impeded the sailors' attentiveness. And so it was that Rawhide Robinson, along with the ship's officers, learned of the shanghaiing of a half-dozen sailors from the *Cordwood*'s ranks. While under the influence of spirits, it seems, six sailors were spirited away to an unidentified location for an unknown purpose.

But all was soon revealed.

As some suspected, the kidnapping was the work of the *Cosa Nostra;* its purpose, ransom for their release.

"It is best you meet the demand if you desire to again see the men alive," the ranking officer of the *Carabinieri* told Captain Howard Clemmons.

"^%@*+$!" came the vociferous reply in a cloud of pipe smoke. "What kind of lawman are you, willing to knuckle under to a gang of criminals?"

"My apologies, *signore.* But in Palermo, we learn to deal in realities. And the reality is, your *marinai,* your sailors, are in the hands of very evil men. Men whose power extends beyond this harbor, beyond this city, beyond this island."

"So?!"

"So, there is nothing to be done, *amico mio,* but pay the ransom to *La Cosa Nostra.* Even then, I fear, the result may be less than satisfactory."

The captain exhaled a contemptuous cloud of smoke into the policeman's face. "What you're saying, then, is that you and your sorry excuse for a police force will not do anything to rescue my men. Need I remind you, sir, that these men are citizens of the United States of America and in service to their country?"

"Of this I am well aware, *signore.* But, as I have said, there is nothing we can do. And,

I declare most fervently, there is nothing you can do other than as I have advised. You are dealing here with forces beyond your reckoning," the police officer said. With that, he stood, adjusted his cap, clapped his heels together, and offered the captain a salute. "And now, *Capitano* Clemmons, as I have work to do, I invite you to leave my office."

Clemmons and Major Benjamin Wayne departed and, on the street outside, met the waiting Rawhide Robinson.

"What's the word?"

Clemmons's tight-lipped reply barely contained the anger evident in his florid face. "Pay up."

The cowboy replied with wide eyes and a slack jaw.

"No help at all," Wayne said. "Says there's nothing they can do. Claims this mob or gang or whatever you care to call it is too powerful. Wouldn't be surprised if they were in league with one another."

Rawhide Robinson tipped back his thirteen-gallon hat and scratched his head, pursed his lips and furrowed his brow. "I got an idea."

"What's that?" the officers chorused.

"Don't look too noticeable-like, but there's a feller over the way leaned up ag'in' a lamp post."

After some shuffling of feet and squirming around to disguise furtive glances, Clemmons and Wayne acknowledged seeing the suspicious character.

"He showed up 'bout the same time we did," said the cowboy. "I had the sneakin' suspicion he was followin' us. Let's find out."

Clemmons said, "What you got in mind?"

"You-all head back to the ship. Unless I miss my guess, he'll follow. I'll go t'other way and slip around behind him — he'll be followin' you and I'll be followin' him. Then we'll see what happens."

With that, the cowboy crossed the street and ducked down an alley, rattled his hocks around another corner, then another and followed the narrow winding street, making his way back to the thoroughfare that led to the seaport. As he suspected, the furtive fellow formerly propped up by a lamp post lurked in the shadows and doorways, stealthily slipping along behind the captain and the major.

Rawhide Robinson was anything but unobtrusive in his cowboy regalia, but he assumed — rightly so, as events will bear out — that the villain's attention was riveted to the officers and he would not be watching his back trail.

As they neared the waterfront, the pursuer closed the distance between himself and his prey, and Rawhide Robinson did likewise, slipping up behind the mobster, prodding him in the small of the back with the barrel of his pistol.

"You hold it right there, you sniveling coyote!"

Clemmons and Wayne turned on their heels to close off any avenue of escape.

"What is it you want?" Clemmons said.

The man said nothing.

"Speak up, man!" Wayne said.

The man said nothing.

Rawhide Robinson pressed the barrel of the revolver into the man's back hard enough to cause his belly button to bulge. With that, with eyes agog and beads of sweat popping out on his forehead, he launched into a tirade of indecipherable prattle accompanied by frantic gesticulation.

"Let's take him aboard ship," Clemmons said. "We'll find someone to make sense of what he's saying."

Once they cleared the gangplank, Rawhide Robinson grabbed a fistful of the man's collar and hefted him onto a hogshead. "Now you sit there till I say you can move," he said.

Within minutes, Ensign Ian Scott appeared with a deckhand in tow, having fulfilled with his usual alacrity the assignment to find a translator.

"See what this vermin has to say," the captain said.

The multi-lingual sailor spoke.

The captured man responded with a torrent and tirade in the Italian language, again accompanied by wild waving of arms and hands. The sailor followed up with other questions, answered with more babbling and flapping.

The multi-lingual sailor spoke. "He says, Cap'n, that they got our six men locked up where we won't never find 'em, and that if we wants to see 'em ag'in, we got to pony up 6,000 *lira* — a thousand apiece."

"#&%^@★!" Clemmons said. "What's that in real money?"

The ever-well-informed Ensign Ian Scott stepped forward. "Exchange rates vary somewhat, sir, depending. But 6,000 *lira* would be somewhere in the neighborhood of 240 pounds sterling, which would amount to about eleven hundred dollars."

"Hmmmph," the captain said. With furrowed brow, he signaled Wayne and Scott and the other officers nearby to gather 'round. A steady murmur arose from the huddle as ideas were exchanged, thoughts conveyed, scenarios explored, and possibilities bandied about. Circling the circle stood a round of sailors attempting to listen in.

Meanwhile, the *Mafioso* atop the hogshead observed the officers, studied the sailors, and saw in the concentrated attention the opportunity to escape. He hopped off the hogshead and headed for the gangplank.

But what he did not see among the inattentive seafarers was Rawhide Robinson, leaning against the starboard rail and watching the detainee's every move. As soon as the captive's shoes hit the deck the cowboy snatched a lariat hanging on a nearby belaying pin, (Note: Ever since Rawhide Robinson's heroic display of reata expertise with the roping of the humpback whale's tail to free the ship from the doldrums, the sailors had taken up cowboy-style roping en masse, practicing the craft as time and circumstance permitted; therefore, reasonable facsimiles of lariats were widely available aboard the USS *Cordwood*.) shook out a loop and after a triplet of spins to build momentum, accomplished a perfect heel catch.

As he jerked his slack, the tripped-up

hostage tripped and hit the deck with a resounding thump that shivered the ship's very timbers. Before the collapsed captive caught his breath, Rawhide Robinson cast his coils over a yard arm and elevated the malefactor until he dangled, head down, above the deck, shifting in the wind. Once the would-be-escapee caught his breath, invective poured forth in a torrent. Even in his upside-down position, wild gesticulations accompanied his vociferations.

"Nice catch, Robinson," Captain Clemmons said. "Now what?"

"Well, now, Captain, I don't know what you-all have figured out with all your palavering. But I reckon if we let that feller hang there for a while, he'll calm right down and assume a more cooperative mood. Then, I'll bet you spur rowels against silver dollars we can convince him to guide us to where they got them sailors hid up."

And so it happened.

The parade, led by the bound bandit, wound through streets and alleys and walkways and lanes. The assemblage of United States Navy officers and sailors, a United States Army officer, and a Texas cowboy attracted no small amount of attention as they wended their way. Long guns bristled like porcupine quills, pistols protruded from

122

belts and holsters, and saps and belaying pins slapped palms, counting cadence as the men marched informally into the seamy side of Palermo.

The Americans all but melted into the weathered stones of the buildings lining the alleyway where their hostage, still nursing a headache, led them. He indicated a rough lumber door inset into a dim archway as the place the sailors were secreted. Captain Clemmons shoved their prisoner into the archway then retreated around the corner. Rawhide Robinson and Ensign Ian Scott hid behind the opposite side of the arch; the captain stood with Major Wayne.

Ensign Scott prodded the *Mafioso* with his rifle barrel, and, as instructed, he pounded on the door. A peephole slid open and the prisoner gave the password — under threat from the Americans that if he tried anything untoward, his next breath would be his last.

The door cracked open, then flung wide when the captain, the major, the ensign, and the cowboy burst through, shoving their captive ahead. A few sailors followed while others, assigned to watch for approaching danger, stayed as much out of sight as possible in the narrow alley.

The two guards in the room were taken

completely by surprise, raising their hands immediately in surrender. Ensign Scott herded them into a corner. Rawhide Robinson laid a boot heel into an inner door, which sprung open to reveal the snatched seamen huddled in the corner of a fetid cesspool of a room the size of a backhouse. Shading their eyes from the shaft of light streaming through the shattered door, the men blinked and squinted until the silhouette of the cowboy in his thirteen-gallon hat came into focus.

"Rawhide Robinson!" some one of them said.

"Thank goodness you found us!" said another.

"Oh, it weren't only me," the cowboy said, staring at the toes of his boots as they scratched and scraped at the cold stone floor. "The captain, and the others, they're here, too."

As if in response to the introduction, Clemmons hollered from the other room. "Let's go, men — on the double and look sharp!"

"I reckon he's right, boys," Rawhide Robinson said. "We'd best beat it back to the boat."

"Ship," Ensign Scott said from the other room.

As they made their way with haste toward the waterfront, shouts and hollers echoed through the streets and alleys as word spread among members of the outlaw gang that a business opportunity was slipping away. Running feet reverberated as the hoodlums hurriedly spread the word and rounded up their ranks to prevent their ransom from escaping.

But, within minutes, the USS *Cordwood* cast off and was underway, with its full complement of officers and crew. And as they drifted out of the harbor, unfurling sails in search of a favorable wind, the abandoned wharf teemed with tempestuous members of *La Cosa Nostra,* venting their frustration at the loss of a payday.

And, as seemed to Rawhide Robinson the norm in the port city of Palermo, the men shouted with their arms and hands as much as their voices.

"Gentlemen, we sail for Smyrna," Captain Clemmons said as the ruction receded. "Our cargo awaits!"

CHAPTER THIRTEEN

With the cargo offloaded and the decks of the USS *Cordwood* vacant, Major Benjamin Wayne pursued the completion of camel quarters with exuberance as they sailed toward Smyrna. With less than a week to complete, the work proceeded apace. The bulkheads that would enclose stalls below decks were completed, and serious construction commenced on the main deck.

Wayne and the sailor crew assigned to the task pored over the officer's carefully considered plans and detailed drawings and as the hours and days passed what could only be called a barn appeared on the main deck. Nearly sixty feet long and twelve wide, each stall in the barn included a porthole for fresh air, as well as a roof hatch that could be opened in fair weather for further ventilation.

"I do declare, Major Wayne, I ain't never seen such plush accommodations for livestock," Rawhide Robinson said. "Even fancy-bred horses don't get no better than this. I've half a mind to move in myself."

Wayne laughed, and advised that while the stable might seem fitting at present, it would be less appealing once permeated with the stench of camels.

The cowboy allowed as how that might well be the case, but that eventuality did not dampen his admiration for the dromedary lodgings. "How did you come by your understanding of what would be needed? I don't reckon I could even guess how to care for camels on a boat."

Ensign Ian Scott, standing nearby, reminded Rawhide Robinson that the appropriate terminology was "ship," not "boat."

"When assigned to this mission, I corresponded at length with counterparts in the French and English armies who had experience utilizing camels in military operations. While they offered invaluable assistance and advice in many areas, no one had experience shipping 'ships of the desert' on ships," Wayne said. "To tell the truth, Mr. Robinson, this is solely my own invention. Nothing of the sort has ever been done before, so far as I have been able to ascertain. It may well prove to be misguided and wrong in every respect."

Rawhide Robinson tipped back his thirteen-gallon hat and contemplated the construction. "I don't believe that will be the case," the cowboy said. "Looks to me like the camels ought to be content so long as their bellies are full."

"I surely hope so. If they are agitated or upset in transit, it could prove unfavorable to their health — and ours. I can only imagine — but imagine I have, from every angle I can come up with — what might happen if a herd of angry camels broke out and rampaged around the ship at sea. I'm not a navy man, but I suspect a mutiny would be a more inviting prospect."

Ensign Scott said, "Mister Rawhide. Major Wayne, follow me to starboard if you will. The men have informed me there's something you might like to see."

And, indeed, it was something to see.

Across a wide expanse of the Mediterranean Sea, fish were flying out of the water and sailing across the sky, slicing back into the sea to rise again, wings unfurled. Several members of the crew lined the rail, entranced. Likewise, the cowboy and army officer.

"What on earth. . . ." Major Wayne whispered.

"*Cheilopogon heterurus.* Mediterranean Flying Fish," the encyclopedic ensign said.

"I have never seen anything like it," Wayne said.

"They are of the family Exocoetidae, and one of many varieties of flying fish," Scott said. "Representatives exist in the warmer waters of most all the oceans."

"Fish with wings. Who'd have thought . . ."

"Actually, sir, the wings are enlarged pectoral fins. That, and other adaptations in the fishes' physical makeup, allow it to lift off the surface and glide for half a minute or more."

"If Rawhide Robinson here had told me such a thing, I'd have written it off as one of the cockamamie tales he regales the sailors with. By the way, Robinson, have you ever seen flying fish before?"

"Only once," the cowboy said with a sly smile, "when I was riding horseback to Hawaii."

Silence hung heavy in the air as the major, the ensign, and every sailor in the vicinity considered the cowboy's claim. He allowed them to contemplate for a time, then continued. "That's an experience I'll have to tell you about sometime. One thing's for sure, though. There's plenty of strange critters on this here earth. Critters with wings that fly, fins that swim, legs that walk, bellies that crawl — why, I've even seen creatures with wheels!"

Flying fish forgotten, the assembled crowd launched a chorus of complaints concerning the veracity of the cowboy's claim. In further discussion, they concurred there were numerous examples of flying, swimming, walking, creeping, and crawling creatures. But the skeptical congregation drew the line at rolling.

"I tell you, it's true!" Rawhide Robinson said.

"Couldn't be!"

"No way!"

"Not a chance!"

"Can't happen!"

So came the replies, along with others unsuitable for repetition. These men were, after all, sailors — famous for a vocabulary as rich as it is rude, coarse, vulgar, impolite, ill-mannered, unrefined, and uncouth.

Rawhide Robinson stuck to his guns. "I've seen it, I tell you, with my own eyes."

"Where?"

"When?"

"How?"

And other such questions rained down.

"You-all calm down some and I'll tell you about it," he said. "Somebody get me a cup of coffee, if you please. On second thought, make it cool water. There's parts of this story that get a man mighty hot."

Following irrigation of his vocal cords and a suitable interval, the cowboy set the scene. "How many of you boys has ever seen a prairie fire?"

A few sailors with roots in the heartland allowed they had.

"Then you-all know what kind of catastrophes one of them conflagrations can cause. Smoke and flames and heat that'll melt the spots off a pinto pony. And them fires move across the prairie faster than a hot Bowie knife through bear grease. Why, you can't believe the country they'll consume.

"As that French feller François de La Rochefoucauld wrote, 'Neither love nor fire can subsist without perpetual motion.' Now, I won't offer an opinion so far as love is concerned, but that Frenchie sure had it right with brush and grass fires. They've got to keep moving to keep burning, and the more they burn the faster they move. And when a wind comes up, like it 'most always does on the plains, that only makes it worse."

"Hold it right there, cowboy!" some sailor said. "What's that you said about some Frenchman?"

"It don't make no never mind. I mention him as the author of a few words of wisdom wrenched from the recesses of my mind to support a point."

"Yeah, but what was his name?"

Ensign Ian Scott jumped into the conversation. "François de La Rochefoucauld. A French writer. Not that it matters, sailor. Let Mr. Rawhide share his story!"

"Yes!" came the call from the chorus of seafarers.

"Well, here's the deal. One time I was punching cows for this high-plains outfit with range in parts of three states. So I can't say for sure which political subdivision was the site of this particular inferno. Like as not, it scorched shrubs and torched grass in all three states. And, the way it was moving, it may well have burned on into several more.

"Anyhow, I was ridin' circle and pushing strays back toward the home range when I seen this curtain of smoke on the horizon. I knew it was trouble, as it stretched side to side far as I could see. Before I could say 'Holy smokes!' the flames peeked over the horizon, chasin' sparks into the sky and eatin' grass off the ground faster'n a gaggle of Canada geese.

"Now, as you would expect, that fire swept

every critter right off the range ahead of it. As I sat there takin' in the sight, jack rabbits started hopping past. Here come whole herds of deer, bunches of buffalo, a passel of elk, a band of wild mustangs, gangs of antelope, and whole herds of cattle. Even little critters was high-tailing it out of there — prairie dogs and pocket gophers, packrats and grasshoppers. And there was every kind of bird you can imagine winging its way away from the flames. There was crows and kestrels, meadowlarks and mourning doves, cedar waxwings and sandhill cranes, burrowing owls and barn swallows. I swear, boys, I even saw a rare loggerhead shrike — more commonly known on the plains as the butcher bird — fly by."

Sailor and officer alike sat riveted to Rawhide Robinson's every word, the fascination with flocks of flying fish forgotten in the intensity of his tale.

The cowboy sipped some more water, removed his thirteen-gallon hat and used his bandana to mop sweat from his brow — perspiration prompted, no doubt, by the recollection of heat from the flames stirred up by his story.

"Now, that's all well and good, so far as critters with legs and wings and such go. But what about them that creep and crawl and slither and slink? Now, I ain't no fan of rattlesnakes, but the fact is the plains are plenty plentiful with them castanet carriers and if you're going to be spending time out there, you got no choice but to put up with them. And the very thought of acres and acres of torched prairie eels is enough to put a feller off his feed.

"As it turns out, I needn't have worried."

Again, Rawhide Robinson paused in his telling to pat his pate dry and run water down his throat.

Again, he allowed the lapse to extend until tension in the crowd was palpable. Crumbling under the pressure, the sailors and officers protested.

"Get on with it!"

"And then?"

"Tell the tale!"

"What happened next?"

And so on.

The cowboy mopped and sipped another time, then talked on.

"Them snakes can't fly, as you know. They can't walk, neither, seeing as how they lack legs. They can slither along plenty fast, as you're sure to learn should one ever take after you or if you try to chase one down. But that sort of locomotion — a word I lately picked up from Major Wayne, by the way — is only good for short distances, and not much help when it comes to avoiding fangs of fire on the prairie.

"So them snakes found another way. At first, I didn't know what I was seeing. Then, I didn't believe what I was seeing. But I'll swear to it as sure as seawater's salty that I seen what I saw.

"And what I saw was wheels."

A collective gasp rose from the assembled crowd with an intake of air so intense it temporarily luffed the sails on the USS *Cordwood*'s masts.

"When I saw the first one of them wheels rolling toward me, I thought maybe somebody in a buggy or wagon was whippin' up the team to escape the flames, hit a prairie dog hole, and jarred loose a wheel.

"But then I saw another one coming. And another. Then another. And still another. Then more. And more. And still more. Pretty soon, there was wheels rolling across that prairie right and left. And they came in all sizes. Some big, some little. Some large, some small. Some short, some tall.

"They was snakes, boys. Snakes. Not only rattlesnakes, but rat snakes, bull snakes, garter snakes, brown snakes, copperhead snakes, bull-nosed snakes, water snakes, glossy snakes, coachwhip snakes, racer

135

snakes, black-head snakes, king snakes, red-bellied snakes, ring-necked snakes, green snakes, king snakes, milk snakes, worm snakes, and all kinds of other snakes I had never seen before nor seen since. And they kept on wheelin' and rollin' and rollin' and wheelin' right along.

"It was obvious what they had done — when they saw they couldn't slither away from them flames, they swallowed their tails and wriggled their way upright and commenced to roll. Worked right well, too. They was outrunning that fire in fine fashion."

Rawhide Robinson rose from his squat against the starboard rail and moseyed over to the water bucket for a refill. After refreshing his parched palate, he feigned surprise at seeing the crowd still assembled. "That's it, boys. That's the story. If you ain't inclined to believe it" — his surmise based on the befuddled looks on the sailors' faces — "I can only say it's as true as any word I've ever spoken. And should you ever find yourself on the high plains out West, you'll notice for yourselves that there are plenty of snakes slinking about, which fact only signifies the accuracy of my account."

"It ain't that, cowboy," some sailor said.

Said another, "Whether your story is true or not, it ain't over."

Now it was Rawhide Robinson's turn to look befuddled. "Whatever can you mean?"

Several sailors spoke at once, rendering Rawhide Robinson helpless to ravel out the thread of the question from the tangle. "Hold on, boys! You can't all talk at once and expect me to hear what you're saying."

One raised his arms, signaling the others to silence. "Here's the thing," he said when he had calmed the crowd. "You left yourself out there on the prairie with that fire bearing down on you. How did you escape incineration?"

"Oh, that," the cowboy said. He tipped back his thirteen-gallon hat and continued. "Well, I had sat there dumbstruck over what was happening for so long that there wasn't any way I was going to be able to ride out of there — even if the horse I was ridin' was a fast one, which he was.

"So I rode to the top of a little rise — you couldn't call it a hill, as there weren't any hills in that country — to wait. When that fire's flames started lickin' at the grass close by, I took down my lariat and shook out a loop. I spun it overhead, feeding it more slack with every turn. Once it got to a sufficient size, I spun out the spoke to turn it to a flat loop and let it drop down close to the ground around me and my horse.

"Then it was a matter of spinning it faster and faster and faster until it whipped up a wind like one of them tornado twisters. That blasting breeze beat back the flames, and held off the heat while I increased the velocity of the rotation till I feared the centrifugal — or is it centripetal? — force would rip my arm right off. But, it didn't — only stretched it out six inches or so. Took seven months, two weeks and four days to shrink back to its normal size, by the way."

"Get on with it!" an impatient seaman said.

"Well, boys, as it happened me and that horse lifted off the earth and rode the vortex of my reata tornado to safety."

With that, raconteur Rawhide Robinson rambled down the nearest hatch, leaving the skeptical sailors scratching their heads and discussing, debating, and disputing the truthfulness of the tale.

Despite the sailors' skepticism, even downright disbelief, in the days to come Rawhide Robinson could not help but notice length after length of shipboard rope converted to lariats, and sailors standing inside circles of hemp attempting to master the art of spinning the flat loop.

CHAPTER FOURTEEN

Whitman Fitzgerald thumbed through accumulated messages, memos, and correspondence. Paper shuffling was the bane of his diplomatic existence and one he routinely avoided. As a result, stacked sheets teetered, tottered, tipped and occasionally toppled atop his desk.

But somewhere among the heaps was a dispatch from the War Department in far-off Washington outlining details of his assignment to assist Major Benjamin Wayne of the United States Army in the acquisition of camels for shipment back to the States aboard the USS *Cordwood,* a naval supply ship under the command of Captain Howard Clemmons.

Not that he had been ignoring the assignment. Anything but. Indeed, the diplomat had pursued it with a passion, as it represented a respite from his usual duties, which were, he had long since realized, mundane.

Or did he mean humdrum? Monotonous, perhaps? Prosaic, pedestrian? Tedious? Tiresome?

Whatever label one chose to attach to the attaché's responsibilities, they were far from exciting. Fitzgerald experienced none of the intrigue, the excitement, the dash and daring, the negotiation and mediation he anticipated when joining the diplomatic corps those many years ago. Instead, here he was assigned to Smyrna. Once an important crossroads in the sprawling Ottoman Empire, a busy seaport linking east to west, Smyrna, like the empire of which it was a part, was past its prime. Much like himself, Fitzgerald realized.

Still, it was a busy place, in terms of trade if not international diplomacy. Its markets were abuzz with business — including the buying and selling of camels. Beasts from throughout the Levant found their way there — whether arriving solely as items of commerce, or in caravans and sold off along with the trade goods they carried. Both dromedaries and Bactrians frequented the sale rings and auction blocks and anyone in need of a camel was easily accommodated.

But assembling a herd suitable for use by the United States Army was no simple task. Fitzgerald, unlike most everyone else in government service aware of the scheme, did not scoff at its prospects. His time at various locations in Levantine cities left him with an appreciation for the abilities of the camel. If properly chosen, trained, and handled, he had no doubt the ungainly beasts of burden would serve the intended purpose of packing supplies across the Southwestern deserts of North America with the same flawless performance they provided in this part of the world.

"Aha!" With the desired document in hand, he dashed from his cluttered closet of an office and hustled off to the corner café to meet his friend Hayri. The Turk's very name — Hayri — meant "helpful man," and it was a moniker well chosen. While yet a young man, Hayri's long years of experience with camels suited him to the task of filling the Army's order.

"I have it!" Fitzgerald said, waving the paper overhead as he hurried across the street and took a seat at Hayri's table. A waiter arrived at the table as soon as the attaché, placing a cup of rich, sweet coffee before him.

"Teşekkür ederim," Fitzgerald said.

"Despite your years among we Turks, your accent remains atrocious," Hayri said with a smile. "A simple 'thank you' in English would be more easily understood than your attempt at Turkish."

Fitzgerald smiled. "Elementary diplomacy," he said. " 'Make every attempt to honor local culture wherever assigned, including obtaining a facility with the language sufficient for everyday use,' I believe is how our government puts it in the handbook."

"My friend, there is wisdom in what your government advises. But 'facility with the language' seems beyond your grasp." Again, the Turk's face widened in a smile. "It can be said that your abuse of our tongue has the opposite effect of what your handbook anticipates."

Smoothing the paper on the table before him, Fitzgerald skimmed its contents. "Between thirty and forty," he said. "That's how many camels the War Department thinks they will need. The actual count will be contingent on how many animals the ship can accommodate." He patted his suit jacket over the outside and inside pockets in an attempt to locate the telegram, then reached under the lapel to pull it from the inside pocket. With a snap of the wrist, the diplomat unfolded the sheet and said, "Says here the *Cordwood* has sailed from Palermo. We've got less than a week."

"It will be no problem, my friend. I have already identified more than twenty animals. We can easily fill out the remainder of the order in a matter of days."

"What about handlers?"

"That has proven more of a challenge. Many of the most accomplished are reluctant to leave our civilized homeland for the wilds of the American West."

"Uncle Hayri —" The soft voice came from a young girl crouched on the sidewalk not far from the table. Fitzgerald had not associated her with Hayri, who he knew to be a bachelor. The girl looked to be in her thirteenth or fourteenth year (the slip of a girl, in truth, was nearly sixteen); not yet a young woman but not far from it. Wide eyes in a lovely face framed by a head scarf, glistened with enthusiasm. "I have said to you that I will go."

"And I have said 'no' young lady. Many times. It is not to be."

"But, Uncle! You know that I know camels better than most men! I have lived among them since birth. I was practically suckled on camel milk."

"A sailing ship is no place for a young girl. And should you survive the perilous journey, living among soldiers and Indians and cowboys and other savages in the Wild West of America is no life for you."

"There are savages enough in our own country!" the girl hissed through tight lips. She grasped the tail of her scarf and flung it over her shoulder as she turned away.

Fitzgerald said, "And who might that be?"

"She is my niece. The daughter of my sister. She and her husband met with an unfortunate accident and are no longer among us. The girl is in my care — a temporary arrangement, until a more suitable accommodation can be made."

"What happened to her parents?"

Hayri leaned closer and lowered his voice. "I called it an accident, but it was not. What she said about camels is true. Her father was a trader, and ran caravans to far countries. His wife, my sister, and the girl accompanied him on every journey. As they embarked on their most recent journey, the caravan was set upon by thieves at their first stopping place. All were killed except Huri. Her mother hid her under a bush before she, herself, was ravaged and killed in a most savage manner. Huri witnessed things no girl should see."

"Huri? That is her name?"

"Yes. Huri. It means 'angel' in our language."

144

"Huri. Hayri. Her name is much like your own."

The Turk laughed. "Only when spoken by one whose accent is as atrocious as your own."

A shadow fell across the table. Fitzgerald looked into the sun to see the silhouette of a pear-shaped man. Beside him, but a step behind, stood a giant of a man who showed little of his face through a thick, coarse beard. Huri crouched even lower. Hayri scraped his chair across the patio's paving stones, sliding it away from the glare of the sun.

"Hasan," he said, with no hint of greeting in his voice. "What brings you here?"

"It is with the American I wish to speak."

Hayri, with raised eyebrows, raised a palm and gestured toward the diplomat. Fitzgerald nodded.

"At the markets, there is word that you are acquiring camels. A significant number of them, I am told."

Fitzgerald nodded.

"I am a trader. I deal in many goods and services. Including camels."

"Yes?"

"I can supply all the animals you need. Superior creatures, all. And at a fair price."

With a nod across the table, Fitzgerald

145

said, "I appreciate your interest — Hasan, is it? — but Hayri here is already at work filling the contract."

Hasan laughed. "You have made a poor decision, sir. This man knows nothing of camels. I can assure you that he will provide only inferior animals."

Again, Hayri's chair scraped across the stones, this time as he stood. The chair tipped over with a clatter. The huge man stepped forward. Hasan laid a hand on his chest and said, "Not now, Balaban. Not now." He looked at the American. "Remember my offer, Mr. Fitzgerald." His eyes shifted toward Hayri and narrowed in a wicked glare. "And my warning." The fat man and the giant walked away.

"Who on earth was that?"

Hayri righted his chair and sat. "Hasan is nothing but trouble. He intimidates and bullies his way into every commercial transaction he hears about. And he hears about most of them, through a network of spies and informants who haunt the markets. To say he is less than honest are the kindest words with which I can describe his way of doing business."

"And the other?"

"Balaban. He is Hasan's protector, as well as enforcer. His name means 'giant' and you can see he is well suited to it. But the evil inside the man far surpasses his body in size."

Throughout the altercation, Huri crouched ever lower, as if trying to melt away into the stone pavement. Her eyes glistened with tears that would not fall.

CHAPTER FIFTEEN

Despite hints of an Aegean Sea breeze sifting through the portholes in Captain Clemmons's office aboard the USS *Cordwood,* the room was close. Suffocating smoke from the captain's pipe irritated Rawhide Robinson's eyes and prompted an occasional cough from Ensign Ian Scott. The miasma he created seemed not to affect Clemmons at all, as it did not keep him from dozing, awakening only when his chin bounced off the hollow between his collar bones.

"Work on the stables is essentially complete," Major Benjamin Wayne reported to the small audience. "In addition to the camels, we will, of course, be loading sufficient fodder for the animals. Sacked grain will be easily stored. Hay will have to be stacked and stuffed into every available cranny and crevice."

Clemmons did not raise his head, but his eyes popped open to look through his brow at Wayne. "You will rely on Ensign Scott for guidance as to that. I will not allow you to create a fire hazard aboard my ship."

"The way I figure it, the camels will need approximately eleven to twelve tons of hay, assuming a ten-week passage."

Clemmons turned his attention to the junior officer. "Mister Scott?"

The young ensign reddened, embarrassed at his unlikely lack of a ready answer. "I am not familiar with the transport of loose animal fodder in quantity. I will make some calculations."

Scott's florid complexion deepened when Rawhide Robinson said, "Why, Ensign Ian! I declare that is the *onliest* thing I ever heard of that you don't know!"

"I suspect we all have much to learn concerning camels and their provender."

Major Wayne slapped the desk and said, "Right you are! My hope is the learning process will be a rapid one. If the advance preparations ordered by the War Department have been carried out, it should be."

Rawhide Robinson hefted a booted foot, grabbed it by the ankle and propped it atop a knee. "So it all depends on this feller in Smyrna with two last names, then?"

"Not altogether. But my superiors in Washington arranged with the Department of State to have their man in Smyrna, Whitman Fitzgerald — two last names, if you will — to assist us. He has been apprised of our anticipated arrival by wire from Palermo. My hope is that he will have already made arrangements with reliable camel merchants to hasten our acquisitions."

"You are aware, Major, that the people you will be dealing with are likely experienced and sharp traders and will drive a hard bargain," Clemmons said.

"I have been so informed. But I trust they will know better than to attempt to take advantage of the government of the United States of America."

Clemmons laughed. "These people don't give a fig about the United States of America. They've been running this part of the world and controlling trade between East and West for centuries. According to their way of thinking, our nation hasn't been around long enough to matter. Be that as it may, if you negotiate well, they will treat you fairly for the most part. Haggling is an art to them. Not only a way of doing business, but a source of enjoyment as well. Your man Fitzgerald should know the ropes if he has been here a while."

"That he has. And we will rely on him if

necessary. But, as I said before, I believe we can negotiate favorably on behalf of our government."

Clemmons only smiled and emitted a final exhalation of fetid tobacco smoke.

"That's all, gentlemen," Wayne said.

Rawhide Robinson took Scott by the elbow and suggested they go topside for some fresh air. From the ship's rail, they watched the Gulf of Smyrna slide by and the seaport city of Smyrna, the most important trade center of Asia Minor, draw near.

"What about this place, Ensign Ian? It amount to much?"

"Indeed it does, Mister Rawhide. As Captain Clemmons suggested, it has been an important trading center for many hundreds of years. It's even mentioned in the Bible — Book of Revelations, if I recall correctly."

"Who lives here? Arabs?"

"Smyrna's longevity and trade networks give it a cosmopolitan population, I am told and have read."

"Cosma-who-litan?"

Ensign Ian grinned. "Cosmopolitan. It's a fancy word that means nationalities don't count for much — 'citizens of the world,' so to speak. Turks, Greeks, Armenians, Jews and others have resided here for centuries.

151

Many others come from many places to trade, both overland and by sea — from Egypt, Arabia, Palestine, Persia, the Caucasus, Hindustan — as I said, many places."

"What sort of stuff do they trade for here?"

"Carpets. Wool. Textiles. Tobacco. Timber. Figs. Raisins. Rice. Spices. Pottery. Olive oil. Opium. Barley. Leather. Cheese. You name it."

"Camels," the cowboy said.

"Camels — let's hope so."

The sailors scrambled about the deck and masts, preparing to heave to and drop anchor in the harbor. Those maneuvers completed, Major Wayne, Rawhide Robinson, and Ensign Ian Scott boarded a boat to be rowed ashore.

"I reckon by now everybody has seen the Stars and Stripes and knows the Americans are in town," Rawhide Robinson said.

"I imagine so," Wayne said. "I hope Fitzgerald is among them and will meet us."

The boat tied up at the quay and the men scrambled up a ladder. Before their legs stopped wobbling on unaccustomed firm ground, a hefty man approached, pushing his way through the busy seaport traffic, ordering others aside and out of his way. Three camels followed, led by a man as large as any the Americans had ever seen.

The portly fellow eyed the arrivals and approached Major Wayne — whose resplendent full-dress uniform signaled his importance — touched fingertips and palms together and bowed.

"Welcome, *beyefendi* — sir. Hasan Hussein at your service," he said, and bowed again. "May I have the pleasure of knowing your name?"

"Major Benjamin Wayne. United States Army."

"Thank you, Benjamin *bey.*"

"How can I help you, Mister — Hasan, is it?"

"No, no, no, no, no, no, Benjamin *bey*! It is I who can help you."

"Oh? How's that?"

"I am told you are in the market for camels." Hasan turned, bowed, and with a smile and sweep of his arm toward the three camels, said, "As you can plainly see, I have camels!"

Again, quayside traffic parted as a silver-haired man in European-style business attire forced his way through, followed by a younger man in local dress, followed by a girl wearing a head scarf.

"Let me pass!" the older man shouted. "Make way!" When at last he broke through to reach the Americans, he presented a sheaf of papers to Major Wayne. "Major Benjamin Wayne, I presume. I am Whitman Fitzgerald of the Department of State of the United States of America. You are expected, sir, and I believe you are expecting me."

"Indeed we are, Mister Fitzgerald."

Fitzgerald turned to Hasan and said, "What is going on here? Hasan, what are you up to?"

With a bow, Hasan said, "Merely doing business. Or, it is more correct to say, offering a gift of these three camels to Benjamin *bey* with the hope that he will engage my services in the acquisition of other camels he may require."

"Nonsense! Your services are not required!"

The Americans on the wharf looked like the pendulum on a clock as their attention shifted from one disputant to the other, occasionally interrupting the rhythm to cast a glance at the giant controlling the camels. As if his hulking presence wasn't intimidating enough, the glower on his brow, sneer on his lips, and anger in his eyes enhanced the menace. The fingers of his free hand tapping the jeweled handle of a lengthy dagger in the sash around his waist added to

154

his fearsome presence.

Rawhide Robinson's attention, however, was on the young girl. As the men argued, she walked among and around the three camels. She stroked their hides, patted their sides, felt their legs, examined their hooves, even peeled back their lips to look at their teeth.

Eventually, the spat reached an impasse. Hasan allowed that he, as much as anyone, had a right to do business with the Americans. Fitzgerald allowed that Hasan was a thief and that his own man, Hayri, should be trusted. Hasan allowed that Fitzgerald's prejudice against him was unfounded. Fitzgerald allowed that Hasan's reputation was well-earned and long established.

And so on.

The army officer brought the brouhaha to a halt with the announcement that the decision was his, and he was not ready to make it. "In the meantime," he said, "we will, with much gratitude, accept Mister Hasan's gift."

The girl's voice was barely more than a whisper, but somehow, some way, it sounded clear and strong, easily heard even in the cacophony of the crowded quay. "Pardon me, sir, if you please. You do not want these camels."

As if tethered together on a string, every

head snapped to attention in the girl's direction.

"Sssssssst," said Hayri, the man who came with Fitzgerald. "Be quiet, Huri!"

The girl stood silent, but firm. Rawhide Robinson tipped back his thirteen-gallon hat and grinned a grin, eager to hear what she had to say.

But it was Major Wayne who asked the question. "Whatever do you mean, young lady?"

"That one," she said, pointing to a camel, "is good. But that one in the middle is old. His teeth say he is well past his prime. Nearing forty years, I should think. And that other one is diseased. He has *surra* — a sickness from biting flies. He looks fine now, but with the *surra* he will soon grow thin and weak. Then he will die."

"The girl knows nothing!" Hasan shouted. "She is but a child!"

"I cannot offer an opinion, as such matters are beyond my experience. But Huri's uncle, Hayri" — Fitzgerald said with a nod toward the man who accompanied him — "who I know and trust, says she was raised among the beasts and knows them well. At the very least, her concerns merit an opinion by an expert with no interest in this affair."

Rawhide Robinson sidled up to Major

Wayne. "Major, I ain't never seen a camel until this very minute and ain't got no idea about them critters," he said, barely above a whisper. "But I can see that girl there knows her stuff. She's got a way with animals, for certain. If I was you, I'd listen to what she says."

Wayne, hands clasped behind his back, head bowed, forehead furrowed, contemplated the complicated circumstances. Then, "Take the camels away, Hasan. We will consider accepting your gift later."

The round man spun like a top and stomped away. The giant stared at each of the men through slitted eyes, gave Huri the same treatment for an uncomfortably long time, then led the camels away, following the wake his master left through the crowd.

CHAPTER SIXTEEN

With the departure of Hasan and his camels, Whitman Fitzgerald suggested the party retire to a corner café for refreshment and to compare notes about fulfilling the mission. Major Wayne concurred and soon Fitzgerald led the way through the crowd.

Leastways it seemed like a crowd. But it was nothing compared to what the group encountered at the bazaar. Jam-packed and pungent, the market resembled nothing like anything Rawhide Robinson had ever seen before. Brightly colored canvas awnings covered rows of stalls separated by narrow passages. They shouldered and elbowed their way through the pandemonium of sellers hawking their wares, buyers bargaining for better prices, the clang and bang and clatter and rattle of moving goods, the cackle of chickens and squawk of caged birds and gabbling of geese, the bleating of sheep and baaing of goats and bawling of

158

cattle. The stench of rotting vegetables and overripe fruit and cooked food, the sting of dung and urine, clouds of smoke from tobacco and cooking fires, a fog of sweat and spices and scents and incense.

The whole of it all overwhelmed the cowboy, accustomed as he was to a calmer existence and quieter life.

"This is smellier and noisier than a stock-yard full of mad cows!" he shouted to Ensign Ian Scott.

"What?"

"This is smellier and noisier than a stock-yard full of mad cows!!"

"What??"

"This is smellier and noisier than a stock-yard full of mad cows!!!"

The young officer shook his head, telling the cowboy with the silent gesture — the only thing that could be understood in all the uproar — that he could not hear him. Rawhide Robinson shrugged his shoulders. After a brief eternity, the group debouched into a packed public plaza that seemed calm and quiet compared to the bazaar. Fitzgerald led the group to his accustomed table at his accustomed open-air café. The diplomat, the army commander, the naval officer, and the cowboy took seats around the small table. Hayri stood to the side while

Huri knelt in the shade of a small tree.

Since introductions, formal and informal, had been left wanting at the wharf owing to the squabble with Hasan, Fitzgerald led out with a round of handshaking.

"Major Benjamin Wayne," he said. "Whitman Fitzgerald."

Then, to the naval officer, "Whitman Fitzgerald. And you are?"

"Ensign Ian Scott, United States Navy, assigned to the USS *Cordwood.*"

"Charmed, I'm sure. Whitman Fitzgerald — and you?"

"They call me Rawhide Robinson, and I reckon you can too. Mind if I shorten up our conversations some by calling you Whit Fitz? Could save us some time."

Fitzgerald swallowed his shock at the implied informality, but rightly assumed it was but a result of the cowboy's rustic background. "Whit Fitz it shall be, Mister Robinson."

"Rawhide. I don't answer to Mister."

"Right you are, then."

He introduced Hayri as a reliable guide, skilled negotiator, experienced camel handler, able acquirer of camel furniture, locator of feed and fodder in quantity, and all-around-man-for-the-job. Hayri, he said, had agreed to accompany the camels to America

160

if the army would guarantee return passage. Huri, he said, was temporarily in her uncle's care and he assured one and all she would not be in the way.

Thick coffee in tiny cups arrived, and Rawhide Robinson rolled the sugary, bitter brew around his tongue. A tray of fancy little cakes and pastries, barely a bite each, reminded the cowboy of his hunger. While the others talked, his sticky fingers made short work of the sweet treats.

Fitzgerald was curious about the political climate back home, the health of the economy, the actions of Congress, developments in the military, even the latest female fashions — that, for his wife's benefit, he said. "I have not set foot on my native soil for several years," he said. "I fear I am now more familiar with this part of the world and related international matters than domestic affairs."

Major Wayne and Ensign Scott traded turns offering facts and opinions on the state of the States. Hayri looked on in silence. Huri, from her spot in the shade, seemed unconcerned. Rawhide Robinson noticed, however, as he periodically licked his fingers and helped himself to more of the seemingly endless supply of sweetmeats, that the girl did not miss a word.

"How about you, Robinson? How do you view current affairs?"

The cowboy swallowed a mouthful of pastry, flushed it down with a swallow of coffee, tipped back his thirteen-gallon hat, hitched his thumbs in the armholes of his vest, and said, "Mostly from the back of a horse."

The State Department man looked confused.

"You asked how I view things, Whit Fitz. 'Bout the only view I've got most of the time is from my seat in the saddle on the back of a horse. Usually looking at a herd of cows. Don't pay much attention to much else."

"Surely you follow politics?"

"Cows don't much care about that stuff."

"The economy?"

"Why, sure, Whit Fitz — I always pay attention to cattle prices."

The diplomat laughed diplomatically, and Major Wayne suggested they turn their attention to the price of camels.

"Indeed. My man Hayri, here — your man, now — has been at work evaluating the market. Hayri?"

The Turk cleared his throat. "Prices now are high, I fear, for it is not the ideal season for traffic in camels."

162

As the man spoke, Rawhide Robinson noticed a man at an adjacent table set his coffee cup on the table and cock his head, turning an ear to the report. He noticed, as well, that the girl Huri noticed the eavesdropper.

Hayri said he had identified some two dozen camels as good prospects, fourteen from one camel trader and ten from another. He named the dealers, and testified as to their reliability, if not honesty. "Like any traders, these men will take any advantage offered," he said. "I will see that any advantage taken will be ours."

Ensign Scott asked about the purchase of hay and grain, and his need to determine the storage space that would be required on the USS *Cordwood* for the unaccustomed fodder. Hayri said it was a problem easily solved and he would escort the naval officer immediately to the hay market and assist with calculations.

Wayne whispered to Scott, wondering if the Turk could possibly be of any help.

"It would not surprise me in the least. Keep in mind that many algebraic equations were either invented or perfected in this part of the world," the ensign said.

Then, to Rawhide Robinson, "Let's get to it. I trust no pilfering pickpocket lifted your lariat as we passed through the bazaar."

"Got it right here," he said, fetching the coils from under his chair.

"We will use the rope as measuring device," Scott told Hayri, who nodded in agreement.

As the men readied to leave, Rawhide Robinson — and Huri — watched the erstwhile eavesdropper hurry across the square and report to Hasan's giant, who was trying to remain inconspicuous in the recesses of an arched doorway.

"That is quite the hat you wear, sir," Hayri said as he walked with Rawhide Robinson and Ensign Scott to the hay market. "Most inconvenient, I should think."

"Hmmph. This here hat — the handiwork of one John B. Stetson, by the way — serves a passel of purposes in my line of work. Where I come from, most everyone covers his head with a lid like this. They're as common back home as them upside-down flowerpots are on men's heads around here."

Hayri laughed. "Fez, we call this hat. And they have indeed become very popular of late. But tell me, what are the purposes of such a immense hat as that?"

"Light a spell and I will tell you-all about it," the cowboy said with a grin. The three men and Huri squatted in the shade of a stone wall and Rawhide Robinson held forth.

"The first thing is that a hat like this one here that I and most every cowboy out West wears is to protect me from the sun. It shines bright on the range, and in lots of places there ain't a tree within a day's ride to shade up under. Keeps the sun off my head, out of my eyes, and off my face and neck. When I take a notion to use my back for a mattress of an afternoon, I jist plop this John B. over my face and it gets as dark as night.

"And if horseback on the range when a thunder gust and gully washer shows up —"

"— A what?"

"— rainstorm — well, this here hat makes a right fine umbrella. It keeps the rain off my face and out of my eyes, and the brim funnels it away so it don't trickle down my collar. Keeps snow off of me, too, and if it gets too cold and windy on my ears, why I fold the brim down for muffs and tie it with my wild rag," the cowboy said with an instructive tug on his colorful bandana.

Hayri — and Huri and Ensign Ian Scott — were speechless.

"And that ain't the half of it. A hat like this makes for a fine bucket when you have to pack water to your horse. It's been a basket when I've picked berries for a bunk-house pie. I even used it to gather henhouse eggs when helpin' out a laid-up sodbuster and his family. It's a signal flag on a roundup, and a flag to start a Fourth of July horserace. You can fan a fire with a hat like this.

"Many's the time I've used it to flail a mad cow in the face to keep her from maulin' me. I'll use it to slap a sulky steed on the backside, lay it upside a stampedin' horse's head to get his attention, and fan a salty bronc till he bucks hisself out."

Now beyond speechless, the audience of three faces looked and listened in identical jaw-ajar enthrallment.

"Not only that, these here hats is good for sweeping — I've swept dust off a buckboard seat, snow off my saddle, and litter off a line-camp bunk. And before entering some-body's abode or calling for a young lady, I use it to beat the trail dust out of my duds."

With that, Rawhide Robinson smiled with satisfaction and tugged at the lapels of his vest. "Can that there fez coverin' your topknot do any of that?"

Hayri pulled off his fez and rotated it around, examining its every inch. "No, sir, it cannot. I confess your head covering is much superior to my own."

166

"Oh, you don't need to feel none too bad about that. Ain't nobody else the whole world over ever come up with a lid as useful as the cowboy hat. John B. Stetson is owed a place in history for the invention of it."

"It is so. To my knowledge, there is nothing to compare."

Like the Turk, the cowboy took off his hat and examined it — only in Rawhide Robinson's case, it was with admiration rather than disappointment.

"What I've told you is just the ordinary, everyday, run-of-the mill uses for my thirteen-gallon hat. It has also served me well in emergencies."

The wide eyes of his attentive audience spurred the raconteur to talk on.

"This one time — out in Wyoming Territory, it was — I was roundin' up cows on this sorry bronc that bucked for fun at every opportunity and no one else wanted to ride him. The ramrod on that outfit figured I was the man for the job. I ain't ashamed to say it, but that ewe-necked, hog-backed, mule-hipped, snipe-gutted, paddle-footed, cow-hocked, rat-tailed, pin-eared, wall-eyed, cold-jawed, hard-mouthed, widow-makin' hay burner was so contrary minded he made punchin' cows a right unpleasant business.

"Fact is, that horse bucked me off regular-like. Not only bucked me off, he pitched me so high I could see clear into next week. Thing is, I was so intent on watchin' him that I didn't pay attention to what else was goin' on around me.

"So, one day, there I was, out on the wide Wyoming plains when a storm blew in without my notice. Them clouds must have been boilin' something fierce, for when I quit watchin' that crow-bait horse's ears to have a look-see at the range thereabouts, I see one of them twisters comin' at me. That tornado was whirling and spinning and sounded like a train.

"There wasn't a thing I could do, as that sorry excuse for an equine companion got scared and sulled up and wouldn't move a muscle — he planted his hooves in that prairie grass like fence posts and the only movement he'd make was to tremble like a tot in a cold bathtub.

"Anyhow, that twister come on and plucked me out of the saddle like a ripe apple off a tree and spun me up into the sky. I tell you, I was so high in the sky that I could see stars in the middle of the day. As you might imagine, when a feller finds himself going up like that — higher and farther than he ever imagined a man could go — he gets to wondering how he's going

168

to get back down.

"Not that he has to worry about it much, you understand, as he's going to come down if he wants to or not. But, as any bronc peeler will tell you, it ain't the falling that's worrisome, it's the sudden stop at the bottom. Then that storm peeled me off like the hide off an orange and before I knew it, comin' down is what I was doing. And fast. I'll tell you, I was comin' down so fast my ears was whistling. Then I got to falling a little faster and my hat brim started to flapping and I got an idea."

Rawhide Robinson waited, as was his wont when regaling an audience, for the tension to reach the breaking point.

"What did you do?!" three voices asked at once.

(Equally enthralled, albeit unknown to the cowboy and his companions, was Balaban the giant, secreted on the opposite side of the stone wall. He bit his tongue to keep from asking.)

"Well, it was like this. I took me a firm grasp on the edges of the brim with both hands and lifted it slowly — ever so slowly — off my head, then stretched my arms up as high as I could reach. As I hoped, that hat filled up with air like a toy balloon and slowed my fall considerably. So much so that I landed right back on that bronc's back so soft and easy-like I made barely a bump."

"Saçmalık!"

"Nonsense!"

"Fasa fiso!"

And, whispered unheard on the other side of the wall: *"Zirva!"*

Rawhide Robinson grinned. "I swear it's true — every word, just as I told it! But that ain't nothin' — let me tell you about the time I got unhorsed crossing a trail herd over the Red River and I used that hat for a boat to keep from drowning —"

"Not now!" Ensign Ian Scott interrupted. "We have work to do."

CHAPTER SEVENTEEN

Rawhide Robinson, Ensign Ian Scott and Hayri huddled among the haystacks scratching figures in the dirt, sweeping them away, then scratching more. Huri lost interest in the computations and calculations and scrambled up the side of a stack of hay for a bird's-eye view of the haymarket and Smyrna's suburbs.

"I have no experience in the field of hay," the ensign said. "So I've no idea how much storage space we'll need aboard ship. We have signed a contract for the twelve tons of hay Major Wayne thinks we'll need for the camels, but I have no idea what twelve tons of hay looks like."

The cowboy offered no assistance. His experience with hay consisted of reluctantly pitching it to penned cattle on occasion. Such chores were considered farm work to top hands, and such work was refused as often as not. But, sometimes it had to be done and Rawhide Robinson was not the man to neglect a necessity where cattle and horses were concerned. Now, that sense of husbandry and responsibility extended to camels. But the numbers and formulas and equations and comparisons and conversions escaped him. Simple arithmetic he could handle. But Scott and Hayri had long since left him in the dust of their stampeding numbers.

It all started simply enough, with the ensign's request to see what a ton of hay looked like so he could establish how much space it occupied. From there, he could extrapolate storage requirements.

"It is simple," Hayri said. "Our Pasha has introduced the metric system of weights and measures in the empire, but they are not yet embraced by the people. So, I converted your units of weight, your pounds and tons, to our *kantar* and *ceki.* What you Americans call a 'ton' is roughly equivalent to four *ceki.* The purchase contract is for hay weighing forty-eight *ceki* — about twelve tons by your measure."

"But I still do not know the volume of that amount of hay, whether tons or *ceki.*"

Hayri had a haymarket attendant fork into a compact pile one *ceki* of hay then squatted in the shade of the tall haystack upon which Huri perched.

Rawhide Robinson pitched out his lariat and he and Scott stretched it taut across the length and breadth of the pile and plumbed its depth — or height — then the ensign scratched some more in the dust.

Huri watched the Americans at work and was aware of her uncle below.

But most of her attention was on Balaban. She watched the giant steal into the haymarket and slip furtively (or so he thought; to Huri, a man of such size attempting to conceal his movements seemed silly) from stack to stack, sneaking glances down the alleyways between in search of something or someone. That someone, the girl realized, being them. She burrowed into the stack to avoid being seen, but not so deep she could not keep an eye on Balaban.

As she watched, the giant saw the Americans then retreated behind a pile of hay. He peered around the opposite side of the stack then drew back when he saw Hayri. Huri hissed and whistled and whispered to attract Hayri's attention, but he was lost in concentration.

Balaban eased across the alley to the next row of haystacks, and Huri watched him appear and disappear in the gaps as he hurried down the row beyond. The behemoth crept across the alley and slithered along the end of the stack below her. She scrambled to the edge and watched him peek around the corner and size up her uncle, still crouched in the shade studying the list, with his back toward the hulking harm.

He crept around the angle and slowly stole up behind Hayri. Balaban froze at Huri's sharp intake of breath and she covered her mouth with a trembling hand, fearing she had been discovered. The giant cocked his head from side to side and looked around. Seeing nothing and hearing nothing more, he shrugged and took another step toward Hayri. Huri could see the huge man's muscles bulge as he readied himself to strike like a snake.

With a shriek and a scream, a yelp and a yell, she jumped off the haystack and landed on Balaban's back and shoulders. Wrapping her arms around his neck and her legs around his chest — as far as they would reach — she squeezed and squealed and squawked and kicked.

Balaban did not know what had hit him. He did not know what manner of attacker was latched to his back. He raised to his full height and spun dumbly in a circle, snapping his head from side to side, trying to catch a glimpse of his captor. Hayri sprang to his feet, watching the big man whirl like a dervish with Huri hanging tight and hollering to raise the dead.

The giant slowed and stopped and found himself staring into the bore of Rawhide Robinson's six shooter.

"Huri, I think you can get down now," he said.

She loosened her wrap on his neck and slid down Balaban's back, thinking all the while what a long way down it was.

"Ensign Ian, take that catch rope of mine and tie this behemoth's hands behind his back. Wrap it tight and twice and tie it double. I suspect that reata would part like sewing thread if he took a notion to test it."

"Done," the young ensign said.

Rawhide Robinson holstered his sidearm and turned to Hayri. "What now?"

The Turk thought for a moment. "We cannot take him to the authorities, as he has committed no crime here. Creeping about like a wharf rat is not illegal."

"But, Uncle Hayri! He meant you harm! I know it!"

"I know it too, my child. Fortunately, you upset his plans before he could carry them out. I thank you for that."

Hayri questioned the giant as the cowboy and ensign looked on, unaware of what was

175

asked or answered. It was clear, however, the questions outnumbered the responses.

"He tells me nothing useful. He will only say his orders are to keep an eye on us and report our activities to Hassan Hussein."

Ensign Scott said, "I believe he intended to put more than his eyes on you."

"Of that there is no doubt. But what to do?" Hayri thought for a moment. "I think our best course of action is to return this man to his master. It may make no difference, but at least he will know we are on to him."

Down the alley between rows of haystacks they marched, lined up like a mother duck leading her ducklings. Before the parade made it out of the hay market, Balaban spun around and charged, bowling over Ensign Scott and knocking Rawhide Robinson and Hayri and Huri aside and to the ground. He loped off down the alley, the rope singing as it burned through the recumbent sailor's hands, searing flesh and muscle as it went.

The men scrambled to their feet to see the giant diminishing in the distance. Before they had time to dust themselves off they watched Huri set off in pursuit. Being fleet of foot, she overtook the lumbering Balaban in what seemed no time, despite the considerable distance covered. Without even thinking about it, she snatched up the tail of Rawhide Robinson's reata, passed Balaban, crossed in front of him, and dropped behind. With the action, she wrapped the lariat around him and as it dropped to his ankles she dug her heels into the dirt and laid back on the rope.

Her nose plowed a furrow in the dust when Balaban's bulk hit the end of the rope and upended her. But the giant, too, lost his feet and hit the ground with a whump that shook the earth.

Before he could catch his breath and regain his feet, the men were on him. This time, they looped the lariat from his bound hands around the giant's neck, and Rawhide Robinson hog-tied and hobbled his feet with his piggin' string. When jerked to his feet, Balaban could still walk with small, shuffling steps. And he was given to understand that it only took a tug on the rope around his neck to cut off his wind.

Again, they set off for town, trooping along in line with Balaban in the lead on his leash. "That is one remarkable young lady," Ensign Ian said, an assessment with which the cowboy agreed.

Said Hayri, "Huri! Hurry to the quay and

see if Hasan Hussein happens to be at hand."

Without a word, the girl disappeared. Before you could say Rawhide Robinson, she was back. "Uncle Hayri, Hassan is not at the quay. However, he holds court at the café."

"Thank you. We will deliver this package to him there, then."

"Hold up a minute, you-all," Rawhide Robinson said.

Ensign Ian tugged the tail of the reata and Balaban stopped.

"Hayri, do you mean to tell me that this girl, who ain't been gone no longer than it takes to milk a cow, has been down to that wharf and through that bazaar and past that coffee café and is back here already?"

Hayri looked at Huri, who looked at the cowboy and nodded in the affirmative.

"Land sakes, girl, you get around quicker than spit in a hot skillet. 'Stead of Huri, from now on I'm-a-goin' to call you Hurry."

"Hurry?" she said. "What means that?"

"Oh, you know. 'Hurry' means pronto. Make tracks. Rattle yer hocks. Go on a high lope."

The girl's still-perplexed look was reflected in Hayri's face.

Likewise confused at their lack of cogni-

178

zance of his clarification, the cowboy looked to the ensign to toss him a life preserver. "Ensign Ian, bail me out here. How would you explain 'hurry'?"

"Hmmm," the young officer hummed through pursed lips below furrowed forehead. "Hurry. I believe Mister Webster would explain it as 'to go with haste,' or perhaps, 'to impel to greater speed.' Then again, you might say to 'hurry' is 'to go as rapidly as possible,' to 'expedite.' "

"I see," said Hayri. "It seems to make sense."

"The way I see it," the cowboy said, "since Huri gets around in such an all-fired hurry, we ought to call her Hurry. Besides, the word fits my Texas tongue better. What do you say, girl? 'Hurry' suit you?"

Unaccustomed as she was to being consulted about anything, the girl grinned and nodded enthusiastically. "Hurry!" she said. "If that is what I do in your language, then that is who I shall be."

Rawhide Robinson smiled. "Long as we're cowboyifying things around here," he said to Hayri, "how's about I call you Harry? It ain't much different, and it don't tangle up my tongue none."

Hayri hesitated only a moment before agreeing.

"What do you think Ensign Ian? Harry and Hurry?"

"I think we had better get back to business. Let's get rid of this colossus Hurry captured and back aboard ship so I can ascertain whether or not we have adequate space for forage storage."

Hasan sat sipping coffee at the café when the procession paraded into the plaza. Rawhide Robinson held Balaban at gunpoint while Hurry unleashed the hobbles and Ensign Scott loosed the lariat from around his neck and wrists. Once he was unbound, Hayri — or Harry, if you please — gave the giant a firm shove in the back to propel him toward Hasan's table. Unfortunately, it did not so much as budge Balaban, significantly diminishing the intended intimidation of the gesture.

Harry launched a tirade at Hasan.

Hasan responded in kind.

Back and forth, to and fro, from pillar to post they parried.

Rawhide Robinson and Ensign Ian Scott looked on, heads ticking and tocking back and forth from one side of the confrontation to the other. They knew the discussion was angry. They sensed the tension. They felt the heat. They recognized the ire. Unfortunately, the combatants battled in their native tongue so neither observer knew what was said.

When Harry turned and stomped off toward the waterfront they followed, certain Harry would fill them in in time.

Hurry hurled a hateful look at Balaban.

He returned the favor, then took a threatening step in her direction.

Hurry hurried away.

CHAPTER EIGHTEEN

Back aboard the USS *Cordwood* over the next day or two Ensign Ian Scott wandered the decks and holds with Rawhide Robinson, stretching the cowboy's lariat into every nook and knothole, cranny and crevice, corner and alcove between hatch and hold to see how much hay they could store where. In a ship designed for crates and kegs and barrels and boxes, finding dry places to pile hay took some doing. Spaces for stacks of sacks of oats were easier to come by.

Confident the ship could comfortably carry the required provender the camels would consume, the men retired to the main deck for some sunshine and fresh air.

They found Major Wayne and Captain Clemmons there, the latter fouling the air with his pipe smoke. From the stink of it, Rawhide Robinson assumed the captain had been shopping at the bazaar and been hornswoggled into purchasing a packet of pipe tobacco of a particularly odiferous Oriental blend. Ensign Scott finished reporting his plans for haystack stowage to the officers as he watched Whitman Fitzgerald and Hayri — Harry — come aboard. The diplomat trod across the deck like a man with a mission.

"What is it Whit Fitz?" Rawhide Robinson said as the man and his companion halted at the assemblage of officers.

"You look troubled," Clemmons said around an exhalation of malodorous smoke.

"Bad news, I'm afraid."

When Fitzgerald did not continue, Major Wayne said, "Well, come on man! What is it?"

"Hasan. Hasan Hussein."

"What about him?" Major Wayne, Captain Clemmons, Ensign Scott, and the cowboy asked in chorus.

"He threatened to upset our operation and I fear he may have succeeded."

"How?" the major said.

"What?" the captain said.

Ensign Scott remained silent, but his crimson complexion implied similar questions.

Rawhide Robinson looked on with interest. "C'mon, Whit Fitz," he said. "Spill it. If you don't, these folks are likely to explode like a bloated cow on a hot August afternoon in West Texas."

Fitzgerald cleared his throat. "As you know, Hasan wields considerable influence in Smyrna. Although he deals under the table and is not altogether on the up and up, he has a hand in much of the business transacted here. And, I am sorry to say, merchants, traders, brokers, agents, importers, exporters, buyers, sellers — even officials of the empire — hesitate to cross him."

Captain Clemmons spat out a mouthful of pipe smoke. "Land sakes man, that is no concern of ours!"

"I am afraid it is, gentlemen. You see, Hasan's influence extends to the camel trade. And he has let it be known that you are to acquire no further camels in Smyrna."

"That so?" Wayne asked Hayri.

"I am afraid it is so. For the past two days, since the affair in the haymarket, I have sought camels to purchase. No one — at least no one with camels of any quality — will even talk to me."

"Surely this Hasan doesn't control everyone!" Wayne said.

" 'Control' might be too strong a word," Fitzgerald said. "But through intimidation and outright threats, his influence affects even the most seemingly insignificant transactions."

"What can we do?"

Rawhide Robinson said, "I say we turn that girl Hurry loose on him. She sure enough made short work of his man Balaban. Whaddya say, Harry?"

The Turk almost smiled. The other men almost laughed.

"Well?" Major Wayne said.

"I am afraid there is nothing more I can do for you here," Fitzgerald said. "But Hayri has a suggestion."

Hayri took a deep breath. "I have cousins. Not exactly cousins as you Americans would say, but close friends and distant relatives, in other places who may help us."

Clemmons said, "Exactly where are these 'cousins' of yours?"

"Many places — most ports of call in the Levant. May I suggest Alexandria, where we will find my cousin Mehmet. He should be able to assist us in acquiring camels there, beyond the influence of Hasan Hussein."

"Remind me how many camels you've got," Wayne said.

"There were twenty-four, but one seller backed out of the bargain for his three camels. So I have twenty-one for you. All good quality."

"That means we'll need another ten, maybe a dozen."

"Yes, sir. We should have no trouble acquiring that number in Alexandria. If we do not find enough quality animals there, we will easily find the remnant elsewhere. Tunis, perhaps, or Algiers."

Wayne mulled it over. Then, "Captain Clemmons — can you sail this ship to those places?"

"Certainly. My orders are that this ship and crew are at your disposal. So long as we are pursuing fulfillment of your mission, we will sail to the ends of the earth."

Conversation shifted to preparations for departure. Hasan would surely use his influence to deny the USS *Cordwood* a berth at the wharf and the loading facilities there. The contracted hay would have to be loaded onto a barge and floated out to the ship in the harbor. Despite Hasan's interference, Hayri was confident a barge could be hired, as one of his many "cousins" operated one that would serve.

As with the ship, Hasan's influence would deny the barge use of the facilities at the wharf, but Hayri assured them they could load hay onto small boats from a nearby beach, row out and transfer it to the barge, from which it would be offloaded to the *Cordwood.*

There was also the question of the camels thus far acquired. Fitzgerald said, "How do you intend to get the camels aboard, Major Wayne? I don't believe swimming them out is an option. Small boats can't carry them to the barge. And even if they could, how to get them from the boats to the barge?"

The question stymied the army officer. Nor did the naval captain, the ensign, or the cowboy have an answer. Hayri offered no help.

"*&@#%$!" said Major Wayne. He clapped his hands and rubbed his palms together. "We'll think of something."

No one, however, had any idea what that might be, who might think of it, or when inspiration might strike. It was furrowed brows all around.

"Hayri!"

The voice was barely heard above the lapping of waves against the hull of the *Cordwood.*

"Hayri!"

Hayri and the others saw a small boat rowing across the harbor toward the ship. Hurry stood in the bow, waving her arms and shouting.

"Hayri!"

"What is it, child?!"

"The camels! The camels!"

Hurry scrambled up the rope ladder and onto the ship, running before her feet hit the deck.

"What about the camels?"

"Sick," the girl said, gasping for breath. "They are sick! You must come at once!"

The boat carried Hurry, Harry, and Rawhide Robinson toward the quay as fast as the boatman could work the oars. Fitzgerald, Wayne, and Ensign Scott kept pace in the diplomat's launch.

The men could not keep up as Hurry hurried to the camel pen. She ducked down alleys in the bazaar, ran through streets, hurried through neighborhoods. But Harry knew where she was going and the Americans had more success matching his pace.

"I declare," Rawhide Robinson said between hard breaths, "Hurry is the name for that gal. I knew it."

They stumbled to a stop, propping themselves on a fence. Beyond the fence rails, the twenty-one camels stood spraddle-legged with heads hung low, pawed at the dust, slinging heads back and forth, lay on their sides with thrashing legs, or slobbered and staggered like a sailor after too much rum. Only a few seemed unaffected.

"What is it, Harry?" Major Wayne asked.

"I do not know. I have never seen such a thing."

Rawhide Robinson tipped his hat back and studied the sick animals. "Looks to me like they got into some locoweed."

"What?" came a number of replies.

"Locoweed. Back home, horses sometimes eat it in the springtime and get to acting loco — that's the Mexican word for crazy. I think that's what happened to these camels."

"But I have never heard of your locoweed. Besides, these camels have been only in this pen. As you see, there is no locoweed or plants of any kind. Only the dust."

The cowboy considered that. "Could be someone fed them something. Maybe not locoweed, but something like it."

Hurry leapt the fence and started pawing through the scattered hay. Harry and Rawhide Robinson followed.

"Here!" she soon said, holding up a sprig of dried plant. "And here!" she said, grabbing more in her other hand.

Once the cowboy and the Turk saw what they were looking for, they, too, started pulling out wads and pieces of the odd plant. Its brittle dryness and dark color said it did not belong with the hay. "I do not know what this is!" Harry said. "I do not know how it got here."

Rawhide Robinson tossed a sheaf of the poison weed over the fence and brushed the residue off the palms of his hands. "I don't know what it is, either. But I can guess how it got here."

"Hasan," said Harry.

"Hasan," Major Wayne agreed.

"Hasan!!" added Ensign Scott.

"&^@)*!" said Whitman Fitzgerald.

Hurry squatted in the dust studying a sprig of the strange plant. "I know what it is. I think I know."

"What?" came the chorus.

"From the East come the two-humped camels. The slow, lumbering ones. I have talked from time to time with their handlers when they come in a caravan. I wanted to understand those strange animals that are camels, but unlike camels —"

"Huri!" Harry said. "What is it?!"

"One of them told me of a plant of many varieties that grows in a faraway place called Mongolia. *Shiir,* he called those plants. He did not know if it has a name in our tongue. The plant makes camels — and goats and horses and sheep — sick like these, if I remember rightly what he said to me. I do not know. But I think this is *shiir.*"

"Mongolia is a long way from here," Major Wayne said. "Who on earth around here would even know about this poison weed, let alone get their hands on some?"

The chorus came at once: "Hasan!"

"I don't doubt it," Fitzgerald said. "He is as ingenious as he is devious. I do not doubt the man's cunning drives him to acquire all manner of tools for accomplishing his evil schemes."

"The question is," Wayne said, "what do we do now? Will these camels recover?"

It was a question no one could answer. Then, Rawhide Robinson said, "If it's anything like locoweed, it could go either way. If they didn't get too much they might pull through. If they ate a lot, they may not get over it, and stay loco. They could even die."

"Is there any treatment?"

"None that I know of. They get over it in a day or two on their own or they don't. Some folks I knew would try to get the horse to drink a lot of water to push it on through. But I don't guess that would work with these critters."

Wayne thought.

And thought.

Then thought some more.

"I guess all we can do is wait and see."

"I will wait. I will see," Hurry said, blinking back tears.

"You will not be safe here," Harry said. "If it is Hasan, he will try again. He will send Balaban to take care of you — and the camels."

Hurry laughed without mirth. "Balaban. That *domuz* does not frighten me. I will stay."

"Yes, he is a pig — but still, Huri —"

"Do not worry, Harry," Major Wayne said. "We will post a guard. I am confident Captain Clemmons will concur. Ensign Scott, will you see to it?"

A snappy salute and crisp "Yes, sir! I will watch over the girl myself, if necessary. And the camels, of course."

Harry looked skeptical. "But the danger —"

"I wouldn't worry none, Harry," Rawhide Robinson said. "If Balaban does show up, I don't believe he could lay hands on Hurry. Besides, I'm fixing to stay here and look after these camels. And I'll feel a whole lot safer knowing that girl's here looking after me."

192

CHAPTER NINETEEN

With the intense heat of his ire, Whitman Fitzgerald feared blisters would rise on the rims of his ears. But neither his florid complexion nor the fire in his eyes affected Midhat Pasha, who sat cross-legged on his cushion sipping tea and sucking smoke from a hookah pipe.

"But you are the Grand Vizier of the Ottoman Empire!" the diplomat said. "Surely there is something you can do!"

"My concerns are much larger than the acquisition of camels by the American army. As you are aware, our empire is teetering on the brink and there are crises aplenty that demand my attention. You must address your concerns to the local authorities. I soon return to Istanbul and my duties there."

"You know as well as I do that Hasan has all of Smyrna in his pocket. No one in this city dares lift a finger against him."

Midhat exhaled a cloud of fragrant smoke and sipped at his tea. The first sign that he may be troubled by Fitzgerald's rant came when he removed his fez and mopped his brow with a silk handkerchief.

"I should think," Fitzgerald said, "that given the political difficulties you allude to, a strong alliance with the United States would serve you well." After allowing the Turk's laughter to subside, he said, "I know you think we are nothing but an upstart nation and that is true in terms of our longevity. But I can assure that America is destined to become a world power."

"We shall see. In another century, maybe two, we shall see." The Grand Vizier assumed the American diplomat would recognize that as a dismissal, but Whitman Fitzgerald did not rise from his cushion or otherwise give ground. He again harangued the Grand Vizier with his complaints, asking — demanding, in diplomatic language — the aid and assistance of the Ottoman Empire in bringing Hasan Hussein to bay.

Midhat said, "Hasan, as you are well aware, is a powerful man. Although I do not deal personally with such trash, he does, as you say, have the attention of local leaders here in Smyrna. We hear of his exploits even in Istanbul. But he is — how do you say it?

— but a flea annoying the ear of the empire. I cannot waste time with such trivialities."

"Surely there is something you can do."

Following more silent and thoughtful sipping and smoking, Midhat Pasha brightened. "It is camels you are after, and camels Hasan denies you — that is so?"

"That is so."

"Then I, Midhat Pasha, Grand Vizier of the Ottoman Empire, shall gift you with a glorious camel! This marvelous beast from the royal stock will put to shame any other camel you shall acquire and represent well the strength of the Ottoman Empire to the people of America!"

"One camel? Only one camel!?"

"Ah, but he is a grand camel, as you shall see. Now I must move along to other business, Mister Fitzgerald. See my assistant to arrange delivery of the generous gift of my magnificent beast. As for further acquisitions, you must do as you must do. Deal with Hasan Hussein as best you can."

The day was growing late when Fitzgerald's carriage rolled away from the palatial estate the Grand Vizier occupied when visiting Smyrna. The gift of a camel did nothing to relieve his sense of failure.

Even as Whitman Fitzgerald failed, Rawhide Robinson found success. But his joy would be short-lived.

The cowboy and Hurry had spent the night tending the ailing camels while sailors stood guard. There wasn't much they could do beyond encouraging the camels to drink, try to calm those who were overly active, and keep the inactive ones up and around.

Hurry's connection with the camels impressed Rawhide Robinson all over again and throughout the night he dogged her heels, asking questions about the beasts and observing her actions. When dawn broke, he believed time — and her ministrations — had done their work and all the animals appeared healthy, or nearly so.

"You fellers might as well go back to the boat," he told the sailors, sleepy from their night duty. "I don't suppose that monster of a man or his master will try anything in broad daylight with me and Hurry standing by. Tell Major Wayne the camels seem to be over the worst of it."

"Yes, sir!" the sailors said with what passed for snappy salutes at that early (or late) hour. As they stumbled off toward the city and the waterfront, Rawhide Robinson settled into the long sunrise shade of a haystack, plopped his thirteen-gallon hat over his face and studiously studied the crown for holes until his eyelids slammed shut and slumber ensued.

Hurry, for her part, propped herself against a fence post meaning to keep an eye on the camels, but that eye — and its mate — soon grew heavy and she, too, dozed until mid-day.

The snort of a camel interrupted her slumber and she leaped to her feet as if on springs. Her action startled Balaban and he dropped the rucksack he carried and pulled a revolver from the sash at his waist. Instinctively protecting the camels, Hurry ducked under the fence rails and ran past the giant, slowing only to kick him in the shin.

Gun in hand, Balaban turned and fired. Hurry seemed to anticipate the shot and dodged at the last moment. Another shot missed as she darted in the opposite direction, and yet another as she dived into a roll, regained her feet, and ducked away again as a bullet kicked up the dust behind her.

The racket awakened Rawhide Robinson, who found his feet with six-shooter in hand. Whether through luck, providence, or skilled marksmanship (Rawhide Robinson believed the first but would claim the last) his shot found its mark — sort of. The giant let loose a bellow as the bullet struck his gun hand, sending the weapon winging through the air. He roared again, grabbed the offended hand, clutched it to his chest and lumbered off at top speed.

"Hurry! You all right?"

The girl dusted off her clothes. "Yes. Balaban is a fool and cannot shoot a gun. He could not hit the wide side of a camel with a bucket of barley."

Hurried footsteps announced the arrival of Major Benjamin Wayne, accompanied by Ensign Ian Scott, Harry, and a handful of sailors from the USS *Cordwood*.

Major Wayne, between labored breaths, said, "Good heavens, Robinson! What happened? We heard shooting."

"Oh, it weren't nothing. That oversized feller of Hasan's dropped by for a visit. We sent him on his way."

"What was he up to?"

"Didn't ask. Truth is, I was napping when he showed up. Didn't dream he'd try anything in the daytime. I woke up when he started throwing lead at Hurry here."

Ensign Ian assured himself the girl was unhurt. Harry checked on the camels. Wayne asked Hurry if Balaban had said anything.

"No, sir, he did not. When he saw me he dropped that haversack over there and started shooting. I was never in any danger.

Balaban is a fool. And inept with firearms."

Rawhide Robinson said, "I don't know how good a shot that goon is, but I don't believe Annie Oakley her own self could shoot that girl, quick as she is. Why, Hurry was bouncing around amidst all them flying blue whistlers like a billiard ball. I swear she plumb outrun some of them bullets!"

"Sir!" one of the sailors shouted, holding the giant's rucksack upside down and shaking out dried stems and leaves.

"Looks like he intended to give the camels another dose of his poison," the major said. "Robinson, did you return fire?"

"I did. I must have hit something 'cause he left here a-cussin' up a storm."

"Major Wayne, have a look at this," Ensign Scott said. "Rawhide, you might want to see this, too."

The young officer stood over Balaban's revolver where it lay in the dust.

"I'd say there's no doubt that you hit him, or where. Look at that."

The cowboy and the army officer squatted over the pistol for a closer look.

"Well butter me like a biscuit!" Rawhide Robinson said.

"I've never seen the like," Major Wayne said.

"It is a wonder," Ensign Scott said.

The sailors and the girl, by now gathered round the spectacle, voiced similar astonishment.

Balaban's pistol looked ordinary enough. But the fact that an index finger was still wrapped around the trigger was extraordinary.

"He'll have a heck of a time shootin' at anyone else," Rawhide Robinson said.

Wonder still hung thick in the air when interrupted — then enhanced — by the tinkling of a bell. Plodding into the camel yard came a beast as big among camels as Balaban among men.

Major Wayne broke the silence of astonishment. "Glory be, what can that be?"

Not only was the camel conspicuous by his size, his accoutrements could attract a crowd. Halter, reins, blanket, saddle, packs — everything was artistically tooled, richly embroidered, bedecked with jewels. It sparkled and shined, glimmered and glistened, flickered and flashed. The shimmering camel stopped and Whitman Fitzgerald stepped out from among the rays, haloed in their glow.

"Well, if it ain't Whit Fitz himself," Rawhide Robinson said.

"I come bearing gifts. Yesterday afternoon, I demanded and was granted an audience with Midhat Pasha, Grand Vizier of the Ottoman Empire who happens to be visiting Smyrna. My request for assistance in reining in Hasan was denied, but in recompense for your present difficulties in acquiring camels, Midhat makes this gift."

The men stared in awe. Hurry hotfooted it over to the camel and stroked its nose, scratched its neck, rubbed its shoulders, and otherwise introduced herself.

"I ain't seen a whole lot of camels," the cowboy said, "but that thing don't look like no camel I ever seen."

"He is a tulu," Hayri said.

"?" came the response from the Americans.

"A tulu. His mother is a dromedary, like the camels we have purchased. But his father is a Bactrian camel — the two-humped variety from the East."

"He's sure enough a big ol' thing," Rawhide Robinson said.

"I make him to be at least ten feet long and seven high," Ensign Ian Scott observed.

"The tulu is known for size and strength," Harry said. "They grow larger than either parent, and their feats of strength and power are remarkable."

"Then why don't folks use them more, if they're so good?"

Major Wayne had the answer to that question from the cowboy, remembering having read of the tulu — also known as a bukht, a bertuar, dromano, dromel, iner, iver, majen, nar, turkoman, yaml, and a variety of other names depending on where you were in the world of camels. "The tulu are no good for breeding purposes. Like the mule, they are hybrids."

Harry said, "I am told they are more popular in other places as work animals. But in the camel markets they are not prevalent."

Whitman Fitzgerald said, "Gentlemen, the animal is yours. If you refuse the gift, an international incident could ensue." He turned and walked away. Two steps later he stopped. "By the way — the man there," he said, pointing at the handler, who was as richly adorned as his charge, "is Ibrahim. He comes with the camel."

CHAPTER TWENTY

Back aboard the USS *Cordwood,* the officers and sailors gathered round to hear of Rawhide Robinson's latest exploits with the camels. But it was not of himself the cowboy spoke, it was of the girl he called Hurry.

"I'll tell you, boys, that girl Hurry is really something. She measures a full sixteen hands high and she's brass plated. She knows camels inside and out and is as brave as any man I've ever seen and would put most to shame in the courage department. Where I come from, we say 'she'd do to ride the river with.' I reckon she'll do to cross the sea with, too — and if Major Wayne don't bring her along to help with them camels, he'll have me to deal with. I swear, Hurry's way with them critters is something to behold. Her kind of knowing is as rare as rocking horse manure."

The sailors murmured and mumbled, groused and griped, groaned and moaned, bellyached and babbled at the prospect of a young girl aboard ship, but the cowboy did not back down. "Boys," he said, "Once you see that girl in action, you'll be as surprised as I am. You'll plumb forget she ain't but a bit of a girl when you come to know her pluck."

Seeing his audience remained unconvinced, Rawhide Robinson related the story of her leaping from the haystack onto the back of Balaban, likely saving her uncle's life. "Boys, she rode that strappin' feller like he was a salty bronc. He spun and he lunged but he couldn't no more buck her off than an Irish girl can than throw the freckles off her nose!"

He told how she put a stop — and a sudden one at that — to the giant's attempted escape. "Whilst all us men was still bouncin' and rollin' around on the ground from bein' upset by ol' Balaban, Hurry was after him. She ran him down like a rope horse and tripped him up like he was a bunch-quittin' beef. She handled that lariat like a regular ranahan, I tell you. You couldn't trip a steer no more neat with a stout horse and a saddle horn to dally to than that girl tripped that brawny ol' bull Balaban, bare-handed and barefooted."

Still sensing skepticism in the crowd, the

cowboy articulated her courage in the face of gunplay, her valor in drawing fire away from the camels, her haste in escaping harm, her audacity in attacking the over-sized aggressor with a swift kick in the shin, her quickness in dodging bullets, her speed in evading hot lead.

"I'll tell you, boys, you'd have to see it to believe it. In all my born days, I ain't seen nothing to compare to that girl Hurry. The only thing I ever saw that fast was a horse I owned once."

For a moment, Rawhide Robinson was lost in reminiscence, recalling said steed.

"Say, did I ever tell you boys about the time I found myself dodging bullets on that horse?"

A chorus of "no" rang out from the crowd, and immediately the men settled in for a tale.

"Here's how it happened. And I swear, every word of it's true.

"We had delivered a herd of Texas cattle to Dodge City and me being the trail boss, I had saddlebags full of gold and the respon-sibility of carrying it to the owners back down in Texas. Somewheres out in Indian Territory, I sensed someone was following me. So I hid out in a little stand of cotton-woods along a creek to see if them hairs was standin' up on the back of my neck for a reason.

"Soon enough, four fellers rode over the rise and from the look of them I could see they was up to no good. They was packin' more iron than Sherman's army, what with long guns hanging from their saddle strings and revolvers holstered to their saddle forks and hanging from their waists. And when I seen that each of them had a pistol in hand, with hammers cocked and fingers on the trigger, it didn't take no Isaac Newton to calculate what they was up to.

"They rode on down to where they wasn't skylined — a sure sign they knew their business — then reined up to look things over. They knowed I was there, but couldn't be sure where so they watched and waited.

"But not for long, sad to say. See, that horse I was on was as friendly as he was fast. And when he sensed them other horses wasn't going to come on down without an invite, he proceeded to send them one. His welcoming whinny, of course, alerted them road agents to my whereabouts. They rode toward them trees and I rode away from them.

"Now, them trees was the only thing in the way of cover for miles around. Out on them plains there are about as many trees as there are on the Atlantic Ocean. So I was about as exposed as a baby's bottom come diaper-changin' time. Them boys mounted a charge, and I kept that horse of mine moving fast enough to keep them from gaining ground. But then, they started shooting."

Rawhide Robinson paused, made his way to a water bucket and dippered himself a drink. He settled back into his place beside the rail, doffed his thirteen-gallon hat and mopped his brow with the wild rag around his neck. It only took a moment for the crowd to reach the borders of their forbearance and encourage, in no uncertain terms, the cowboy to commence the continuation of his tale.

"Patience, boys, patience. Now, where was I?"

"You just said, 'But then, they started shooting'," an audience member offered.

The raconteur rubbed his chin, adjusted the lay of his vest, flicked a fleck of dust from the toe of a boot. "Did I say how fast that horse I was a-ridin' was?"

There came a chorus of affirmative, if impatient, answers.

"Well, with their hardware smokin' and them wantin' to send me to heaven to hunt for a harp, there weren't a thing I could do but run. So I did. With all the lead in the air, that horse soon got the idea. And once he hit his stride, them bullets didn't bother us a bit."

Once again the cowboy waited.

Soon, an exasperated sailor spoke: "Why not? You're not going to tell us you outran them bullets are you?"

"Land sakes alive, no! There ain't a horse ever lived could outrun a bullet fired from a gun. But that horse ran fast enough that those lead pills was more like floating past than flying by. I could have reached out and grabbed them — which I did a time or two but gave it up as they was too hot to handle. So what I did was, I lifted my lid" — which he demonstrated — "and set to swatting them bullets out of the air," he said, flailing his thirteen-gallon hat as he re-enacted the race. "I whacked them away, swiped them aside, walloped them hither and yon, slapped them sidewise, and otherwise disposed of the danger."

"Absurd!" someone said.

"Balderdash!" said another.

"Claptrap!"

"Drivel!"

"Eyewash!"

"Flapdoodle!"

"Garbage!"

"Hogwash!"

208

"Impossible!"

And so on, all the way down the alphabet.

"It's true, boys, as sure as I'm sittin' here. Looky here now — here's irrefutable proof." He reached into a vest pocket and pulled out a perfectly pristine plumbum projectile, fired from a forty-five. "Here's one I caught. Kept it as a keepsake."

"Poppycock," a sailor said. "That could have come from anywhere! You coulda yanked it out of a cartridge this very morning!"

"Well, then, if you won't believe that's one of them bullets I caught, look at this."

They looked. They saw. There was Rawhide Robinson's pointy finger wiggling through a hole in the brim of his thirteen-gallon hat.

"That, boys, is one that got away."

"%^$&#*@(!"

CHAPTER TWENTY-ONE

Sailors and Turkish laborers scurried around on the beach on the shore of the Smyrna Strait some ways away from the seaport — and the influence and interference of the interloper Hasan Hussein. Ensign Ian Scott ordered the crews about as they measured and sawed, hefted and hammered, arranged and assembled. Harry was on hand to interpret orders and relay instructions to the native laborers.

Rawhide Robinson looked on with wonder as the boat from the *Cordwood* carried himself and Major Wayne to the beach. The oarsmen expertly ran the boat aground and one leapt out to drag the boat further ashore then secured it with a line hitched around a stake driven into the sand.

"Major Wayne, sir," Ensign Scott said with a snappy salute. "Thank you for coming. I believe you will find my arrangements for loading the camels aboard the *Cordwood* capable of accomplishing the task."

The major watched the men working. "You've certainly got these men busy, Ensign."

"Yes, sir. They are intrigued with the project, our men and the Turks alike. Like me, they are excited at the prospect of seeing their handiwork in action."

"As am I, Scott. As am I."

Rawhide Robinson said, "Me, too, Ensign Ian. How is it you're fixin' to get them camels aboard the boat, anyhow?"

"Ship."

"Ship — boat — floatin' barn — whatever you call it, them hay stackers and grain sackers are near finished and we're all a-wonderin' about the camels."

Harry stepped forward. "Major Wayne, Mister Robinson —"

"— Rawhide —"

"— Mister Rawhide — seldom have I seen so inventive an undertaking. Ensign Scott's scheme will prove up to the task, I am certain. I, too, cannot wait to see it in action."

"All well and good, gentlemen," Wayne said. "So tell us how it works."

With effusive excitement and expansive enthusiasm, Ensign Ian Scott led the small assemblage from one lumber pile to the

211

next, from one labor crew to another, from sea to shore, from sawdust to sand. He pointed out the place the barge would tie up offshore near the beach. He showed them the "camel car" — a rectangular box slightly longer and wider and higher than a camel — and pointed out how it had been necessary to enlarge the crate to accommodate the oversized tulu. He demonstrated the solid bottom of the box, the fully enclosed sides, and how the ends, hinged at the bottom, dropped to the ground and created shallow ramps. He displayed the axles and wheels — pilfered from freight carts at the wharf — upon which the car would ride. He exhibited a modification to the wheels — a wooden circle a couple of inches larger around than the wheels, fastened to the ends of the axles to cover the outside of the wheel.

And, finally, the young officer revealed the genius of his scheme: parallel strands of planks, joined together, narrow edges at top and bottom, and tied side-by-side with crosspieces to form a set of rails on which the car would roll — in effect, a short-line railroad to carry the camels.

"We'll stake one end of the rails to the beach, attach the other end to the barge with a simple tongue-and-groove arrangement, heft the car onto the rails, lower the gate, load a camel, and roll it from the beach to the barge by means of applying manpower to these push rods affixed to the sides of the car. We shall rig a crane aboard the ship to hoist the camels to the deck, and again to the lower deck as necessary."

"Ingenious, Ensign Scott," Major Wayne said.

"Thank you, sir. We are confident it will work."

Rawhide Robinson said, "Has anyone asked the camels what they think?"

"What!?"

"I'll admit it's a pretty fancy plan. But most critters I've dealt with have a mind of their own. I suspect camels ain't no different. They might not want to go for a ride."

"You are right, of course. We will not know how the camels will react until the time comes," the ensign said.

Harry stepped forward. "Mister Robinson —"

"— It's Rawhide, Harry —"

"— Begging you pardon, Mister Rawhide, I show to you the camel car, constructed with solid sides so a camel cannot see out and become alarmed or anxious concerning his circumstances. We will also consider blindfolding the camels. In my experience,

213

what a camel cannot see, he does not fear."

The cowboy mulled that over for a moment, then agreed. "I reckon you're right, Harry. Leastways that works with horses. Even the orneriest bronc will stand still for darn near anything if he's got a wild rag wrapped around his peepers. But when you pull off them blinders, watch out."

Harry smiled. "It is so, Mister Rawhide. But we shall have on board the ship a secret weapon to mitigate any such difficulty, if not eliminate the threat altogether."

Major Wayne raised his eyebrows and widened his eyes.

Rawhide Robinson tipped his thirteen-gallon hat back off his brow, wrinkled his eyes and laughed.

"Secret weapon?" the cowboy said.

"What am I missing here, gentlemen?" the major said.

"He's talking about Huri — Hurry, if you'd rather," Ensign Ian said with a smile.

Harry nodded his affirmation. The officer looked no less perplexed.

"I get it," Rawhide Robinson said. "Hurry will meet the camels once they get to the boat —"

"— Ship —"

"— ship, dadgum it — and with a little pattin' and scratchin' and strokin' and a few kind words, she'll calm them right down. I reckon she could put them right to sleep, if she was of a mind to."

"Hmmph," said Major Wayne. "I know you think highly of her, Robinson, but she's but a girl."

"She's a girl, all right. But that don't matter none to them camels. I've seen her work her magic and I ain't ashamed to say she's taught me plenty about handling camels already. And I reckon there's a lot more she'll be teaching me."

"We set sail for Alexandria once the camels are aboard. Any future education will have to come from Harry. The girl won't be coming with us."

"Harry's a fine hand with a camel, I'm sure," Rawhide Robinson said with a nod to the Turk. "But that little gal's got something extra. If we don't take her with us, we ain't nothin' but a bunch of fools."

"But Robinson, I say again, she's but a girl!"

"That she is. Besides that, she's brave. Trustworthy. Loyal. Courageous. Smart. Dedicated. Helpful. Honest. Resourceful. Shrewd. Reliable. I could go on, Major, but you get my drift. She can handle them critters better than any ten men. Besides that, she likely saved my skin — and her uncle

Harry's here. Ol' Balaban would have had us toes up and sleepin' under dirt sougans if not for that girl. I say she goes with us."

"Unfortunately, you are not the one who gets the say, cowboy. The decision belongs to the United States Army."

Ensign Scott cleared his throat. "Major Wayne, sir — if I may?"

"Speak freely, Ensign."

"With all respect, sir, I believe the navy has a say, as well. And I am all for bringing the girl."

"The navy surely has a say in the matter — but that will be Captain Clemmons's say, not yours."

"Yes, Major Wayne, sir."

"And I am given to understand there are certain taboos about females aboard a military vessel — let alone a young girl."

"That, too, is true. There may be some dissension among the men. And it would be an unprecedented eventuality for the USS Cordwood to have a girl aboard. . . ."

"Is there something else, Ensign?"

"Well, sir, we are — or will be — after all, carrying a cargo of camels. So, the unprecedented, the unusual, the uncommon, even the unimagined surely must be reconsidered where this voyage is concerned. If I may say so, sir, hints have already been dropped

216

among the men about the possibility of the girl sailing with us."

"What!? Who has been dropping such 'hints' as you call them?"

"I can assure you it was on an informal basis, sir. Rawhide Robinson suggested — no, I should say strongly recommended — that the girl accompany us when talking with the sailors recently."

The army officer turned his attention to the cowboy. "And how did they react, Robinson?"

"Some scoffed at the thought. Some didn't seem none too bothered by the notion. Them as has seen Hurry in action is all in favor. Them sailor boys recognize a hand when they see one."

"Ensign Scott, what do you think Captain Clemmons's thoughts on the subject might be?"

"Wouldn't dare say, sir."

"Hmmm. . . ."

"But, sir, if you will pardon my saying so, if we approach the captain with a unified front, I dare say he may be amenable. If not, I believe he could be persuaded."

"Unified front? I'm not sure I am persuaded myself, let alone join your unified front."

Rawhide Robinson said, "Aw, c'mon.

Hurry ain't of a size to do any harm. And she could sure as shootin' do lots of good. Come down to it, you'd be better off to leave me behind and take her."

"I'm sure it won't come to that, Robinson."

Major Benjamin Wayne, hands clasped behind his back, paced up and down the beach for a moment or two, head bowed in thought. He stopped in front of the waiting ensign, cowboy, and camel handler.

"Harry, we have not heard your thoughts on the subject. What do you say?"

"Huri is family. It is my responsibility to see to her well-being. Arrangements have been made for her care by distant relatives here in Smyrna. While such would be acceptable, I — and my late sister — to Allah we belong and to Him is our return — would much prefer she stay with me. There is nothing before us — here, upon the seas, or in your America — that my Huri cannot face with courage and meet with success."

"You gentlemen seem to be in agreement. And determined. I shall take the matter under advisement and discuss it with the captain." Wayne smiled and clapped his hands together. "Now, let's see if this contraption of yours works, Ensign Scott! Let's load some camels!"

"We will be ready at first light, Major."

"Then we had better make arrangements to caravan the camels to this place, and alert Captain Clemmons of the schedule. Let's get back to the ship."

The major and Rawhide Robinson climbed back into the boat and Ensign Scott joined them for the return trip. Harry would return to the city overland at the end of the day's work to see to the movement of the camels and, come morning, lead the caravan to the jury-rigged loading contraption.

The Americans' venture had, by now, caught the attention of many in Smyrna. Curiosity compelled a goodly number of citizens to follow the procession come the morning. Joining the parade in his official capacity was Whitman Fitzgerald. Also in the crowd — and also in an official capacity, it could be said — was Hasan and his henchman Balaban, carrying a bandaged hand in a sling.

The parade reached the beach where, as if by magic, an assemblage of colorful awnings had sprouted in the night, shading vendors and their offerings of food and drink and small, festive American flags on sticks for the arriving crowd. Even spyglasses, binoculars, telescopes, opera glasses, and other seeing aids were available for rent to those

219

wishing a closer view of the bizarre — and, most thought, absurd — operation.

Offshore, the USS *Cordwood* lay at anchor with Captain Clemmons and crew on board to hoist the camels from the camel car. Hurry stood by to calm the camels once they arrived. Ensign Scott supervised operations ashore, with a handful of sailors and Harry.

The operation experienced a minor hiccup when the Turkish workmen who signed on to help disappeared into the crowd with the arrival of Hasan and Balaban. But, anticipating such an eventuality, the ever-industrious Ensign Scott had already assigned sailors to the work. Major Wayne was on hand to see to the well-being of his camels, while Rawhide Robinson lent Harry a hand wherever and whenever he could. Assistance from the aloof and indifferent Ibrahim was questionable as his interest seemed limited to the tulu.

Harry opted for the safety of the blindfold and he and the cowboy walked the first camel into the car without incident, accompanied by a chorus of "oohs" and "aahs" from the intrigued crowd. Sailors manned the handles affixed to the car and waded into the surf, pushing the car along the rails. It rolled easily to and onto the barge and the camel stepped aboard without incident. When the barge held a sufficient load of dromedaries, the sailors released the end of the rails and the oarsmen propelled the barge to the ship.

The crowd milled in excitement as the shipboard crane rigged by the navy engineers went to work. A cheer went up with the first camel and intensified as it swung over the ship's rail. The barge returned when empty, the sailors rejoined it to the rails, and the operation was repeated.

"Congratulations, Major Wayne," Whitman Fitzgerald said. "Your scheme appears to be a success. Many in Smyrna — including Hasan Hussein — considered it a fool's errand doomed to failure, but you have proved them wrong."

Indeed, Hasan, having seen enough, started back down the path to the city with Balaban in tow.

Wayne watched him go. "It would have been so much easier had not that infernal Hasan pulled his invisible strings to deny us a berth at the wharf," he said. "But it seems Ensign Scott — who deserves credit for all this — has dealt the final blow in our conflict with that hoodlum and his hooligan. We will soon set sail and trouble you no further. Your assistance has been and is much appreciated, Mister Fitzgerald."

"I can only apologize for my inability to effect a more satisfactory fulfillment of your mission. Unfortunately, Hasan's power is stronger than my ability to overcome. You can rest assured my efforts to eliminate his evil influence will continue. My reports to Washington will reflect his meddling, along with the refusal of the Grand Vizier to intervene. It may well affect relations between the United States and the Ottoman Empire."

"All that is beyond my ken, Mister Fitzgerald. As for my reports, they will state that you did your best and your contributions were uniformly positive."

"Thank you. Now, if you don't mind, I will take my leave. There are duties at the office that require my attention."

The men shook hands and the army officer offered a smart salute in parting. From somewhere among the camels came the voice of Rawhide Robinson: "So long, Whit Fitz!"

Throughout the morning, the cowboy and the Turk cinched a sling around each camel's belly, wrapped a blindfold around its eyes, and escorted it into the camel car. The camels rode the rails, rode the barge, rode the crane, and landed on the deck of the

USS *Cordwood,* and the operation repeated itself, without a hitch, until every dromedary was aboard.

Captain Clemmons and Hurry (who, by the way, was now an official member of the expedition following a late-night pow-wow between the captain and the major) and the crew aboard ship experienced smooth sailing — so to speak — as well. The girl was able to keep the camels calm and under control upon arrival, as expected, and helped see to their stowage in their shipboard stalls.

All went without a hitch — with one exception: the tulu was too tall.

Ibrahim pitched a fit when he came aboard, complaining and caterwauling and clamoring, but since he had no English he was largely ignored. The resourceful sailors simply sawed a spacious slot in the ceiling of his stall and added a cupola-like extension to accommodate his too-high hump. The tulu, who the sailors named Tulu, seemed happy with the arrangement.

Even as the last nail was driven, the USS *Cordwood* weighed anchor and left the Strait of Smyrna to set sail for Alexandria in search of more camels.

CHAPTER TWENTY-TWO

Hurry's hurrying and scurrying around the ship, inside and out, set Rawhide Robinson's name for her — Hurry — in stone. She and her uncle Harry soon improved their adequate, if hesitant, ability to communicate with the crew and caught on to the American idiosyncrasies of the English language in no time.

Poor Ibrahim, however, had no English and his aloofness — and lack of interest — stalled his assimilation. But when it came to communicating with Rawhide Robinson and his arcane cowboy lingo, Ibrahim was at little disadvantage compared to Harry, Hurry, or even — on occasion — the other Americans. After months at sea with the rustic westerner, the sailors still, on occasion, found themselves befuddled, bewildered, flummoxed, flabbergasted, perplexed, nonplussed, confounded, and confused by cowboy argot, jargon, idiom, and slang.

Rawhide Robinson was asked, "This, in my hand, is it a lariat or a reata?"

Rawhide Robinson replied, "Well, it's both. 'Lariat' is a cowboy way of saying *la reata,* which is the Mexican way of saying rope. Reata, lariat — all the same. 'Course it's sometimes called a twine, a lass rope, lasso, ketch rope, seago, gutline, string, cable, choker, maguey, a skin string —"

"— But how do you know?"

"I don't know how you know. You just know."

And this simple question: "Food?"

"Chuck. Grub. Bait. Vittles. Muck-a-muck. State doin's. Throat ticklin's. Them's your general terms. If you're palaverin' about some particular comestible, it could be anything from axle grease to whistle berries, fluff-duff to huckydummy, sow bosom to bear sign, sinkers to cackleberries — I gotta quit talking about food. It's making my stomach think my throat's been cut."

"What?"

"Oh, you know — I'm a mite gut shrunk — wolfish — narrow at the equator — my belly button's bouncin' off my backbone —"

"Hungry, you mean?"

"Why, sure — in a manner of speaking."

Rawhide Robinson: "Harry, what is it you

225

call a bunch of camels?"

Harry: "Caravan is the common term. Sometimes flock."

"That's it?"

"That is all. Why?"

"Seems a mite slender. Horses, now, out where I come from, might be a bunch or a band or a herd or a remuda or a cavvy or remounts or the saddle band or plain 'hosses.' "

"It is too much!" Harry said.

"Well, there's a lot of horses. So you need a lot of words to talk about them. You got your caballo and your cayuse, your bronc and your broomtail, your mustang and your mockey, your pony and your plug, and so on.

"Then, of course, you got to be able to identify a horse by what he's good for. Say, a cow horse or a cuttin' horse or rope horse or night horse or Sunday horse or top horse or circle horse or last year's bronc, if you catch my meaning.

"And how in heaven's name could you discuss equines without considering their physical characteristics? Some of 'em's clear-footed and some puddin' foots. You find 'em cold-jawed, coon-footed and cow-hocked. They might be fiddle-headed or hogbacked. Head shy, jugheaded, ewe-necked, or mule-hipped. They might be snorty or whistlers or cribbers.

"Thing is, when you get to chin-waggin' with your saddle pals, a man's got to have a vocabulary to make himself understood."

Someone said: " 'Understood' is a relative term."

Another said: "I have no idea what you are talking about."

And another: "What language is that you're speaking, anyway?"

And still another: "A horse is a horse."

Rawhide Robinson, as is the wont among cowboys, stuck to his guns. "Maybe so, maybe no. You could say a boat is a boat, for all that. But sometimes it's a ship."

The time the cowboy spent schooling Turks and sailors alike in cowboy lingo paled in comparison to the hours and days he spent learning about camels. Some of his education was formal. At Major Wayne's request, Captain Clemmons assigned a handful of sailors, under the able leadership of Ensign Ian Scott, to help Harry, Hurry, and Rawhide Robinson care for the camels. Ibrahim resisted all efforts of assistance with the tulu, but Wayne was having none of it.

"What's the matter with the man?" the army officer asked Harry.

"He did not want to leave Turkey. His life

227

with the Grand Vizier was soft, and held much status. He thinks now he is below his station. He has no interest in associating with infidels. He is homesick. Ibrahim will care for the tulu as he is under obligation by his master's orders, but beyond that he vows he will not cooperate."

"#&^$%*!" Wayne said. "We'll see about that!"

Harry and Hurry, on the other hand, leapt into their role as teachers with high spirts and enthusiasm. The first day the USS *Cordwood* was underway to Alexandria, they led a camel onto the open deck where studious sailors and a curious cowboy encircled it.

"What's the matter with its knees?" one sailor asked.

"There is nothing wrong," Hurry said. "Why do you ask?"

"They ain't got no hair on them. Looks all scuffed and rough and wrinkly."

"Oh, I see. The camel, he lowers himself to the earth by first kneeling on the knees of his forelegs. When he rises, his knees are the last to leave the earth. They are much used, and so the knees are protected by the thick skin."

Another sailor: "How much water can these camels keep in that hump?"

Harry: "Oh, my friend, there is no water

in there."

"But they say that's how come they can go so long without water!"

"Not so. I am afraid the hump is filled with fat. That is all."

And another: "I heard tell they can walk on sand. What keeps 'em from sinkin'?"

Harry lifted the camel's front foot. The sailors gathered around, with Rawhide Robinson elbowing his way among them for an unobstructed view. Harry pointed out the leathery pads on the bottom of the hoof, and told how they spread when the camel walked, providing a wider surface area.

"Like snowshoes, then," said a sailor from the North Country.

"Snow shoes?" Harry said, looking perplexed.

"Well they're these wood frames maybe three, four times the size of your foot with webs of rawhide laced across. We strap on our shoes when we go out in deep snow."

"I suppose it is much the same principle," Harry said.

"About them hairy ears and all them eyelashes," another sailor wondered.

"Ah, yes," Hurry said. "You have noticed their ears are covered with hair inside and out, and they have two rows of eyelashes. In a windstorm, this protects them from blowing sand. In a sandstorm, humans wish for the same."

Then she told the pupils, "But that is not all! Watch this!"

The girl tickled the camel's upper lip — which wiggled and waggled on either side of its split middle. As the sailors laughed, she blew on the beast's muzzle, prompting oohs and aahs and chortles and chuckles when the camel slammed its nostrils shut.

"You see!" Hurry said. "The camel can also close his nose to keep out the blowing sand!"

The revelation drew a round of applause from the appreciative Americans.

Harry said, "A marvelous animal, the camel. Much superior to the horse."

"Now hold on there," Rawhide Robinson protested. "These here camels might be fine for fending off a sandstorm, but they ain't no horse. Why, a horse is noble looking — splendid and stately standing still and beauty to behold when ambulating. These creatures look like whoever invented them was booze blind and dizzy drunk. Why, they're so ugly if one of them looked in a mirror he'd scare himself plumb to death. God his own self must have been playing a joke on mankind when He created camels and again when He had old Noah unload these beasts from his ark. Better than a horse! Hmmmph!"

Harry smiled the kind of sympathetic smile reserved for the addle-brained and hopelessly ignorant. "You shall see, Rawhide Robinson. You shall see."

Hurry defused the situation with a simple whistle.

Somehow, the camel understood the signal and lowered its knees to the deck then folded its hind legs double and squatted on them.

"Climb aboard, cowboy!"

Skeptical but always game, Rawhide Robinson hitched up his britches, grabbed a hank of camel hair at the front of the hump as he jumped and swung a leg over. As he lit, Hurry whistled a different command and the camel hefted its front end, its hind end, then, again, the front with Rawhide Robinson leaning expertly with the motion.

"How's the weather up there?" a sailor said.

"It's a mite breezy," the cowboy said from his perch atop the dromedary. "But I reckon a man could get accustomed to ridin' high like this."

Harry said, "As with a horse, the camel's back is much more comfortable when saddled."

"I sure hope so. It's a mite spiny up here. Besides trying to keep from slidin' down the slope."

But learning to ride a camel was not on the agenda aboard the *Cordwood.*

"Robinson get down from there and stop this nonsense!" Major Wayne said as he clomped across the deck. "I have developed procedures concerning the camels. You men look sharp and pay attention."

The major outlined a precise and detailed set of orders for camel care. He ordered one sailor to be on watch at all times, continuously making the rounds through the stalls on deck and those below deck. He ordered the camels fed and watered daily at three o'clock in the afternoon; to wit, one gallon of oats, ten pounds of hay, and one gallon of water for each camel at each daily feeding. In addition, the camels were to receive a weekly ration of salt.

"Men, the grooming of these animals is your responsibility as well, and I can assure their ablutions and toilette will far exceed your own. The camels are to be currycombed and brushed for no less than a half hour each and every day."

The sailors groaned.

"The legs and feet of every camel are to be washed daily."

The sailors moaned.

"With soap."

The sailors mumbled.

"Stalls are to be mucked out and cleaned daily."

The sailors grumbled.

"Harry will instruct you in all other aspects of their care. I will make unannounced inspections routinely. Should anything out of the ordinary occur, I expect to be informed post haste. My assignment is to transport these camels, and the others we will be acquiring, safely to the United States. It is a mission I take with the utmost seriousness and I am relying on you men to facilitate its success. Captain Clemmons has assured me of your cooperation. Are there any questions?"

"Sir, suppose I am spat upon by one of the camels?" a fastidious sailor asked.

"I can assure you — and Harry will agree — that eventuality is highly unlikely."

Another sailor: "Supposing one of them steps on me, sir?"

"Mind where you put your feet. Avoid putting them under the camel's hooves and you will be fine."

"Sir, why so much water? I hear tell they don't drink much water," came the question from another sailor.

"There is truth in what you have heard. Camels can go for extended periods without water — but, like you, they will drink when drink is available."

A burly, bearded, brawny sailor said, "What about the girl, sir?"

"What about the girl?" Wayne said.

"Well, sir, you said the man there, Harry, was to tell us what to do. Does that apply to the girl, too? Will we be takin' orders from her?"

Hurry blushed at the attention but stood her ground.

"Orders, no," the major said. "Advice, yes. Instructions, certainly. Guidance, of course."

"But she ain't but a little bit of a thing."

"Granted. But her experience with camels far exceeds your own — or that of any other person on this ship save her Uncle Harry and, perhaps, Ibrahim. Don't dismiss what she tells you."

"Still and all, she's a girl."

Rawhide Robinson stepped forward. "Listen here, sailor. I don't know much about camels but I've been tendin' cow critters since you were in nappies and horses before that. So I know a thing or three about animals. I've told others this and I'm a-telling you — Hurry has a way with

234

camels and you'd do well to pay attention to what she says."

"Hmmmph."

"I'll tell you this, too — if you cross her, she's likely to clean your plow. I've seen with my own eyes this little gal get the better of a better man than you. And if she don't knock your ears down a notch, I'll likely do it myself if you give her any trouble."

"What're you, cowboy? Her protector?"

"Not likely. She don't need me watchin' over her."

"Enough of this!" Major Wayne said. "As I said, Captain Clemmons assured me of the cooperation of every one of the sailors who volunteered or were assigned to this task. I expect nothing less. If this young lady's presence upsets you unduly, you are welcome to seek re-assignment. I'm sure swabbies are —"

An explosion and shower of seawater interrupted the major's discourse, followed by another blast and more of the Mediterranean raining down.

"Pirates!" came the cry from the quarterdeck.

CHAPTER TWENTY-THREE

As the raining-down seawater dissipated, Ensign Ian Scott rushed to the rail, seeking the source of the shots over the USS *Cordwood*'s bow.

"Holy mackerel!" he said and hustled toward the captain's quarters but met Clemmons on his way to the quarterdeck.

"Did I hear cannon fire, Ensign?"

"Indeed you did, sir."

The befuddled captain raked his fingers through his hair, reset his peaked cap, and sucked on his unlit pipe. "Are we under attack?"

"Those were warning shots over the bow, sir. No hurt or harm. But you won't believe what's firing on us."

Clemmons stared at the junior officer, his anticipation at a low boil. "Well, Ensign Scott — are you going to tell me?"

"It's a xebec, Captain! A xebec!"

"Xebec? Are you sure?"

"Yes, sir. Absolutely."

"I was under the impression the only xebecs still afloat were in Mediterranean maritime museums."

"Yes, sir. But it is a xebec all the same."

"Do you suppose the Barbary pirates have returned after all these years, as well?"

"Couldn't say, Captain. But whoever it is out there, they are coming after us."

Clemmons eyeballed the attackers through his telescope. "Well I'll be. A xebec. Knock me over with a feather. . . ."

"Is that an order, sir?"

"Don't be daft, Ensign Scott. I suppose we should see what they want. Heave to," he ordered the helmsman, and sent an officer to see to the ship's four twenty-four pound howitzers and the arming of the sailors.

Major Benjamin Wayne stomped onto the quarterdeck as the ship hove to. "Captain! What the hell is going on?"

"We're about to find out," Clemmons said as he watched the xebec draw closer, its sails assisted by oarsmen.

"We're stopping. Why?"

Clemmons explained in as few words as possible that, as a supply ship in peacetime, the USS *Cordwood*'s armaments were scant. Fleeing would be futile, as the smaller, trimmer xebec could easily outrun them. "And it appears they have the firepower to blow us out of the water should they so choose."

"So what's your plan? Let them take over the ship?"

"I doubt it will come to that. I shall allow them to come aside and ascertain their intentions. If they are pirates, they most likely assume an American military supply ship will make a fine prize. Once they understand what our cargo consists of, interest will diminish."

"And if it doesn't?"

"If they attempt to seize the ship, we will, of course, resist. We'll give them a taste of our lead and steel long enough to allow us to hoist our sails and be underway."

"But you said they could outrun us!"

Clemmons smiled. "True enough. But if my seamanship is good enough — and I believe it is — we'll put ourselves in a position to run them down. That ship of theirs is delicate — a twig compared to our tree trunk. We'll smash them to smithereens."

Sailors scrambled around on the main deck seeing to their duties, unaccustomed though they were to hostility on the seas. But all were soon armed and dangerous and ready to meet whatever threat presented itself.

When the xebec came alongside the *Cordwood,* Captain Clemmons was at the rail.

"Permission to come aboard, Captain," came the call across the water from the pirates.

"Permission denied. State your business."

"I wish you no harm. It is your cargo we seek — we have no wish to damage your ship or injure your men."

"Cargo, you say? We carry nothing of value — only the ship's stores."

The pirate captain laughed. "You underestimate me, sir. Although a humble Levantine, I am not such a fool as to believe a United States Navy supply ship would sail around the Mediterranean empty."

"And yet it is so."

Triggered by some unseen signal, grappling hooks sailed from the pirate ship, seeking purchase aboard the *Cordwood.* No sooner had they taken hold than the rail of the navy ship bristled with rifles, handguns, and swords as nearly all forty of her officers and enlisted men — and Rawhide Robinson and Harry — stood ready to repel any attempt at boarding.

"Aren't you going to cut those lines?" Major Wayne asked Clemmons.

"Not yet. For the time being, I want to keep them close. They are unlikely to fire

239

their guns while alongside. And, as you see, we have the high ground, and likely a more lethal complement of small arms. If they storm us, we will repel them, cast off, and unleash the guns or ram them. I assure you, Major, despite appearances there is little danger in our present situation. It's treasure they want, not a fight."

"I wish I shared your confidence, Captain. But since the cargo on this ship is my responsibility, I am concerned."

Clemmons laughed, prompting the turning of heads all along the rail — and aboard the pirate ship — to see who found humor amid the tension.

The pirate captain again demanded to board and again Clemmons turned aside the demand. "I assure you, there is nothing aboard this ship that would interest you. We are on a specialized mission and carry no cargo of any value to you."

"I do not believe it! I will see for myself. Throw down a ladder at this instant!"

"Not on your life. If you so much as attempt to set foot on my ship you are a dead man."

"And if you do not allow it, my friend, you are a dead man. As a matter of fact, you are already a dead man and do not know it." The brigand gave orders to his seamen in a language no one aboard the *Cordwood* understood and the pirates brandished their weapons. The sound of ratcheting hammers rolled along the *Cordwood*'s rail in response.

But as the men shouldered their rifles and readied their revolvers, several of them felt themselves crowded from behind — nudged and shoved, jostled and jolted, bumped and butted.

Surprise rippled through the pirate ranks as, all along the naval ship's rail, sailors were shunted aside and the heads and necks of dromedaries stretched over the bulwark to stare down placidly at the attackers. The shock and awe the camels caused soon turned to laughter. For while the pirates were not unfamiliar with camels, seeing the animals on the high seas was an unfamiliar and unexpected eventuality.

The surprise and laughter retreated briefly before returning as the giant tulu shouldered his way between Captain Clemmons and Major Wayne. The camel, so tall he loomed over all but the sails, bent over the rail and let loose a rich, resounding, rumbling, resonating, reverberating burp.

Hilarity erupted on both ships and continued through at least three strident demands for "Silence!" from the pirate captain.

241

The laughter died down after a bit and the buccaneer boss demanded, "What is the meaning of this?!"

Captain Clemmons smiled. "This, my friend, is our cargo."

"Camels! Camels are your cargo?"

The navy officer nodded.

"What kind of fool would put these smelly, stinking animals aboard a ship? Are you crazy?"

Captain Clemmons did not respond.

Major Wayne did not respond.

Rawhide Robinson did not respond.

Hurry, however, did. She scrambled from her place on deck into the rigging and, dangling there, presented the pirate a piece of her mind.

"Quiet! Do not speak so of these noble beasts! *You!* — You! — you, who are lower than a steaming heap of camel dung have no cause to speak ill of useful animals. You are nothing more than a common thief. Less than an animal yourself!"

The pirate captain reddened and with the ring of steel, drew his cutlass from the jeweled scabbard at his waist and stepped onto the rail of his ship.

"I shall have that lass's tongue for such impertinence!"

Rawhide Robinson extended his arm to

its full length, centered the bore of his Colt revolver on a spot an inch above and between the buccaneer's eyes. "Stand right there," he hissed. "You twitch a single hair of that scraggly mustache of yours and I will put smoke in your face and a window in your skull as sure as we're both a-standing here."

With fire still smoldering in his eyes, the pirate sheathed his short sword and addressed Captain Clemmons. "Do I have your word as a gentleman that these — these — these camels are your only cargo?"

Rawhide Robinson responded. "He don't owe you his word on that nor any other subject. He done told you once already. Now you had best put aside any notions you have of causin' us any more ruckus and get that boat of yours out of here before I ventilate you."

Tulu put a period (or exclamation point if you prefer) at the end of the cowboy's soliloquy with a repeat performance of his exemplary eruction.

With the alacrity of obeying an implied command, sword-wielding sailors aboard the *Cordwood* sliced through the pirate ship's mooring lines and watched the xebec slowly drift away, then watched the oarsmen maneuver the ship into a running wind as other hands furled the lateen sails and the sleek ship fairly slid across the sea.

As the *Cordwood*'s officers and sailors scurried about getting the ship underway again, Harry and Rawhide Robinson helped Hurry stow the camels in their stalls under the shed on the main deck.

"Hurry!" Captain Clemmons shouted after issuing his orders.

The girl sidled over to where the captain and Major Wayne waited. Harry and Rawhide Robinson hustled over in case Hurry required defense of her actions, or support of same.

"Young lady," the captain said with a wrinkled brow. "What on earth prompted you to turn out the camels like that?"

She shrugged. "I thought an impasse was near and sought to avoid it. It was my belief that a display of something as surprising as ships of the desert on the deck of a ship at sea would astonish the pirates and convince them to leave us be."

Hurry studied the furrowed foreheads of the military leaders but could read nothing there. (Had they been camels, on the other hand, their every emotion, intention, determination, resolution, reflection, rumination, cogitation, and contemplation would be as clear as crystal.)

244

"Young lady, you listen to me and you listen good —"

"— Now you hold on a minute there, Cap'n!"

"Robinson, hear me out! As I was saying, Hurry, your actions during our recent imbroglio were — how to put it? Inspired, to say the least. Inventive. And, most of all, effective. Were you a sailor or officer under my command I would recommend you for honors — a medal for meritorious service, at the least."

Major Wayne said, "I concur completely. Despite my years of military service, I saw no way out of those difficulties short of bloodshed. Your performance was bold, and as the captain says, inspired."

Hurry hardly had time to blush before Ibrahim clawed his way out from under a pile of coiled lines — his hiding place, as it happens, during the pirate attack — shouting and hollering and engaging in all manner of histrionics, most of which were directed at Hurry.

"What's he saying?" Rawhide Robinson said to Harry.

"He is angry that Huri handled his camel. He says she has no business doing so, as the tulu is his responsibility. He says she is not capable of controlling his animal. He says

she is not worthy to lay hands on it. He says
—"

Rawhide Robinson had heard enough, albeit second-hand. He clomped across the deck in his high-topped, high-heeled cowboy boots on a beeline for Ibrahim with his forefinger shaking with every step.

"Now you listen here, you cowardly cur! You ain't got enough sand in your craw to make a camel close his nose! Why, there's a yellow streak down your spine so wide it wraps all the way around to your brisket! There you was, hidin' in the shade of the wagon whilst Hurry was savin' the day!" he said, all the while backing Ibrahim up step-by-step with his pointer finger stopping near enough his nose with every shake he could feel the breeze.

And he continued. "Compared to this here girl, you ain't fit to muck out these camel's stalls. She'll do to ride the river with, but I wouldn't spit on your sorry hide if it was afire. Why, if it was up to me, I'd drop you over the side just to see if your swimming is as pitiful as your pluck."

And he continued. "If I hear tell of you uttering one cross word at Hurry or raising your voice or even so much as lookin' at her cross-eyed, you'll have me to deal with. I ain't a violent man by nature, but I swear

246

on my dear departed mother's grave that I will stomp a mudhole in you then walk it dry," he said with a final wag of his now-weary index finger at the cowering Turk.

"Translate that!" he said to Harry.

Harry smiled. "There are no words for what you say. But I think he gets the point."

"Ensign Scott!" Captain Clemmons hollered. As he waited for the junior officer, he said to Harry, "You may not be able to translate that cowboy vernacular, but make this clear to Ibrahim: his cowardice, laziness, and all-around contemptuousness have earned him a day in chains." Then, "Ensign Scott, escort Ibrahim to the brig. He is to be confined for twenty-four hours on a diet of bread and water."

Ensign Scott saluted the captain.

Harry deciphered the captain's words for the fuming Ibrahim.

Ibrahim erupted in angry protest, but bit off his objection with the mere rise of Rawhide Robinson's digit.

Before the young officer carried out his assignment, he inched up to Rawhide Robinson and tapped him on the shoulder.

"What is it, Ensign Ian?"

"Rawhide, when you were talking to that pirate, you told him to 'get his boat out of here,' or words to that effect. I am obliged

247

to tell you that a xebec is a ship, not a boat."

The cowboy contemplated — if only for an instant — employing his powerful pointer in Ensign Ian Scott's direction.

CHAPTER TWENTY-FOUR

As the sun sank slowly in the west, Rawhide Robinson hunkered down on the deck of the USS *Cordwood,* savoring a cup of coffee and contemplating the day's events. Several sailors and some officers likewise sat, stood, settled, squatted, spraddled, and scrooched around. Conversation, naturally, chewed over the confrontation with the pirates.

"Say, cowboy," one said. "You ever before found yourself in a standoff like that?"

"Oh, sure. That little tiff didn't amount to much compared to some I've seen."

"Pshaw!" another sailor said. "That weren't no 'little tiff.' I was afeared the shootin' would start anytime!"

"He's right," said another. "That was a pretty dicey business."

"Yeah. Had it been any worse, some of us wouldn't have survived."

Rawhide Robinson smiled. "Sure. But the shootin' didn't start. The time I'm a-thinkin' of, the lead was flying like a swarm of mosquitoes. The fact that I wasn't perforated like a screen door was downright lucky."

"Well, tell us!"

"What happened?"

"Where?"

"When?"

"Why?"

"How?"

Wiggling down into a more comfortable crouch, Rawhide Robinson tipped back his thirteen-gallon hat, swallowed the last sip of his stimulating liquid refreshment, and heaved a long sigh. "It's like this," he said.

"One time I and a crew of Texas drovers took a mixed herd up into the west end of Colorado to stock a ranch there. The place was owned by some nob from Scotland who had more money than he knew how to spend. Thing was, he had a brother down in Texas who had even more money. And it was that Texas brother's ranch that supplied the stock. Anyway, we got the cattle to Colorado without incident and I was fixin' to mosey on back to Texas with the herd money in my saddlebags — gold coins, it was, along with some bank notes and drafts and other such items of legal tender — when that Scotchman asked me for a favor.

"He had this shotgun, see, that was a family heirloom he wanted me to carry back to his brother. Oh, it was quite the piece of weaponry — double-barreled eight-gauge goose gun, it was. Weighed about as much as a yearling steer, it did, and the bores in those barrels looked wide enough to drive that same steer through. Darn near the size of those in the cannons on this here boat, they was. The metal on that gun was engraved with these real pretty swirly curlicue designs and polished all shiny, the wood carved and crosshatched and buffed to a glossy gleam. It had twin triggers and —"

"Enough with the gun, already!" an impatient sailor interrupted.

"Tell the story!" another said.

"Get to the shootin'!" said another.

"Boys! Boys!" Rawhide Robinson said. "In the immortal words of the great Bard of Avon — I believe it was in his play *Hamlet* — 'Upon the heat and flame of thy distemper sprinkle cool patience.' I'll get to it in due time, so you-all just relax and enjoy the ride. Now, where was I?"

"Nowhere, yet!" a still-impatient sailor complained.

"You was gettin' ready to go back to Texas," one, more helpful, offered.

"Right. So I was. Well, then, here's what

251

happened. I stowed that shotgun in my saddle boot and headed for the high country, wanting to see what had become of Pike's Peak and all the mining camps and such since I was there last.

"I was rambling along through the Sangre de Cristo Mountains when I came across this high mountain valley. Oh, it was right pretty — tall trees all around, a nice little lake, grassy meadows — well you get the picture, I guess. What I didn't know until I broke out into an open place was that there was a road agent convention goin' on at the same time. One whole end of that valley was chockablock with criminals —"

"Baloney!"

"Bunk!"

"Balderdash!"

"Blarney!"

"Bull!"

"It's true, boys, sure as I'm sittin' here. Call it what you will — desperado rendezvous, confab of crooks, highwayman assemblage, outlaw powwow, robber rally, bandit clambake — it don't much matter what handle you attach to it. The fact is, most every man — and more than a few females — in all of the West with larcenous leanings had showed up there to do what folks do at such gatherings. I'm tellin' you, it was a regular congress of corruption.

"What I didn't know when I rode into that nest of vipers was that they knew I was coming. Somehow, the holdup hotline had put out word that I was afield with saddlebags full of abundance. So, they were laying for me.

"Before I knew it, I was seeing spots before my eyes — and every spot was the hole in the muzzle of a firearm aimed right at me. Now, I ain't one to shun a fight when fighting is called for. Nor am I a man who'll take a hand in a rigged game. So I ain't ashamed to say I turned tail and told that horse with the rowels of my spurs that it was time to run.

"And run we did, down that mountain valley with bullets buzzin' around us like a horde of hornets. Just when I thought we had the hundreds of them outlaws on my tail outrun, others started angling down out of the timber on every side, throwing lead as thick as the others.

"With them hemming us in thataway, there wasn't nowhere to go but into that little lake I told you about. So me and that horse splashed into that oversized puddle so fast we didn't have time to sink or swim before shoring up on this little island out in the middle.

"I thought to keep going right on across the island and into the water and exit the lake on the opposite shore. But, wouldn't you know it, them outlaws had the place surrounded. Every time that horse poked his snout out of the timber, a solid wall of slugs, balls, bullets, shot, and shrapnel would drive us back.

"Well, boys, it was as plain as the brand on a barbered beef that I was in a bad jackpot. And I couldn't see no way out of it short of cashin' in my chips and meetin' my Maker. Which I wasn't of a mind to do at the time.

"So, I set in to thinking. I contemplated and cogitated. Ruminated and reflected. Deliberated and speculated. Studied and scrutinized. Mulled and mused. Considered and concentrated.

"By and by, I had an idea," Rawhide Robinson said.

The cowboy chronicler then lapsed into a silence as pensive as that of a man pondering the expanse of eternity. Eventually, the sailors' impatience heated up to the temperature of annoyance, emitted a steam of irritation, then boiled over into exasperation. In answer to their irate pleas, he proceeded.

"I could see there was no way I was getting off that island and onto the shore.

Neither that horse nor I was likely to sprout wings, so we couldn't fly off that island. We couldn't go over and we couldn't go across and we couldn't go around and we couldn't go up. That left down."

"Down?"

"Down!?"

"Down," Rawhide Robinson said. "Here's how. I loaded up both barrels of that eight-gauge shotgun — each chamber took a cartridge about the size of a can of peaches . . .

"I mounted up and took a firm grip on that firearm . . .

"I spurred up my horse and set off across that island quick as we could caper . . .

"I jumped that horse off a ledge and into the lake . . .

"It all happened so fast them bandits on the beach didn't have time to do anything about it. 'Course they figured they didn't have to do anything about it, as I would soon be swimming to shore where they would waste no time relieving me of the small fortune in my saddlebags. But, instead, as I said, we went down."

"Down!"

"Down?"

"Down. Soon as we hit the water we started sinking, and we kept sinking and swimming and swimming and sinking until we hit bottom. So there we were, me and that horse, sittin' in the basement of said lake. And there, in that aqueous cellar, the genius of my plan was revealed."

"Well?" said a sailor.

"And?" said another.

"Then?" said yet another.

"Then," said Rawhide Robinson, the waterlogged raconteur, "I aimed that double-barreled eight-gauge shotgun at the seafloor, wrapped a finger around each trigger and let loose both barrels at once."

After a moment of tense silence a chorus of sailors, as if on cue, said, "What happened?!"

"What happened is, that goose gun blew a huge hole right through the bottom of that lake. Opened up a drain as slick as pullin' the plug out of a bathtub. The water whirled and swirled and funneled down the drain like it does, and took me and that horse and the shotgun and the saddlebags full of money right along with it.

"Next thing I knew, I was spit out into a river. Turns out, after going down, down, down that drain we ended up in the San Luis Valley and that river was the Rio Grande itself. So, we floated along all the way down to Texas. As the aforementioned

Shakespeare said, 'All's well that ends well.' "

The audience sat silent, completely overwhelmed.

Except for one particular officer: "One thing, Rawhide."

"What's that, Ensign Ian?"

"You said earlier the bores in those shotgun barrels looked 'Darn near the size of those in the cannons on this here boat.' "

"Yes, I do believe I did say that."

"I needn't remind you, sir, that the USS *Cordwood* is a ship, not a boat."

CHAPTER TWENTY-FIVE

Rawhide Robinson, Major Benjamin Wayne, and Ensign Ian Scott stood at the rail of the USS *Cordwood* as Alexandria hove into view. Harry, Hurry, even Ibrahim (now free from confinement and behaving himself, if only reluctantly) and every sailor and officer not otherwise occupied did likewise.

"It is unfortunate the great lighthouse of Alexandria no longer stands to greet us," came a wistful observation from the young ensign. "Or the library, for which the city was once famous."

Rawhide Robinson said, "I've read bits and pieces here and there about this place, but can't say I know much of anything about it."

"For a thousand years, this was one of the most important cities in all the earth. The Greeks and the Romans controlled much of their empires from here. Shipping, trade, culture — Alexandria had it all."

"How came it to be here?"

"Founded by Alexander the Great, some three centuries before the time of Christ."

"Alexander the Great — him, I've heard of."

Major Wayne laughed. "As have I — and, I suppose, every soldier the world over. Even today, his abilities as a fighting man are studied. His campaigns were part of the curriculum and drilled into us at West Point, and I suspect they still are and always will be. Alexander used camels in his armies — there weren't many of them in this country before he came along. Let's hope there are plenty of them here now, and that we can acquire what we need."

Within a day, Captain Clemmons arranged a berth at the Port of Alexandria and docked at the wharf. Already, Harry had located Mehmet, a cousin of sorts and trader in Egyptian cotton and other goods. As soon as the gangplank dropped, the Turk and his cousin, with Hurry, Wayne, and Rawhide Robinson tagging along, were abroad in the city on a camel hunt.

Results were disappointing. Old camels were plentiful. Sick camels were available. The supply of lame camels was ample. Camels afflicted with mange were obtainable. Quantities of unsound camels were inexhaustible.

All the camels, of course, were represented by their sellers as prime, pristine, and excellent in every respect. "Reminds me of an old horse trader I come across one time in my travels," Rawhide Robinson said as they stopped to talk on the fringe of the raucous bazaar.

"Don't recollect the name his momma gave him, but 'Pink' is what he went by. I'm here to tell you that boy had larceny in his soul and would do most anything to sell a horse at a healthy profit. He might not out-and-out lie to a feller, but he'd stretch the truth farther than a soakin' wet reata in a rainstorm.

"Why, he'd pull a shoe off a lame horse and try to convince you it limped on account of it threw a shoe. I saw him one time shove a sponge up the nose of a wind-broke horse to keep it from whistling. A horse could be a-layin' there so dead Saint Peter already had a saddle on him and Pink would suggest he was havin' a nap. Weren't no limit to what he'd do to shift a horse, and I suspect most of these camel traders is cut from the same bolt of calico."

"You're probably right, Robinson," Major Wayne said. "Tomorrow's another day and we'll see what it brings in the way of camels."

A ruction in the bazaar drew the men's attention and they saw Hurry scurrying down a narrow alleyway with a man in Bedouin robes hot on her heels. The girl yanked down the awning on a jeweler's stall to slow her pursuer, then leaped over a table displaying fabrics and leathers and upset it in his path. Traders roared and shoppers shouted as the race wreaked havoc in the aisles and alleys of the market.

"Huri!" Harry hollered.

Hurry managed to stay a few steps ahead of the man at her heels. Rawhide Robinson noticed her slow from time to time, then duck or dodge or quicken her step to remain a fingernail's length outside his reach. "I'll be darned," he said. "That gal's toying with him. He ain't never goin' to catch her."

"But why is he after her?"

Hurry ducked out of a passageway and ran toward them.

"I don't know," the cowboy said. "But I reckon we're about to find out."

The girl ran past so fast a breeze fanned the men. Seconds later, the Bedouin raced by and Rawhide Robinson stretched out a booted foot and tripped him up. Before he stopped tumbling, Major Wayne was upon

261

him, pulling him upright and wrenching his arm behind him as a restraint. Hurry circled around and joined them, smiling at her erstwhile pursuer. While he was barely able to draw breath to curse her, Hurry showed no sign of the race.

Harry's cousin Mehmet questioned the Bedouin, his answers coming in gasps. Others from the bazaar gathered round, many pontificating and pointing at the man. The man, they said, was a slave trader. While his attempt to capture Hurry was unsuccessful, they had long suspected him of kidnapping other girls in similar fashion to trade them away to the harems of desert sultans.

The uproar attracted the attention of a policeman patrolling the bazaar and Major Wayne turned the Bedouin over to him.

"Huri!" Harry said. "Huri —" he said, unable to find any other words.

Major Wayne took up the task. "Young lady, what on earth were you up to? We didn't notice you slip away. You must stay with us. Obviously, it is not safe for an unaccompanied girl here. Tell me, what were you doing wandering off?"

Not looking the least bit apologetic or agitated, Hurry looked the major in the eye and said, "I went looking for *Adana kebab.*

I grow weary of your insipid American food."

"Adana kebab?"

Harry explained it as a dish popular in Turkey and throughout the Levant, consisting of spicy and savory skewered minced meat.

Rawhide Robinson laughed. "I know what you mean, Hurry. But don't you fret none. Once we get to Texas, you'll find plenty of provender piquant enough to prickle your palate."

"In the meantime, young lady," Major Wayne said, "you stay with us. Otherwise, you will be forbidden to leave the ship. I'll put you in chains if necessary."

Hurry grinned. "As the Bedouin wished to do?"

"Hmmmph," Wayne said.

His warnings, threats, and admonitions were ineffective, however, for as soon as the major, Rawhide Robinson, and Harry stepped off the gangplank and onto the wharf early the next morning to meet Mehmet and continue the quest to acquire camels, Hurry came running down the wharf toward them from the direction of the city.

"Major Benjamin Wayne!" she shouted. "Mister Rawhide Robinson! Uncle Hayri! I

263

have found them!"

"What are you talking about, young lady? What have you found?" Major Wayne said.

"Camels! The camels!"

Rawhide Robinson laid a hand on the girl's shoulder. "Simmer down, Hurry, and tell us about it."

Hurry hitched and shifted her *salwar* — baggy trousers tight at the ankles — and jacket, disheveled from running. She swallowed hard and took a deep breath. "Last night a caravan of *Dyula* traders arrived from Al-Fashir. I have spoken to them. They will sell some of their camels. The camels are tired and thin from the long crossing of the desert, but they are sound and their health is good."

It took the men a while to overcome their surprise. "I suppose we ought to go see these camels," Major Wayne said upon regaining his composure.

He and the others hurried to keep up with Hurry.

The situation at the Dyula camp on the outskirts of Alexandria was precisely as Hurry described it. The camels had crossed the immense Sahara and the effects were evident — all were tenderfooted, tired, and thin.

But careful examination proved Hurry's

assessment. The animals were in fine fettle, healthy and sound and suffered from nothing that could not be cured by rest and relaxation, fodder and water.

"Heaven knows there will be plenty of time for that aboard the *Cordwood,*" Major Wayne said.

The men examined the caravan at length, studying feet and legs, teeth and toenails, humps and heads, eyes and hides. They compared and contrasted, discussed and disputed, ranked and rated, and agreed on seven mature but young camels. Upon seeing their selections, the Dyula leader laughed.

"What do you find funny, my friend?" Harry asked. "Do you disagree with our choices?"

"Not at all. You have chosen well."

"Then what is the reason for your hilarity?"

"It is the girl," the Dyula said. "Last night, within minutes and by firelight, she selected the same animals!"

Harry gasped. Mehmet gulped. Major Wayne choked and coughed and had trouble catching his breath.

Rawhide Robinson only smiled.

"The girl," the Dyula said, "has a rare gift. I am a man of many years, every one spent in the presence of camels. Never have I seen such an affinity with the animals. For the girl, I will give these seven camels and three others besides."

"Oh, no, my friend! It is not possible," Harry said. "She is of my family, and I have a sacred responsibility to care for her until she is of an age to marry."

The Dyula nodded. "I have gold from Bambuk, kola nuts from the Sudan, and textiles from Timbuktu to offer. And do not fear — among our people many suitable husbands will vie to espouse the girl. Including my sons."

"No. I am sorry. Your generosity is appreciated. But Huri will remain with me."

Rawhide Robinson and Major Wayne looked on as Mehmet and Harry negotiated a price for the camels. The back-and-forth conversation involved a patois of languages, none of which the Americans understood. But they trusted Harry and his cousin to strike a favorable deal and they returned to the USS *Cordwood* late that morning with seven dromedaries in tow.

Unlike the machinations in Smyrna, the loading in Alexandria was simple — the camels trod across the gangplank from the wharf to the deck of the ship, arousing the curiosity of everyone on the quay, then disappeared through the hatch and down the ramp and were ensconced in stalls in the hold within minutes, content with the hay and grain and water and respite from their labors they found there.

By evening, the USS *Cordwood* cast off and set sail for Tunis, where the Dyula trader assured them they would find a few more camels of quality to complete their cargo.

But, in Tunis, the expedition would find much more than the animals they sought.

CHAPTER TWENTY-SIX

The USS *Cordwood* sailed along the coast of North Africa, venturing into deeper waters of the Mediterranean to bypass the Gulf of Sidra, following a more direct route toward the *Halq al Wadi,* the seaport for the city of Tunis.

The earlier experience with pirates prompted Captain Clemmons to keep a careful watch. Eyes were peeled around the clock to detect the presence of Barbary Pirates or other Corsairs, who historically sailed their xebecs out of Tripoli and Algiers, each coastal city lying well within striking distance of the *Cordwood*'s course.

But the voyage proved uneventful, with the officers and sailors going about their routine duties. Rawhide Robinson spent his time with the camels, building familiarity with the beasts by helping the assigned seamen with feeding and grooming. He quizzed Harry and Ibrahim for information when occasion arose. The girl Hurry, however, was where he looked first and foremost for knowledge and understanding.

He asked about the personalities and disposition of camels. About training and handling. He queried the Turks concerning breeding, gestation, and the birth of camel calves. About lactation and weaning. He inquired about sleep habits and preferred periods of peak activity. Proclivities concerning sociability and solitude. He asked about halters and hobbles, saddles and packing, loading and hauling.

And he questioned them concerning a hundred, maybe a thousand, other details about the animals the army expected him to integrate into the Wild West. The knowledge in Rawhide Robinson's head swelled to such an expansive size it took all the room in his thirteen-gallon hat to contain it.

Still, being the curious sort he was, the cowboy risked another onslaught of knowledge as they sailed into Tunis. "Well, Encyclopedia Ian," he said to Ensign Ian Scott, "tell me all about this place."

The eager and informed young officer was not in the least bit reluctant to enlighten Rawhide Robinson and the others who gathered around on the foredeck. "Tunis," he said, "is an ancient city — settled perhaps 8,000 years ago, although of course no one knows for sure.

"Owing to the city's location, the Berber culture here has been influenced over the years by people from the Sahel and sub-Saharan Africa as well as Europeans and Levantines. Phoenicians, Romans, Vandals, Byzantines, Arabs, and Ottomans have all held sway here at one time or another. Of late — within the last century, say — Tunis has been invaded by Algerians, Venetians, the English, and the French. According to what I have read —"

"— What *haven't* you read?" some sailor interrupted.

"Hush up and let the man talk," Rawhide Robinson said.

"According to what I have read," Ensign "Encyclopedia Ian" Scott said, "the French are very much in evidence today, and the city has grown — perhaps as many as 100,000 people live here today."

"I don't much care about how many folks call this place home," the cowboy said. "So long as there are a few camels for sale."

With the history lesson complete, the officers and crew went about the business of landing the ship at a slip at the seaport. At first opportunity, teams of camel shoppers from the ship passed through the *Bab el Bahr* — sea gate — and into the city and the bazaar seeking suitable animals for acquisition. Major Wayne accompanied the intransigent Ibrahim, Ensign Scott was assigned to accompany Harry, and Rawhide Robinson rattled his hocks to keep up with Hurry.

The girl's well-tuned nose for camels led them to a private pen tucked away from the histrionic hawkers and hustlers at the camel corrals connected to the bazaar. After wandering among the ungulates, Hurry, Rawhide Robinson, and the dromedary herdsman squatted in the shade of a mud wall. The cowboy could only shave a stick of firewood into a toothpick with his well-honed Barlow knife as Hurry and the man talked. He had no idea what they were saying, but given his opinion of and experience with the girl, he had no doubt she pressed the trader hard concerning the qualities of and expected compensation for the camels — and that she would negotiate a favorable price to present to Major Wayne.

Hurry could not resist stopping at the bazaar for another dose of Levantine cuisine to offset the decidedly dull diet dished up daily aboard the ship. She nosed out a food vendor who catered to her favorite flavors and, after gobbling a goodie to take the edge off her taste buds, handed something that looked like a fried pie to Rawhide Robinson.

"What's this?"

"*Brik.* It is meat, vegetables, and egg in pastry. Here," Hurry said, handing Rawhide Robinson a small cup of a red pasty sauce. "Dip it in this."

"What's this?"

"*Harissa.* It is made from red peppers, so mind your tongue."

"Horsefeathers! I been funneling chili down my gullet since long before you were born. Why, I've et stuff that'll make your teeth sweat and singe your esophagus."

With that, he dunked a corner of the brik into the harissa and scooped up a ponderous glob of the sauce and chomped off a substantial chunk of the sandwich.

With that, he went wall-eyed.

With that, his face turned the color of the harissa.

With that, perspiration popped from his pores and puddled around his boots.

With that, his tongue sizzled to a crisp.

With that, his teeth seared the inside of his lips.

With that, his stomach swelled as the steam inside sought escape.

With that, the hairs on his head scorched the innards of his thirteen-gallon hat.

With that, a blistering blast of his breath blew through the bazaar and elevated the ambient temperature like a *Sirocco* blustering off the Sahara.

"Yeeeehaaaaw!" he said upon regaining control of his faculties. "That's good stuff!"

And he took another bite.

Hurry laughed until tears ran down her face as she watched tears run down Rawhide Robinson's face as he masticated his second mouthful.

Then another.

And another.

And yet another and another, until finishing his brik and the same again, Hurry munching right along with him, bite for bite.

Their stomachs full and appetites sated, the plethoric pair plodded off to the port, where Major Wayne and Ibrahim awaited them aboard the *Cordwood.*

"Where's Harry and Ensign Ian?" the cowboy asked.

"No sign of them as yet," the major said.

"Any luck with camels?"

"Not any you could classify as good. Ibrahim and I found only jaded and unsound animals among the traders we encountered. Tunis may be a bust and we shall have to

273

sail to Algiers for suitable specimens."

"Oh, I think not," Rawhide Robinson said. But before he could offer an explanation, they were interrupted by cacophonous caterwauling coming down the quay.

"What the #$*&!@?" Major Wayne said.

"Why, I do believe that's Ensign Ian and Harry," Rawhide Robinson said.

Major Wayne: "Yes, and unless I miss my guess they're both drunk as sailors."

Rawhide Robinson: "Yep. They do look to be a bit wobbly on their pins."

Captain Clemmons joined the choir: "The both of them appear to be three sheets in the wind."

"They look like they couldn't lie down without holding on."

"I'd say they're sloshed, sozzled, soused, and snockered all at the same time."

"Indeed. They appear to be tacking, but unable to navigate."

"Tanked up, for certain."

"I don't believe they could hit the ground with their hats in three tries."

"They do seem to have more sail than ballast."

"They definitely have a snoot full."

Accompanied by song and laughter and stagger, Ensign Scott and Harry made their way across the gangplank — threatening to topple with every stumble — and tottered onto the deck. As Captain Clemmons came into focus through the fog, the young officer attempted a salute but his hand missed his forehead altogether. The second try resulted in a thumb in the eye, prompting a giggle fit from Harry.

"Ensign Scott!" the captain said. "Have you been drinking on duty?"

"No, sir. Not a bit. Nary a drop. None. Nada. Sir."

Again, Scott's reply launched laughter on Harry's part, and the ensign joined in. He thought better of the hilarity and again saluted. "Only the sweet mint tea of Tunis. Sir."

That, too, spawned more mirth from Harry.

Now, Ibrahim entered the fray with a tirade both long and loud. No one, of course, save Hurry — and Harry — could fathom a word of it. Throughout the harangue, Harry attempted, unsuccessfully, to keep from laughing, which further inflamed Ibrahim.

"Hurry, what's he carryin' on about?" Rawhide Robinson said.

"He is saying Hayri is an infidel, an unbeliever. That he is no better than the *giaour,* the *kafir* — that Hayri is as bad as you

American heathens."

"But why?"

"Followers of *Muhammed* consider alcohol an abomination of Satan. Intoxicants are forbidden by the holy book, the *Kuran.*"

And still, Harry snickered and sniggered until Ibrahim wound down and stomped off to secrete himself in Tulu's stall, whose company he preferred above all others. This, too, amused Harry, who laughed so hard he collapsed on his backside into a tall coil of rope. Unable to extricate himself, he chuckled and chortled and tittered and giggled at his situation until slipping into somnolence with a smile on his face.

Ever after, the amused Turk was known as Happy Harry.

Meanwhile, Ensign Ian Scott was coaxed to coherency by cup after cup of coffee and he related the tale behind their unintended intoxication. It seems the two had succumbed to the hospitality of a disreputable camel trader who invited them to share tea as they discussed business.

"He must have spiked our tea with spirits of some sort," the ensign said. "Although I did not detect it. The tea was so sweet with sugar and mint it effectively disguised the intoxicant. I assure you, Captain Clemmons, sir, we had no intention of imbibing.

276

Not myself, and certainly not Harry, who would never willingly partake of liquor under any circumstance."

The young officer, with his faculties nearly fully restored, rose smartly to attention and snapped off a salute so sharp you could shave with it. "My apologies, sir. Whatever punishment you see fit to administer I shall willingly accept. I beg, however, that you spare Harry from suffering any consequences from this unfortunate circumstance."

Clemmons assured the ensign there would be no penalty for what he perceived an unfortunate accident. Major Wayne concurred, and offered the hypothesis that the camel merchant might have assumed the men carried cash with which to purchase camels, and intended to incapacitate and rob them.

With the shipboard merriment moderated, Major Wayne accompanied Rawhide Robinson and Hurry to the out-of-the-way camel corral to complete the purchase of four dromedaries the girl and the cowboy had chosen. The camels were soon secured aboard the USS *Cordwood,* bringing to thirty-two the ship's store of camels, and they set sail, at long last, for the United States of America.

But not before Rawhide Robinson and Hurry hurried back to the bazaar for another heaping helping of harissa, shoveled up with a savory serving of brik.

CHAPTER TWENTY-SEVEN

The USS *Cordwood* had barely squirted through the Strait of Gibraltar when Hurry hustled and bustled about the ship in search of Rawhide Robinson and Ensign Scott. "Come!" she said, tugging on the cowboy's sleeve and beckoning to the ensign. "Come quickly! It is time!"

"Time? Time for what?"

"Come! You will see!"

They followed the girl — clomping along quick time to keep up — down the hatch to the lower deck. They caught up to Hurry as she veered off into one of the camel stalls. The cowboy instantly saw what so excited the girl.

"Well sakes alive on a half shell!" he said. "We're having us a baby!"

"A baby?" Ensign Scott said. "A baby!"

The camel in the stall lay on her side, the calf's forelegs, head, and neck well on the way. Happy Harry, squatting at the camel's rear, smiled. "It is so."

Hurry sat at the new mother's head, scratching and stroking her neck as she grunted and groaned. Happy Harry grabbed the calf's forelegs and pulled, helping mother and baby along. Once the calf's shoulders emerged, the rest came slipping and sliding out like a gush of water from a well pump.

"It will grow up to be a bull," Harry said. The mother was soon upright and kneeling as Harry dragged the calf toward her head so she could nose it about.

"How soon before the little critter gets up?" Rawhide Robinson said.

Hurry said, "Like the foal of horses or a calf from cattle, it will stand within the half hour."

"I suppose he will be wobbly on those long and skinny legs," the ensign said.

"It is true. But he will soon be walking well and even running — if he finds room here."

Harry said, "The mother will be on her feet in minutes. I am surprised she is not up already. Then, the little one will find his first nourishment."

"How come that little feller ain't got a hump?" the cowboy said.

"In a few months, when he starts eating

more than milk, it will form," Harry said.

"But are not the tufts of hair already there where the hump will be already handsome?" Hurry said. "He is a beautiful calf. I shall call him 'Okyanus'!"

"Okyanus?" Rawhide Robinson said. "What's that mean?"

"In your language you would say 'Ocean.' I name him that because he is born here, in this ship on the ocean."

"A fitting moniker, if you ask me," Ensign Ian said. "We had best give Major Wayne the news."

The news surprised the major. "A calf? Where on earth did a calf come from?"

"Oh, the usual place, Major — I'd have thought a man of your years would have an understanding of such things!" Rawhide Robinson said.

"Hmmmph."

"The mother is one of the camels we picked up in Alexandria, sir," Ensign Scott said. "No telling, of course, who the father is — it would be a bull she met up with a year or more ago down in Africa somewhere."

"Did we expect this?"

"Oh, sure," the cowboy said. "I ain't never been a nurse nor a midwife to no camel before, but I've seen enough cows and mares at their work that I recognized the signs."

"I confess it was a surprise to me, sir," the ensign said. "Hurry may have dropped hints, but I did not pick up on them. I am somewhat embarrassed by it."

The calf soon became the pet of every man aboard. Within days it wandered the ship at will, getting up to no end of mischief. It chewed up shoes and clothing. It gnawed the finish off the ship's woodwork. It tangled and scattered ropes and lines across the decks. It left unpleasant surprises in the most surprising places.

Still, the sailors fawned over Okyanus. They fed him from their meals at mess and spoiled him with pilfered sugar. They played endless games of tug-of-war with any piece of fabric, rope, sailcloth, belaying pin, or any other piece of anything the calf could get its lips around that came to hand. They chased at tag and ran races. They even napped together, the camel using sailors to pillow his head and sailors using Okyanus as a pillow.

One day Rawhide Robinson cautioned the crew. "You boys best be careful messin' with that camel calf. You know, sometimes baby critters get confused if they spend too much time with something that ain't its own kind

— they get to thinkin' it's one of them, instead of one of what it is."

"Oh, pshaw!" some sailor said. "Ain't no way that could happen."

Ensign Ian, standing nearby, cleared his throat and injected himself into the conversation. "I'm afraid Mister Robinson is right, sailor. It is a phenomenon called 'imprinting.' As far back as ancient Rome, a farmer named Lucius Moderatus Columella taught other agrarians that if they wanted to add tame ducks to their flocks they should gather duck eggs in the wild and place them under domesticated setting hens. The ducklings would hatch, believing the hen was their mother, and grow up with many of the habits and behaviors of Gallus domesticus along with their naturally acquired Anas Platyrhynchos behaviors — or, in common language, the imprinted ducks behaved, in many ways, as chickens."

"Well I'll be," said one sailor.

"I don't believe it," said another.

"I'd have to see it to believe it," said yet another.

"I've seen it," Rawhide Robinson said. "That's how I knowed to bring it up."

The sailors voiced their doubts:

"Poppycock!"

"Hogwash!"

"Bull!"

"I seen it all right," the cowboy contended. "It wasn't a cock and it wasn't a hog and it wasn't no bull — but it was a cow."

"A cow!?"

"A cow. Well, a heifer, to be exact."

"How, now, the cow?" a sailor asked, inviting Rawhide Robinson the raconteur to tell yet another of his tales. The cowboy required no further encouragement.

"I was workin' a line camp for a ranch in the Rocky Mountains this one time. It was spring and I was watching over a herd of longhorn cows up in the high country — a herd, as it happened I had driven up from Texas the summer before.

"But it was spring then, and most all them cows had calves by their sides. One morning one of them cows dropped a late calf then wandered off and left it with nary a care. After a day or three I noticed that cow was overflowin' with milk and knowed its calf must be missing. I searched high and low and here and there and hither and yon and from Dan to Beersheba for her baby but couldn't find it nowhere, nohow, noway.

"Then one day I was a-sittin' on a ridge above this pretty little meadow when an old sow bear wandered out of the timber. Not far behind her come a cub. Not far behind that, lo and behold, came that heifer calf."

"Balderdash!" said a disbelieving sailor.

Another concurred, with "Claptrap!"

"Bunkum!" said another.

"I swear as sure as I'm sittin' here it's the truth," Rawhide Robinson said. "Here's what I figure must have happened. See, them bears generally has two cubs and that sow must have lost one. Feelin' all motherly and such and missing one of her little ones, when she stumbled onto that lost baby calf she must have figured it was better than nothin'. And, of course, that calf not knowing any better went along.

"I saw them bears now and then through the summer, and darned if that longhorn calf didn't get to thinkin' it was a bear! Why, it'd nose around in the duff rustlin' up acorns to eat, and paw logs apart and lap up the bugs and grubs and worms there. I tell you boys, one of the strangest things I've seen in all my born days was watchin' that heifer calf up to her ears in a honey tree suckin' up that sweet nectar."

"Twaddle!"

"Ludicrous!"

"Drivel!"

Despite the onslaught of disbelief, Rawhide Robinson pressed on.

"Them's the facts, fellers, like it or not.

When fall came, things got stranger still. Bears, you know, they hibernate all winter long — crawl into a hole and sleep the winter away. Before they do, of course, they've got to lay on enough fat to last. So them bears — and that heifer — was eatin' everything in sight like there was no tomorrow. I swear, that heifer got two years' worth of growth in only a few weeks!

"I don't know what happened next, on account of we took the cows down off the mountain. But I reckon that heifer found a cave somewhere and hibernated like the bear she thought she was."

"You never saw it again?" an intrigued sailor asked.

"You don't know what happened?" another wondered.

"Is that the end of the story?" someone said.

"Well, come spring we — me and a ranahan from the northern plains who went by the name of DW — took the cows back up to that high country. Me and DW was out in the timber layin' in firewood for the cookstove when we heard some kind of ruction off in the trees.

"You may not believe it, boys, but it was that selfsame heifer! It had woke up from its long winter nap and, like a bear comin' out of hibernation, it was as hungry and grouchy as it was ravenous and ornery. And I'll tell you this — over the winter that heifer's horns had grown a good two feet on either end. All that fat it had packed on in the fall had turned that yearling calf into a full-grown bovine!

"Me and DW watched it paw around in the dirt and horn apart logs looking for bear grub and DW got curious. 'What do you suppose that cow's doin', Rawhide?' he asks me. I says, 'That ain't no cow, DW. I know it looks like one, but it thinks it's a bear.' 'A bear?' he says, and I says, 'A bear.' 'Well,' says DW, 'it sure is actin' like a bear. A right surly one, at that.'

"All that conversation attracted the attention of that heifer-bear and it reared up on its hind legs and took to lookin' around and sniffin' us out. Then it lets out a beller — sounded for all the world like the roar of a bear — and starts in to pawin' the ground. 'I think it's gonna come after us,' DW says. 'I do believe you're right, DW,' I says, and drops my ax. I says, 'I'm for gettin' out of here!' 'Why that's plumb foolish,' DW says. 'You can't outrun a bear.' So I says, 'I don't have to outrun the bear, DW — I only have to outrun you!' And with that, I lit out of there."

Rawhide Robinson took a moment to catch his breath. But the sailors, breathless though they were in their excitement, were also impatient, and encouraged the cowboy to continue.

"What happened?!" one asked.

"What did that bear do?!" asked another.

"You ran off and left DW?!" someone said.

"Did it get DW?!" someone wondered.

"Well!?" a chorus inquired.

After a suitable interval, Rawhide Robinson continued. "Not to fear, boys. Me and DW both got out of there unscathed. Here's what happened.

"That heifer-bear was comin' after us with blood in her eyes, crashin' through the timber a whole lot faster than me and DW could ambulate. Before long, we could feel hot breath scorching our backsides and we both figured we were goners.

"Then, with a crash and a bang and a boom and a clatter, that heifer-bear came to a screeching halt, its horns embedded in a pair of trees too narrow apart to allow passage. Plumb stuck, it was. And none too happy about it, I'm here to tell you. It pawed and stomped and ranted and raved until it wore itself out.

"Me and DW, we went about collectin' our firewood and got it stacked nice and neat back at the line shack. Then we cut a handful of docile steers out of the herd and drove them into the woods where that heifer was held captive by its own fractiousness. They milled around and nosed around and nuzzled around that heifer-bear and otherwise got acquainted.

"The presence of them steers somehow awakened that heifer to the fact that she was bovine rather than bear. Once she was thoroughly convinced of her species — and considerably calmer — we chopped down the imprisoning trees and released her into the herd.

"Last I heard, that cow was still alive on that ranch and dropping good calves every spring. And, so far as I know, there ain't a one of them ever been born thinkin' it was a bear."

The sailors sat quiet, contemplating Rawhide Robinson's tale.

But the silence was soon shattered with a shout from Ensign Scott: "All hands on deck!"

Chapter Twenty-Eight

So entranced had the sailors been with Rawhide Robinson's narrative that they failed to notice a squall line coming on a collision course with the USS *Cordwood*. The officers and sailors on duty, of course, were already at their work to prepare the ship for the storm and the erstwhile audience joined the arrangements like cogs in a clock that kept perfect time.

Rawhide Robinson, Happy Harry, and Hurry hustled about the decks readying the camels for the storm. They checked and made firm their halters, secured the tie ropes, and used whistles and words and taps and tugs to get the camels to their knees. With a lower center of gravity, the animals would more easily ride out the rocking and rolling and plunging and lunging and dipping and dropping of the ship that the winds and waves would soon cause.

His work done, the cowboy watched with

mouth agape as the sailors scrambled up and down and across the masts and yards manipulating lines and sails. Others quick-timed it up and down the hatches, through the holds and over the decks, accomplishing their assigned tasks. Orders and instructions flew on the wind like seafoam as the storm intensified — much of it in a language Rawhide Robinson did not recognize:

"Take in sail!"

"Ease the sheets!"

"Reef the gallant!"

"Batten down the hatches!"

The building wind blew orders apart until the cowboy, bracing himself to stay upright on the rolling deck, heard only fragments as they blustered by:

"— robands —"

"— jackstay —"

"— braces —"

"— clewlines —"

"— buntlines —"

"— tacklines —"

"— sheetlines —"

Then Hurry, who should have been below, tugged on his arm. He bent low to hear her holler, "Okyanus! Okyanus!"

"Okyanus? What about Okyanus?"

"I cannot find him! He is not with his mother!" she said as she tug, tug, tugged on his arm.

"Did you check the other stalls down there?"

"Yes! Everywhere!"

"You looked in all the corners and crannies?"

"Everywhere!"

"You're sure?"

"Yes!"

Rawhide Robinson lifted his thirteen-gallon lid — which took a fair amount of tugging, snugged down as it was in the high wind — and scratched his head in contemplation.

"Hurry, I'll find him. You best get below. This wind will likely blow you right away or a wave wash you overboard, small as you are."

"No! I will not be concerned for my own safety while Okyanus is in danger!" she said before darting off through the spindrift.

"Hurry! Hurry!" the cowboy hollered helplessly, his shouts shattering in the wind and wafting away. He snatched up a coil of rope from a locker and tied a honda in the end, fashioning a makeshift lariat to catch the little camel if necessary — if he could find it in the confusion.

He stumbled and staggered and slipped and slid around the pitching deck, poking into every possible place the camel calf might be secreted. Every time the landlubber thought he had found his footing, the bow of the ship would plow into another wave, upsetting his balance. With the ship pointing into the wind as much as the captain and crew could accomplish, the impact of the waves striking the hull was somewhat diminished, but the blow was still significant enough to spill the cowboy onto the planks.

No sooner would he recover and regain his feet than the *Cordwood* would pitch upward to climb the swell and pause precariously on the crest before sliding steeply and swiftly into the coming trough. "*$*#)$*%!" he said to himself. "I would lots rather be chinnin' the moon on the hump of a jack-knifin' head-boggin' end-swappin' bronc!"

Rawhide Robinson no sooner got his pins back beneath him after yet another in a long line of nose-first visits to the wood when his prey plummeted past in a yawping panic with a howling Hurry hot on his heels.

He thrust out an arm and caught Hurry by the collar, lifted her off her feet and stuffed her into a locker and slammed the lid shut, then set off in pursuit of Okyanus.

The calf glanced off gunwales and

bounced off bulwarks and caromed off coamings with the cowboy chasing after. He saw his shot and took it about the time a monster wave battered the ship, and Rawhide Robinson's backside met the deck as he reeled in his slack. The catch slowed the stampeding camel calf only for a moment, and, with nothing to dally to, the cowboy could only hang on as Okyanus towed him across the slippery deck.

Then the camel ran past the mainmast and Rawhide Robinson managed to veer to the opposite side. He slowed. He stopped. He ducked around the mast, taking a rough-and-ready dally, then tied off to a cleat. He was reeling in the terror-stricken calf and having a time of it when the escaped Hurry arrived. (How she broke out of the locker, by the by, remains a mystery to this day.) She paused only to kick the cowboy — albeit lightly — on the shin, then ran to Okyanus, embracing the camel calf and calming it.

The pair of people kept the calf constrained while the cowboy, in sailor parlance, "took a bight in the line," around the camel's neck, passed it back through the honda and looped it over Okyanus's nose, creating a temporary halter with his lariat. The camel handlers considered taking the calf below to the comfort and care of its mother, but the pitching deck and whipping wind and splashing waves and sloshing water forbade the preferred course of action, so they tucked the camel into the first stall on the main deck they could get to. Rawhide Robinson manhandled the door open against the wind and Hurry urged the baby inside.

Tulu, whose home they invaded, gave only a backward glance and continued chewing his cud as uncaring as if he were kneeling in soft sand on a calm desert day.

"There is so little room," Hurry worried. "Will not the large camel crush Okyanus?"

"I don't believe so," Rawhide Robinson said. "It's going to take more than this storm to move Tulu. Besides, with less room to rattle around in, I think the little feller will be safer here. We might as well ride it out right here ourselves. I don't fancy goin' back out there if we don't have to."

The USS *Cordwood* sailed through the storm for hours, which seemed to Rawhide Robinson like days. He feared every wave would smash the ship to splinters the size of cactus thorns and every wind gust roll her over like a tripped steer and every cloudburst flood her like foam filling a beer mug. But when the seas calmed somewhat and the wind died down to a gale and waves subsided to the size of hills rather than mountains, he dozed off, exhausted, in the cozy confines of Tulu's stall. Hurry and Okyanus likewise snoozed, serenaded by the lullaby of Tulu chewing his cud as rhythmically as the tick-tock of a clock.

Sunlight filled the stall when Ibrahim opened the door. Rawhide Robinson jumped to his feet as if on springs. Hurry sat up, rubbing her eyes and gathering her wits. Okyanus slept on and Tulu chewed his cud, giving his keeper but a bored backward glance.

Ibrahim started shouting. He screamed and shrieked and squawked and screeched. He bellowed and blustered and barked and bawled. By the time his tirade reached the level of howling and hueing and hooting and hollering, every member of company and crew not otherwise occupied had gathered around.

During the rare occurrence of a lull in the tongue-lashing, Rawhide Robinson said, "Happy Harry, what the heck is he haranguing me about?"

"He is most unhappy with your presence in the quarters of his camel — the camel he *thinks* is his, I should say."

"I gathered as much as that. But why?"

"He believes the presence of an infidel — which is you — exposes his charge to evil. He says Tulu, who is of royal blood and lineage, is dishonored by association with the calf, which is of lowly breeding and thus unclean. He expresses the opinion that Huri, being but a female and a child, is inferior and her proximity may corrupt Tulu."

Ibrahim's uproar eventually wound down, but not before Major Benjamin Wayne and Captain Howard Clemmons were called to the scene to restore order. The infuriated Turk would listen to no one else:

He had resisted Rawhide Robinson's requests to pipe down.

He had ignored Happy Harry's appeals for calm.

He had brushed aside Ensign Ian Scott's demands to desist.

He had disregarded Hurry's calls for quiet to avoid upsetting Okyanus.

He had pooh-poohed the pleadings of several sailors to shut up.

When Ibrahim refused to even acknowledge the military officers' orders to put a cork in it, Rawhide Robinson drew his trusty six-gun from its holster, pointed it skyward, and dropped the hammer. The unexpected explosion surprised all to silence, including Ibrahim.

Once the officers had a grasp on the situation at hand, they lit into Ibrahim like hogs on a slop trough.

"Ibrahim, these camels are the property of the United States Army. Tulu is not your property, and your responsibility for his care is neither more nor less than that of the others. You will stop pretending he is your personal charge or you will be put ashore at first opportunity," Major Wayne said.

"Ibrahim, this ship is under my command and you have upset order and harmony for the last time. One more rumpus, one more uproar on your part and I will have you in chains!" Captain Clemmons said.

"Ibrahim, Mister Robinson and the girl were doing no more than their part to protect the lives of the camels. Which is more than you did, I am told, cowering in your quarters while others secured the animals. Another such dereliction of duty, and I shall request Captain Clemmons and his crew keelhaul you!" Major Wayne said.

"Ibrahim, while you are not a sailor and thus somewhat shielded from military discipline, you are, nevertheless, required by laws, statutes, rules, regulations, protocols, practices, procedures, edicts, decrees, conventions, concords, and any and every other such ruling to do your part to contribute to, and do nothing to hinder, the orderly operation of this ship. I may well take under advisement Major Wayne's suggestion to have you keelhauled! Or, perhaps, I shall seat you in the bosun's chair and let you dangle for a spell between the devil and the deep blue sea!" Captain Clemmons said.

After hearing Happy Harry's none-too-happy translation of the officers' harangues, Ibrahim seethed. He stewed. He sweltered. He smoldered. He frothed. He fumed. He foamed. He bristled and boiled and burned. Roiled and rankled, flamed and fizzled, chafed and — well, suffice it to say that while he remained angry he uttered not another word.

And so, yet another storm had passed.

CHAPTER TWENTY-NINE

After the big blow blew itself away and the huge waves wore themselves out, the voyage across the Atlantic was uneventful. Beyond uneventful, it was tedious and tiresome. Monotonous and mundane. Boring and banal. Dull and dreary. And downright wearisome.

One afternoon as the USS *Cordwood* sliced through the sea in winds so favorable the ship all but sailed itself, Rawhide Robinson, as was his wont, determined to lift the spirits of the sailors with another tale of bravery and daring in the Wild West.

"Say, boys, how many of you-all have ever been to San Francisco?" he asked by way of introduction. Many of the seamen responded in the affirmative, as San Francisco Bay was a common port of call for military and commercial vessels plying the waters of the Pacific Ocean.

"Years ago," he said, "I was working on a

ranch on the west slope of the Sierras some ways east of there. I was out hunting stray cattle one day and followed the Merced River up into the mountains. After riding a while upriver, the hills started closing in and I found myself in a narrow canyon. The sides were some steep, but not so much a cow couldn't graze them — and there was good grass everywhere. I spied cattle on the hills here and there and rode up and pushed them down, but left them along the river as I figured to collect them on the way back down the canyon, like you do on a gather.

"The farther upstream I rode the prettier that place got. Grass and wildflowers carpeted the slopes, with clumps of trees here and there, and that clear cold stream clattering across the rocks in the riverbed. Would have been a nice place to start a spread, if only that canyon had any spread to it — but, for those who know your letters, it looked like a vast letter 'V' with no room in the bottom but for the river."

"Is this story about anything?" some impatient sailor asked.

"As the disciple James says in the Good Book, sailor, 'Be patient therefore, brethren.' So you reel in your tongue and mind your manners. I'll get to it in my own good time."

"#*%&%," the antsy seaman whispered.

301

"Now, then, where was I?" the cowboy inquired. But it was a rhetorical question as the raconteur well knew the status of his story. "A little ways farther up that canyon, I caught a whiff of woodsmoke so I knowed I was not alone. After a while I encountered the source of the smoke, which was, as I assumed, a campfire.

"But it was not your ordinary campfire. Fact is, it was bigger than your average bonfire. It was mostly down to coals, as the day was well advanced, but you could still see the logs was the size of trees. And a nearby stack of firewood — stack of timber, more like — bore that out. The ax sticking out of a stump had a handle nearly as long and broad as that mizzen-mast over there —"

"Piffle!"

"Hooey!"

"Tommyrot!"

"Twaddle!"

— came a chorus of reactions from suspicious sailors.

"I tell you it's true, boys, and that ain't the half of it. The boot tracks around that camp was the size of a buffalo wallow. Layin' there was a frying pan of a size you couldn't wrap a lariat around and a coffee cup you could bathe an elephant in. Boys, there was a stack of bones there that looked to be the remains of entire elk and deer, gnawed on like you would a roast chicken. And there beside them bones was a toothpick you could use for a wagon tongue.

"Once I'd took it all in, I rode on up the canyon. I wasn't sure I wanted to run across whoever made that camp, but when you're a-huntin' cows you cover the country no matter what. It's The Cowboy Way."

Rawhide Robinson took to his feet and ambled over to a water keg and dipped himself out a dollop of refreshment. "I declare, fellers, the salt in these sea breezes does give a man a mighty thirst."

"C'mon, cowboy! Get on with it!" someone said. Other irked listeners agreed, offering similar encouragements.

"Well, I rode on up the canyon and soon could see disturbances in the stream bed. There were piles of boulders here and there along the river and dug-out places along the bank. Then I spied there in a clump of trees the worn-out head of a miner's pick the size of a railroad engine. It all told me that whatever else this man was, he was a prospector lookin' to strike gold — of which there has been a mighty amount found in them mountains, I don't have to remind you.

"After a while I could hear digging — a shovel biting into the riverbank — then what sounded like water sloshing in a trough. Then I rounded a bend and I seen him."

Again, Rawhide Robinson paused for effect, and again the audience urged him on.

"There he was. There wasn't no mistaking it. You couldn't miss that man if you was blindfolded. I tell you, he was so big he'd make that feller Balaban back in Smyrna seem small. He was panning out what I'd heard him digging, and that gold pan was the size of — well, I've seen lakes that was smaller. When he'd slosh that water around in that pan, it'd make waves near the size of them in that storm we had a while back.

"Then he saw me. I don't know if he figured I was a claim jumper or what, but he came roarin' out of that river like a grizzly bear with an angry boil on its backside. Grabbed up that giant-size shovel and came after me with real intent and malice aforethought. I spun that horse around and switched directions like a bank shot on a billiard ball. That immense miner was on my heels and chopping down at me with that spade every step of the way. And every time he stabbed at me with that shovel he'd peel a slice off the side of that canyon. It went on that way a fair piece down that ravine till he must have decided I wasn't no threat to his claim and not likely to pay a return visit. And he was right, I'm here to tell you."

Again, the cowboy chronicler suspended his story.

"That's it?" one sailor asked.

"That's the end?" another wondered.

"That's all there is?" still another inquired.

"Well, that's the most of it," Rawhide Robinson resumed. "When that gargantuan gold digger started back to his claim I reined up on a ridge to rest my horse. Like me, he was wound as tight as a dally around a saddle horn so we stopped for a blow and to regain our equilibrium.

"I sneaked a peek back up the canyon to make sure that monstrous mucker was still making his way back to his placer place and laid eyes on a sight so sublime my brain thought my eyes was playin' tricks on me."

"What?"

"What was it?"

"What did you see?"

"I'm telling you boys, where once there was nothin' but a steep-sided canyon — which are as plentiful as prospectors in all them mountain ranges out west — I was lookin' at a valley the like of which you've never seen. Or, far as that goes, nobody had ever seen, until that very minute.

"That rock washer's shovel had sheared off the sides of them mountains until they was, well, sheer. Lining that new little valley on both side was cliffs reaching straight up to the sky. They looked so smooth and slick a spider couldn't get a foothold with any one of his eight feet. Little creeks and streams that used to run down them side hills to meet the river was now waterfalls that looked to be a mile high. Plumb precipitous, them parapets was."

"I don't believe a word of it," a skeptical sailor said.

"That can't possibly be so," a cynical seaman said.

"You'd have to show me before I'd believe it," said a sailor who happened to hail from Missouri.

"Ensign Ian!" Rawhide Robinson hollered, hailing the young officer who happened to be nearby. "I was a-tellin' these doubting Thomases about a place I seen out in the Sierra Nevada mountains of California. Being such an educated and well-read feller, maybe they'll believe you. You ever hear tell of a place called Yosemite?"

The young ensign did not hesitate even a moment. "Why certainly," he said. "Yosem-

306

ite is well known for its spectacular scenery and geological formations. It is named for a band of Indians who once lived in the area — those Indians, by the way, called the place 'Ahwahnee.' While I have not visited Yosemite myself, I have read several accounts by travelers who marvel at its giant cliffs and magnificent waterfalls."

"See," Rawhide Robinson said with a sly smile. "Just like I said."

The speechless sailors, of course, offered no reply.

With a wink, the cowboy spraddled his legs, leaned back against a bulkhead and tipped his thirteen-gallon hat down over his eyes for an afternoon nap, rocked to sleep by the gentle rolling of the USS *Cordwood*.

CHAPTER THIRTY

The Port of Kingston on the island of Jamaica was busy, bustling, boisterous, and hurly-burly with much hubbub, buzz, fuss, and flurry. On any given day, one could locate ships from the seven seas, six continents, and four corners of the earth berthed there. Hurry, ever curious and constantly on the hunt for unfamiliar and exhilarating opportunities, was in heaven.

The USS *Cordwood* stopped over there to refresh and replenish supplies and stores for the last leg of the journey home, and the sailors and officers were given shore leave. Likewise, Rawhide Robinson, Happy Harry, Hurry, and even ornery Ibrahim were free to come and go at their pleasure.

After a quick canvass of Kingston, Hurry hatched an idea. She hashed it over with Happy Harry. Recounted it to Rawhide Robinson. Conversed with Captain Clemmons. Mentioned it to Major Wayne. Elicited Ensign Ian's approval. All gave their blessing to the notion — even expressing admiration for her entrepreneurial spirit — and pitched in with the few preparations required.

Several sailors assisted by disseminating information up and down the wharf and in the streets and squares of the city. Word spread. Excitement mounted. Interest accelerated. Eagerness expanded. Anticipation enlarged. Enthusiasm increased.

And the curious from throughout Kingston congregated. Stevedores and roustabouts, sailors and seaman, slaves and servants, sales clerks and shopkeepers, tradesmen and chambermaids, peons and pencil pushers, beggars and bankers, the prostitute and the parvenu, the filthy rich and the merely filthy all lined up to board the *Cordwood* to see the wonders there — wonders never before seen in Kingston, despite its standing as one of the world's most cosmopolitan seaports.

A steady stream of people paraded up and down the gangplanks and through the gangways, and into Hurry's hamper went admittance fees in coin and currency from across the continents: dollars, drachmas, and ducats, pounds and pesos, rupees, reals, and rubles, francs and florins, escudos and schillings, wén and mon, lira and guilders, tael and thalers, all these and more aggregated, accumulated, and amassed in the basket.

Those awaiting entrance were eager, those departing pleased. None was disappointed and none regretted the price of admission. Some saw fit to shell out for a second, even third and fifth opportunity to experience the exotic allure offered aboard the ship.

Plenteous people — nay, a plethora of patrons — paid for the simple pleasure of filing past an exhibition representative of the USS *Cordwood*'s unusual cargo. They were first exposed to a few ordinary drome-daries which, to the viewers, were an extraordinary sight. Hurry and Happy Harry stood by to answer inquiries concerning the camels — their propensities and proclivities, appearance and appetites, behaviors and habits, idiosyncrasies and peculiarities, and more.

But the best was yet to come.

The pinnacle of the performance, the high point of the exhibition, the pièce de résistance of the display was the disparity, the disproportion, the contrast and comparison of the species provided by the side-by-side spectacle of Tulu and Okyanus.

One large, one small. One short, one tall.

One massive, the other minute. One tiny, one towering. One enormous, the other diminutive. One capacious, one picayune. The distinctions were both amusing and educational, and the audience enjoyed each aspect. It is impossible to say which of the pair proved more popular — the stately Tulu or the cute Okyanus. Regardless, all who regarded the assemblage retired gratified.

It should be mentioned, as well, that even the ordinarily ornery Ibrahim got into the spirit of the occasion and elevated the experience for the audience. He outfitted Tulu in his royal accoutrements and he, himself, dressed in the finery he had worn when parading around with the pasha's camels during Ottoman excursions, activities, and exhibitions. The colorful silks and satins, fringes and fandangles, beads and baubles, embellishments and adornments added to the enjoyment of all.

Through it all, enjoyment of a different kind visited the *Cordwood*'s crew. Officers and sailors alike were given shore leave while awaiting the resupply of the ship and the hosting of the ungulate exhibit. The grog shops of Kingston enjoyed their presence and patronage — especially in light of the fact that their usual clientele was obsessed with dromedaries — and the men enjoyed a respite from shipboard routine.

Rawhide Robinson, no stranger to adventure, enjoyed roaming the streets of Kingston and the surrounding countryside. Like any cowboy, he never walked when he could ride, so ride he did. A rented horse from a local livery served him well. He dusted off a rented saddle, strapped on his spurs, buckled on his chaps, snugged down his thirteen-gallon hat and lit out to see the sights.

The presence of an American cowboy in Kingston was every bit as peculiar as the camels aboard the *Cordwood,* and Rawhide Robinson drew curious stares everywhere he ventured. Pelted with questions, engulfed with appeals, overwhelmed with interest, the horseman was ever polite and accommodating while making every effort to escape the scrutiny.

He rode to the top of Strawberry Hill to enjoy panoramic views of Kingston and the Blue Mountains. He rode the skittish horse across the cast-iron bridge over the *Rio Cobre.* He rode out the peninsula — the *Palisadoes* — to Port Royal to visit the ruined Fort Charles. He rode through Spanish Town to appreciate the architecture. He rode anywhere the wind took him, delighted to be back in the saddle after months afoot and at sea. He only wished for a herd of cattle as the itch to return to his accustomed career was overwhelming. Even so, the simple act of being aboard a horse and feeling the wind whip his earlobes as he loped the island pony up and down the beach brought abundant pleasure and, in the circumstances, was as good as it was going to get.

Alack and alas, Rawhide Robinson was reminded of the truth of Chaucer's words: "There is an end to everything, to good things as well." And, all too soon, he was back aboard the USS *Cordwood*. Which, in itself, when seen through a wider lens, when taking a broader view, when looking at the big picture, when seeing a larger perspective, in the grand scheme of things, was good — no, great — news.

For it would only be about a week until the wandering cowboy would once again set foot on the soil of his beloved Texas.

CHAPTER THIRTY-ONE

By the time the Matagorda peninsula came into view, Rawhide Robinson had all but crawled out onto the bowsprit of the USS *Cordwood* to get a glimpse of his homeland. His enthusiasm was infectious, and Hurry was as excited as her cowboy friend. The ship heeled into Pass Cavallo, leaving the Gulf of Mexico and entering Matagorda Bay. Indian Point, at the entrance of Powderhorn Bayou, was the destination, home to the port of Indianola.

As soon as the ship dropped anchor and a boat was lowered to take Captain Clemmons ashore to make arrangements for a berth, Rawhide Robinson, with an eager Hurry in tow, cadged a seat in the launch. The girl watched with amusement as the cowboy scrambled up the ladder ashore, dropped to his knees and kissed the quay.

"I've been away from home for months and months and I am plumb overjoyed to be back in the good old U.S. of A!" he explained. "C'mon, Hurry!"

The unlikely couple drew more than a few curious glances as they hustled along the wharf toward the town of Indianola. The wharf and the streets were busy and bustling. Boxes and barrels, crates and kegs, drays and wagons, pushcarts and carriages, and — in vast numbers and large quantities — cotton bales were everywhere.

Before long, Rawhide Robinson slid to a halt at the feet of a street vendor and flipped her a coin. A wide grin spread across the cowboy's face as a cloud of aromatic steam rose when the woman lifted the cloth covering a clay pot.

"They're called *tamales,*" he explained as Hurry curiously eyed the corn-husked bundle he handed her. "They taste like heaven."

She nibbled cautiously at the husk.

"No, girl! You don't eat that part. Here, peel it back," he said as he demonstrated. "Now, take a chomp on that."

Still careful, she mouthed a morsel of *masa* while Rawhide Robinson gnawed off half his tamale in a single bite. Soon she, too, was wolfing down the comestible with enthusiasm. "It is good!" she said.

Another coin brought another serving of

the treats.

Then another.

Hurry hungered for yet another, and looked longingly back at the vendor as she hurried up the dusty street in Rawhide Robinson's footsteps. His path soon veered into the open door of a cantina and before Hurry sat down, he called for chili.

Again, the girl studied the sizzling stew and stack of toasty tortillas with trepidation. And again, she was soon scooping and shoveling and dipping and dunking with enthusiasm. While the savor and flavor, the spices and seasonings, the textures and tastes were far removed from her favorite Levantine vittles, she appreciated the piquancy and pungency, and the way her tongue and throat tingled from the tang of chili peppers.

It was much the same with the burritos and enchiladas, the tostadas and tacos, the guacamole and frijoles. Hurry was soon overstuffed and eager for more. Instead, the plump pair waddled to the town square and shaded up under a *ramada* for a rejuvenating nap.

The *Cordwood* was going about the business of tying up at a slip when the contented cowboy and gratified girl returned to the wharf. Hurry regaled Happy Harry with reports and reviews of the local cuisine as she and he and Ibrahim and Rawhide Robinson and the assigned sailors groomed the dromedaries for the final time aboard the ship. Major Benjamin Wayne arrived as the halters were hung on the camels, coming back aboard after securing accommodations for the animals and contacting his superiors at the War Department to report the safe arrival of the cargo.

"Robinson, Harry, come with me if you please," the major said.

They met in Captain Howard Clemmons's quarters, where the officer and Ensign Ian Scott were already huddled in a cloud of Clemmons's pipe smoke.

"Welcome, gentlemen," Clemmons said. "Major, the matter we discussed has been dealt with. I have been in contact with the Navy Department by telegraph. It is all arranged."

"Excellent," Wayne said. "Robinson, Harry, this involves you, which is why I invited you here."

Rawhide Robinson looked at Happy Harry.

Happy Harry looked at Rawhide Robinson.

Rawhide Robinson and Happy Harry looked at Major Wayne.

Major Wayne looked at Captain Clemmons.

Happy Harry and Rawhide Robinson looked at Captain Clemmons.

Captain Clemmons said, "The matter at hand pertains to Ensign Ian Scott."

Captain Clemmons, Major Wayne, Rawhide Robinson, and Happy Harry looked at Ensign Scott.

"Ensign Scott," Clemmons said, "has requested detached service from the United States Navy and his request has been granted."

"Ensign Scott," Wayne said, "has requested temporary assignment with my command to continue assisting with the camel operation."

"This news makes me happy!" Happy Harry said.

"Why, that is right good news!" Rawhide Robinson said. "I'm tickled pink to think of Ensign Ian as our cock-a-doodle-do."

Ensign Scott looked flummoxed.

Happy Harry looked baffled.

Captain Clemmons looked confused.

"Cock-a-doodle-do?" Major Wayne said. "What does the call of a rooster have to do with it? What are you talking about?"

"Oh, I'm sorry, Major. It's cowboy lingo. Lots of times, the big man on a ranch, say

318

the owner or manager, is the *jefe* or 'old man' or ramrod. That would be you, meanin' no disrespect. Second in command, the foreman, he'd be the *segundo* or straw boss — or, sometimes, cock-a-doodle-do. Sounds like that'll be Ensign Ian from here on.

"I am of the opinion that this here youngster has proved himself a good man and worthy of the title, frivolous as it may seem to you what ain't cowboys. But for us in the saddle, it signifies his being a good man. Means he's dependable. A man you can trust. When workin' cattle there's a thousand things can happen, and 999 of them's bad. So, you want the man givin' orders to be willing to step up and handle whatever comes.

"But there ain't none of that makes no never mind. Let's leave it that it'll be good to have Ensign Ian along as cock-a-doodle-do of this here outfit."

Ensign Scott crimsoned with the compliment and despite his voluminous vocabulary could find no words for the occasion.

"Good enough," Wayne said.

"I might add," Captain Clemmons said, "that Ensign Scott is no longer Ensign Scott — he has been promoted to lieutenant junior grade, and should hereafter be addressed as Lieutenant Scott."

"Well done," said the major.

"Good show!" said Happy Harry.

"Well! Congratulations are in order, Ensign Ian," Rawhide Robinson said.

"That's 'Lieutenant' Ian," the newly promoted officer said.

"All right Lieutenant, Robinson, Harry — let's see to the animals," Wayne said, and the men paraded off to the main deck of the USS *Cordwood.*

"You know, Ensign Ian," Rawhide Robinson said, looking around at the ship that had been his home these many months. "I'm gonna miss this old boat."

"Ship," the young officer corrected. "And it's Lieutenant."

"One question — your request to stick with the camels wouldn't have anything to do with our girl Hurry, would it?"

The newly minted lieutenant said not a word, but turned the color of a copper penny.

Major Wayne walked up and down the rows of camels arranged on the deck, each with halter and packsaddle in place, as if inspecting infantry troops. He seemed pleased with the successful accomplishment of this phase of his mission. The ship had left the Levant with thirty-three healthy camels and arrived on American shores with thirty-four — albeit one of them being but a youngster.

"Men," he said to the sailors handling the camels, "your service to our cause is most appreciated. You have, on this mission, undertaken duties most unfamiliar — even unique — in the annals of naval history. Your performance has been exemplary."

As the major addressed the men, one, if listening carefully, could hear an occasional sniffle, an uncomfortable cough. The odd tear could be seen tracing its path down a ruddy cheek.

"We ask one final assignment of you. Corrals have been acquired to hold the camels across town, which will require marching them through the heart of Indianola. You men are to assist with the maneuver. Again, your meritorious service has been much appreciated."

"Sir?" a sailor said, snapping a salute.

"Yes, Sailor?"

"What will become of the camels after that, sir?"

"We will hold them until a cavalry escort arrives from Camp Verde. They should be underway tomorrow and we will expect them in about a week's time. The camels will then be taken to Camp Verde along the military road — a journey of some 200 miles. Once we arrive there, orders will come down from the War Department for deploying the camels. Mister Robinson, Harry, Ibrahim, and the girl will stay with us and oversee the training of army camel handlers and packers at Camp Verde."

Within minutes after the completion of the major's remarks, the cleated gangplank connecting the *Cordwood* to the wharf repeatedly sagged and rebounded under the weight of the camels plodding across, their shifting weight causing the ship itself to rock in the still waters of the harbor. Once the dromedaries were offloaded and assembled on the wharf, Major Wayne gave the order to proceed. The camel caravan set off in single file, with Hurry handling the halter rope of Okyanus, bringing up the rear behind Tulu.

The end of the procession had yet to reach the streets of Indianola when all hell broke loose.

It started with the chickens scratching and pecking around in the dust and dirt of the streets of Indianola. As soon as the camels came in sight, the fowl flipped out. The birds went berserk. The cluckers went loco. The hens went as mad as a hatter and the roosters went round the bend. They flapped and flailed, squawked and screeched, ske-daddled and skittered through the streets — and, of course, chickens gone cuckoo only contributed to the cacophony and confusion created by the camels.

A hitch of six mules on a freight wagon parked at a warehouse loading dock spooked and tore off up the road, scattering traffic as they went.

A pair of saddle horses at a hitch rail panicked, ripping the crossbar from the rail and ran off, yoked together by the flopping pole.

A cart capsized when the donkey drawing it decamped, spilling a load of melons into the street.

A buckboard bashed into a porch post, collapsing the roof.

Saddle horses bucked and ran away. Hitched horses upset their conveyances. Dogs barked. Burros brayed. Pigs squealed. People yelled and yelped, scampered and scuttled, hid and holed up, flopped and fainted.

Major Wayne, leading the caravan causing all the commotion, could only continue on. Never, not once, had the notion that such tumult could result from the mere presence of camels occurred to him. And so, like a good soldier, he marched on through all the ruction and rumpus. The camel handlers, likewise, ducked their heads and carried on.

The camels plodded along, calm and uncaring, placid and passive.

"Hold it right there!" came a booming command, loud enough to be heard over all the hubbub. Standing in the middle of the street, shotgun in hand, stood a tall Texan with a star tacked to his chest.

Major Wayne signaled a halt.

"What in Sam Hill is goin' on here? What're you doin' with them critters?" the lawman hollered.

"They are camels, Marshal."

"I can see they're camels. I seen 'em in picture books. What're they doin' in my town?"

The major told the law enforcement officer that the camels were the property of the United States Army and would be billeted in town while awaiting escort to Camp Verde. A gathering crowd craned to hear the conversation.

"Are you nuts? You ain't keepin' no camels around here. I won't have 'em tearin' up the town."

Major Wayne turned and studied the caravan for a moment then told the officer, "As far as I can see, Marshal, my camels haven't torn up anything. I'm sure you'll agree they are well-mannered and altogether docile."

"Look around, soldier! Them camels might not've made this mess, but they sure as shootin' caused it!"

"I am sorry, sir, but I cannot be responsible for the behavior of those not under my command. Your citizens and their livestock are to blame, not my camels."

"*$&#^!" the marshal said. "I suppose you're right. But it never would've happened were it not for them ugly animals!"

"Ugly?" Major Wayne bristled. "*Ugly?!* These animals are noble beasts in service to our country."

The crowd's many members, chortled and chuckled, tittered and tee-heed, giggled and guffawed, snickered and snorted.

"These camels are owed your respect, sir," the major said to the marshal, and turning to the crowd, continued as a military officer accustomed to giving orders and being obeyed: "And the respect of every other person in this city!"

The crowd laughed.

"Ha!" came a voice from the throng. "They look like somebody's idea of a joke!"

"Gangly-legged, ewe-necked monstrosities," another hollered.

"Besides that, they stink!"

"What are they good for, anyway?"

The major held a gloved hand aloft, signaling for silence. The insults and jibes faded. "The United States Army went to great lengths and considerable expense to acquire these camels."

Again the crowd laughed. Again, the major raised a hand for silence.

"Our intention is to use them as pack animals to supply isolated forts and military outposts in the southwestern deserts."

"Pack animals?" someone hollered. "Ha! They look like they'd tip over!"

The crowd laughed.

Rawhide Robinson stepped forward and hitched his thumbs into the armholes of his vest. "Now you folks listen to me," he said. "These here camels is fine animals."

The crowd laughed.

"Get a horse!" an anonymous voice yelled from the throng.

"I been on more horses than most of you folks have seen," the cowboy said. "I got nothin' against horses. I *like* horses. These camels ain't horses and nobody expects them to be. When it comes to hauling a load, they're better than horses. So you-all ought to quit makin' chin music till you know whereof you speak."

The crowd laughed.

Happy Harry and Major Wayne huddled with Rawhide Robinson for a moment as taunts, mockery, and opprobrium from the crowd continued. Happy Harry stepped aside and signaled Ibrahim to bring Tulu to the front of the line.

Rawhide Robinson said, "All right, you all, we'll just see what a camel can do. As I remember, these here cotton bales you got stacked up all over the place weighs about 500 pounds apiece. Is that right?"

Several voices from the crowd answered in the affirmative.

"Any of you-all got a horse could pack one of them bales?"

The congregation replied in the negative.

"How about a mule?"

Again, voices from the throng agreed that no mule could carry a cotton bale.

"I suppose if you had a good, stout horse or mule well-broke to the pack saddle he could maybe haul half of one of them bales. That about right?"

The crowd concurred.

"Hey, you!" Rawhide Robinson hollered to a man sitting on a cart drawn by a yoke of oxen. The cart carried two tight bales of cotton. "Drive that cart over here."

The curious crowd "oohed" when Ibrahim led the giant camel up and "aahed" when, at his command, Tulu knelt, then squatted, in the street.

"Now," the cowboy said, "how about a bunch of you fellers with strong backs come over here."

The volunteers grunted and groaned one of the cotton bales out of the cart and hefted, hauled, and humped it to Tulu's side.

The crowd watched with bated breath, save a few who expressed concern for the camel. When Rawhide Robinson requested the strong men move another bale to Tulu's opposite side, the crowd stirred even more.

Some worried the camel would be injured under such a load.

Others maintained the camel would not suffer as he could not possibly shift so much weight.

Still others were amused at the very notion of the demonstration.

Hurry, meanwhile, acting on her own hook as was her wont, circulated through the assembled onlookers taking bets on the camel's ability to haul the load. Backed by the money obtained from her sideshow in Jamaica, she took any and all wagers.

Under Ibrahim's direction, the bales were secured to Tulu's pack saddle, one on each side.

"He ready, Harry?" Rawhide Robinson said.

Happy Harry and Ibrahim exchanged a few words and Harry said they were ready.

"Well, folks, you are the first citizens of this here United States to witness the worth of camels," the cowboy said.

He nodded at Ibrahim, who spoke to Tulu.

The intake of breath among the crowd was so pronounced that the air pressure in Indianola dropped; the silence so loud the command from Ibrahim seemed to echo in the stillness.

Tulu raised to his front knees.

He elevated his hind quarters and stood on his hind legs.

He straightened his front legs and stood.

The crowd exhaled in unison, then, again with unanimity, gasped as they regained the breath held so long. Otherwise, the camel's ability to rise with the 1,000 pounds of cotton strapped to his back rendered them speechless.

But when, with a few clicks and clucks from Ibrahim, Tulu walked off with the load as if it weren't there, exclamations spread through the throng, increased in volume to qualify as cheers, then burst forth full-fledged as hurrahs and huzzahs, ovations and acclamations, exuberance and accolades.

The caravan fell in and the camels trailed Tulu along the thoroughfare. All, that is, save Okyanus — who followed Hurry back through the crowd and frolicked as she collected her bets.

day," Rawhide Robinson said, "but there

CHAPTER THIRTY-TWO

The caravan made it to the corrals without
incident — save the occasional spooked
horse or startled pedestrian. Once the
camels were cared for and the sailors-cum-
camel-handlers dismissed with many thanks
and sent back to the USS *Cordwood,* Happy
Harry took Major Wayne aside for a talk.

"Robinson, Lieutenant Scott — can I have
the pleasure of your company," the major
said after the palaver with the Turk. "Ibrahim and Hurry, you may as well join us."

"What's on your mind, Major?" Rawhide
Robinson said. "Besides your hat, I mean."

"Harry here has suggested we not wait for
the cavalry escort from Camp Verde. Rather,
we should set out on our own. He says we
could be at Camp Verde before the troops
get here. We may have to take it slow for a
couple of days as the camels aren't fully fit
after laying around on the ship all this time."

"They will regain their strength in no

time," Happy Harry said. "With so little to carry, the animals will soon be able to travel more than forty of your miles in a day."

"Them camels might walk that far in a day," Rawhide Robinson said, "but there ain't no way I can ride shank's mare that far!"

"Shank's mare?" Happy Harry asked. "What is shank's mare?"

"Well, it's a way of saying I'm afoot. We ain't got no horses and I sure ain't walking all that way, so we can't leave here till we find us some mounts."

Happy Harry laughed.

Hurry giggled.

Major Wayne grinned.

Even Ibrahim, whose lack of English allowed only snatches of understanding, smiled.

Rawhide Robinson said, "What's so funny?"

Happy Harry waved a broad gesture toward the corralled camels. "Look around, cowboy! We have a wealth of conveyance. There will be no need of horses, or your 'shank's mare' as you call it."

"But them camels is pack animals!"

"True enough. But they are well trained and can be ridden as well."

Rawhide Robinson lifted his thirteen-gallon hat and raked his hair.

He kneaded his chin.

He scratched his whiskers.

He pursed his lips and wrinkled his brow.

"Well," he said, "I ain't never been aboard no camel but for about half a minute, and that was a mistake. But I have often boasted of being a bronc peeler who could ride anything with hair on it, so I guess I am game. How's about outfits? We can't ride them pack saddles."

"We have a few riding saddles as well as the pack saddles among our furniture," Happy Harry said. "We will show you."

Major Wayne left for town to acquire traveling provender for his small command, with instructions to prepare for a dawn departure. The cowboy and the naval officer watched as the Levantines broke out the riding gear.

"Why, they look like benches with pillows on top," Rawhide Robinson said.

He was right. The dromedary saddles had four flat wooden legs, wider set at the bottom and tapering inward to attach to the seat, which was but a slightly dished platform topped by a thick pad. From the front and rear rose a small horn, or post.

"There ain't no stirrups, and that apple ain't nothin' I'd want to dally to. But if that's how you sit a camel I reckon I can do it."

"These are but simple saddles for every-day riding," Hurry said. "Come and look."

She led him to Ibrahim's unpacked tack.

"Would you look at that!" he said of the contraption the Turk was buffing and burnishing, shining and smoothing.

Hurry said, "It is a fancy saddle. Very expensive. Only pashas and sultans and rich men like the Grand Vizier who Ibrahim was with can afford such finery. Especially such a large saddle for a camel like Tulu."

Tulu's saddle featured a high backrest and, up front, an equally high extension that flared into three prongs. The upholstered saddle itself and the heap of pads and blankets stacked next to it were exquisitely woven and richly embroidered, with tassels and fringe and other decorations. The cowboy doubted the fancies would be of much use on Texas trails, and Ibrahim must have concurred for he packed most of the finery away and kept only the essentials at hand.

Happy Harry and Hurry showed Rawhide Robinson and Lieutenant Ian Scott the ropes, haltering and leading out a camel, commanding it to kneel on its belly. They laid a pad atop its hump and hefted a saddle atop the pad, demonstrating proper placement. When the camel stood at their cue, they explained the cinch that secured the saddle.

"Ain't much different from a center-fire rig," the cowboy said. "What do you think, Ensign Ian?"

"It's lieutenant. My horseback experience pales in comparison to yours, and my experience aboard a camel is nonexistent. But I am confident I can adapt to the circumstance."

"Then let's saddle us up a couple of these critters and get forked."

And so they did.

While the feel of the seat and the moving camel beneath differed considerably from his accustomed kind of mount, Rawhide Robinson soon adapted to the motion. The most difficulty came with the reins — the camel was not trained to neck rein — to respond to a gentle shifting of the reins in the desired direction — and that required him to saw with both hands as if handling the lines on a harnessed mule pulling a plow.

The naval officer slopped around a little finding his balance in the saddle, but soon enough gained control of himself and then the camel.

Ibrahim sat in the shade and looked on

without reaction. Happy Harry and Hurry trotted around offering encouragement and advice.

"Open the gate," Rawhide Robinson said.

"Where do you wish to go?" asked a genuinely flummoxed Harry.

"I can handle this camel-riding business all right, but I can't countenance my pins dangling down thisaway. Goin' to town to get me some stirrups."

Happy Harry seemed skeptical of turning the cowboy loose on the streets aboard a valuable camel, but opened the gate nevertheless.

Being a seaport town, no saddlemaker had set up shop in Indianola. But Rawhide Robinson ferreted out a livery stable with a hostler who handled repairs and between the two of them, fashioned a pair of makeshift stirrups and leathers from an abandoned stock saddle. With his feet in stirrups the cowboy felt more comfortable and rode with more confidence. Curious onlookers were treated to a few fancy turns and figure-eights in the street, and with a few clicks and clucks of the tongue and a tap with a quirt, the camel squatted in front of a hitch rail and lay there while Rawhide Robinson wet his whistle in a saloon. Coming out, he again impressed the assembled curiosity seekers when he stepped into saddle and cued the camel to stand, with its unorthodox unfolding of knees and ankles and elbows as it arose.

As had happened earlier, the presence of the camel on the streets scared the horses and mules, upset the chickens and dogs, and frightened more than a few of the people. In consideration of their safety, he did not linger longer, and set out for the temporary dromedary domicile at the edge of town.

Riding a camel differed from forking a horse in more ways than one, the cowboy soon learned. Unlike the clip-clop-clip-clop-clip-clop of horseback hooves, the dromedary's footfalls were all but silent given its padded two-toed feet. Urging the animal into a mile-eating trot as he was accustomed to do with horses, Rawhide Robinson discovered the camel knew no such gait. Instead, it set to pacing — a rolling gait altogether unlike a trot. Rather than fore and rear legs striding opposite one another, the limbs on either side of the dromedary worked in unison. Horses could be taught to pace, and the cowboy had ridden such, but with the camel it was the natural way of moving. As he swayed from side to side atop the pacing ship of the desert he could almost imagine he was back aboard the ship at sea.

Major Wayne was back when Rawhide Robinson arrived at the corral, and all hands were at work emptying supplies from a merchant's wagon and dividing them into piles for packing. Only a few of the stronger camels would have a load to carry, and that a light one. Most would be weighted only with empty packsaddles.

Happy Harry outlined the next day's order of march.

"In an unfamiliar place, the camels will not attempt to stray from the caravan," he said. "They will follow the camel ahead wherever led. In our country, caravans are divided into groups of fifteen to twenty animals, with a handler assigned to each group. We are six, with only thirty-four camels, so each must watch over only the camel we ride and perhaps five or six others. It will be easy. Major Wayne knows the path we must follow so he should take the lead. Six camels will follow, then myself, then five camels ahead of Ensign Ian —"

"— Lieutenant —"

"— followed by six, then Huri, then five ahead of Mister Robinson —"

"— Rawhide —"

"— then six camels and Ibrahim at the

rear. Such an arrangement, I do believe, will prove comfortable."

The end of the discussion revealed the fly in the ointment in the planned march. For while Major Wayne had laid in supplies, no one among the party had any experience beyond the rudiments of camp cooking. Other than kindling a fire and boiling coffee, they could do little more than stare at the sacks of flour and corn meal, bags of beans and spuds, slab of bacon and pack of jerky, airtights of tomatoes and peaches.

The ever-resourceful Rawhide Robinson recommended they gnaw on jerky and open cans of tomatoes for supper. He, meanwhile, would saddle up and head back to town for a more permanent solution.

He soon returned with a wobbling, wiggling, whooping woman behind him, her arms wrapped so tight around his waist his backbone made ripples and ridges on his belly. When the camel knelt, she slid off to the rear, staggered a step or two and sat down with a whump that raised a billow of dust. She moaned and groaned, fussed and fretted, and fanned her florid face with flying fingers. Her strawberry hair was mussed, her bonnet askew, her apron awry. One sock was bunched around the ankle and even the freckles on her face seemed out of order.

Ensign — Lieutenant — Ian Scott hurried over and helped her to her feet. "Are you all right, ma'am?"

"Well I declare! I never! I swan!" she stammered and stuttered and sputtered. "To think a proper lady like myself would be aboard such a beast! And astride, no less!"

The woman caught her breath and regained her wits and lit into the provisions with a vengeance. As the major, the lieutenant, Happy Harry, Hurry, Ibrahim, and Rawhide Robinson looked on in slack-jawed awe, she magically turned a good share of the groceries into pre-cooked food that would travel — pots of boiled beans and stew, sacks of corn dodgers and biscuits, slabs of fried bacon and roast beef, all packed and wrapped and stored and stowed for the trail ahead.

During the hustle and bustle, Rawhide Robinson drew Hurry aside and watched a smile spread across her face when he lifted the lid of a wicker basket he brought back from town, revealing a generous stash of tamales.

"Well, ma'am, I reckon I had best be gettin' you back to town," Rawhide Robinson said when all was in order and the major had generously compensated the cook with currency courtesy of the United States Army.

"Not on your life! You lured me aboard that monstrosity once before but you'll not do it again!" She hiked up her skirts and said, "I'll find my own way home, if you please!" and stomped off toward town.

Ever the gentleman, Ensign — Lieutenant — Ian Scott trotted off after her, escorted her safely home and returned to find everyone asleep, with more than a few of his companions serenading the stars with snores. He rolled himself in his blankets and drifted off to dreamland, knowing that dawn would arrive all too soon.

CHAPTER THIRTY-THREE

The road out of Indianola northwest to San
Antonio was a well-traveled trade route,
linking the seaport to the old city and then
far into Mexico and the city of Chihuahua.
The camel caravan traveled without incident
— if you don't count the hysterical horses,
maniacal mules, runaway wagons, and ag-
gravated travelers they encountered along
the way.

Nothing seemed to upset the camels.
Shrieking wheels, screeching brakes, over-
turned drays, distressed draft animals, bellowing bullwhackers, mad muleskinners,
and scattered cargo made nary a dent in the
dromedary's disposition. The animals plodded along chewing their cuds as if they were
the road's only occupants.

But the catastrophes the camels caused
did slow the progress of the parade. The
animals repeatedly squatted at the side of
the road in respite while Major Wayne,

Lieutenant Scott, Happy Harry, Hurry, Ibrahim, and Rawhide Robinson righted wagons, reloaded freight, calmed crazed critters, and re-harnessed and hitched ill-tempered teams to help freighters get back on their way. All the delays meant the train was lucky to make twenty-five miles a day — considerably less than the accustomed distance for the animals.

And so they met the oncoming cavalry escort from Camp Verde near the end of the fourth day of the journey. The detachment was under the command of a second lieutenant fresh out of West Point who still struggled to stay aboard a horse, so it was Sergeant Donald O'Donnell who ramrodded the outfit.

Once the troopers espied the caravan in the distance, O'Donnell ordered the bugler to blow the call to canter, anticipating a brash spectacle of military gallantry.

The military mounts snuffled nostrils at first sniff of the camels.

The horses went wall-eyed at first sight of the dromedaries.

The cavalry equines trumpeted in terror as they drew near the outlandish animals.

The formation fell apart in chaos as startled steeds stopped and wheeled, quivering geldings galloped away in disarray, panicked ponies paid no heed to reins or bridle bits, and alarmed chargers upchucked riders right and left.

The camel *caballeros* halted the caravan and sat atop their unruffled rides as pandemonium proliferated around them. Try as they might, they could not contain their laughter, which upset the tangled and twisted and tromped and trampled troopers all the more.

The addled cavalry officer could not function, so Sergeant O'Donnell strode through the turmoil hollering orders, dispatching every trooper on two feet to pursue the fleeing four-footed hayburners. While the cavalry righted itself, Major Wayne and his minions assembled the camels into a compact group, uncinched the saddles and settled the animals on the ground, where they lazily watched the military maneuvers and contentedly chewed their cuds.

"Who's in charge of this %^#*@ bunch of beasties?" Sergeant Donald O'Donnell screamed, striding into the camel collection with sweat streaming and spit flying.

"That would be me, Sergeant," Major Wayne said, fiddling with the tie strings on his camel saddle.

"You infernal eejit! You —"

"That's 'infernal eejit, *sir*'," the major

said, turning to meet the stampeding sergeant.

O'Donnell snapped to attention, turning even more florid in the face, far beyond the normal rosy hue further enhanced by the afternoon's anger and exertion. "Major Wayne, sir! Sorry, sir! I lost my head, I'm afraid."

"That's all right, Sergeant. Get your men and mounts sorted out, calm yourself down, and we'll try again."

"Yes, sir!" As the sergeant stomped away, he saw Rawhide Robinson halfway reclined against the side of a camel, whittling on a stick. "You!" he said, sliding to a stop and aiming a quaking index finger at the cowboy's face. "You!"

Rawhide Robinson looked up and grinned. "How you doin'? Sergeant O'Donnell, ain't it?"

The sergeant steamed and stammered. "You! It ain't no surprise to me to see the likes of you responsible for all this uproar!"

"Me? I'd have to say it's your fault, Sarge. Had you not woke me up from a happy nap and dragged me off to Fort Brown all those months ago, I'd be off punchin' cows someplace."

The sergeant steamed and stammered.

"By the way, this outfit you're with came

345

down from Camp Verde. How is it you're not at Fort Brown still?"

"Got transferred, you eejit! It happens. Had I known I'd end up in the company of you and these — these — these stinking, slobbering excuses for animals I'd have asked to be re-assigned to hell instead!"

"Why are you so down on me? We only just barely met back then, and only for a minute or three."

"It don't take me long to spot a trouble-maker, boyo. You don't have to drink a whole bottle of whiskey to know if it's bad! I could see with my eyes shut you were naught but a sassy, disrespectful, no-account cowboy."

"Well, I reckon you've a right to your opinion about me. But I'm a-warnin' you right now, Sergeant Bogtrotter, you mind your tongue when talkin' about these here camels. You don't know nothin' about them, so you ain't entitled to no opinion."

The sergeant steamed and stammered. "You impertinent —"

"— Sergeant!" Major Wayne interrupted. "Get back to your duties!"

"Yes, *sir!*"

It took a while, but the troopers eventually rounded up the horses and picketed them safely away from the camels. Their mess was no better than the caravan's as they, too, were living on trail food out of haversacks and had not brought cook nor supplies along. Curious about the animals they were sent to escort, the troopers filtered into the camel camp to look them over and question the handlers about the beasts.

The assemblage, satisfied for now on the subject of dromedaries, sipped coffee and shifted the conversation to encounters with other odd animals.

One soldier, who had spent time in the mines of the South American Andes, climbed the camelid ladder from vicuña to alpaca to guanaco to llama.

Another, formerly an able-bodied seaman on a merchant ship, told tales of wallabies and kangaroos.

They heard of narwhals and capybaras, hippopotamuses and sloths, the platypus and the ostrich.

"You've read 'bout every bit of ink ever been put on paper, Ensign Ian," Rawhide Robinson said. "I reckon you know lots of oddball animals."

"It's lieutenant. And, yes, I have read about remarkable fauna found on every continent." He entranced the audience with wombats and aardvarks, fruit bats and ring-tailed lemurs, mandrills and manatees, jaguarundis and giraffes until winding down. "How about you, Rawhide. You've always got a story to tell."

"Oh, no, Ensign Ian —"

"— Lieutenant."

"— Lieutenant Ian. Plenty of other folks to carry on the conversation. Ain't no need to hear from me."

"Aw, c'mon, cowboy," a trooper said. "What's the strangest critter you ever come across?"

"Well, if you insist," Rawhide Robinson said. He refilled his tin cup at the campfire pot, settled back against the pad on his camel saddle, blew the hot off his coffee and took an experimental sip, and tipped back his thirteen-gallon hat.

"All right, already," an impatient soldier said.

"Get on with it!" said another.

"We ain't got all night."

"The bugler'll be blowin' taps if you don't get a move on!"

The cowboy sipped his coffee. "Take it easy, boys. I'm thinkin'. And having thought it over, I'd have to say the strangest animal I ever encountered was an armadillo."

"Armadillo! They're as common as cow flop here in Texas!"

348

"Now, take a tater and wait, trooper. I ain't meaning armadillos in general. I'm talking about this one particular armadillo I met one time."

Again, he paused to lubricate his talking apparatus with hot coffee.

"Well, what about it!?"

"Here's what happened," Rawhide Robinson said once the tension was taut enough. "I was gatherin' strays one time on this ranch in Arizona Territory. Might've been New Mexico, come to think of it. Fact is, I was so far south sometimes I might've been in Old Mexico —"

"C'mon, cowboy! It don't much matter where you were. What about the armadillo?"

"Don't get all het up. I want to make sure what I'm sayin' is the truth. So, anyhow, there I was, all by my lonesome and out in the middle of a million miles of nowhere sittin' next to a campfire much like this one. It was so quiet out there it got a mite uncomfortable — no bugs chirping, no coyotes howlin', no nothing.

"Then, real easy like, I hears this singing. Real soft — so soft I wasn't sure it was there at all. Bein' the curious sort, I perked up my ears to listen and stepped out into the desert in the direction that sound was a-comin' from. There was a full moon that night, so it was near bright as day. Soon enough I was sure it was out there — but I wasn't sure where.

"But I reasoned out it was coming from somewheres in this jumble of rocks. So I started to clambering around in there, stopping every step or two to listen. It got to where it sounded like that song was comin' up right from underneath my feet. And I'll tell you, boys, it was about as sad and mournful a song as I've ever heard. In Spanish it was, so I couldn't catch it all. Besides, it was some strange kind of Spanish, it was. Not like the border lingo I was used to, but sort of old-fashioned, or something. A lot more of a lisp to it, see, and more rolling of the R —"

"— Oh, for heaven's sake! Tell the story! We don't care about no lesson is the finer points of the Spanish language!"

"Listen here, soldier — I'm telling this story the way I'm telling it. Take a lesson from these camels here and calm down. Now, where was I?" Rawhide Robinson paused for a moment to collect his thoughts.

"Right. That singing was coming right out from under the rock I was standing on. So I hunkers down and starts to pokin' around and sees that this boulder was wedged in a crack and whoever it was that was singing was down in that little cave or crevice or whatever. That stone wasn't so big I couldn't shift it, so that's what I did. When I rolled that rock off, I looks down that hole and there's this armadillo lookin' back at me."

"What!?"

"That can't be true!"

"You're pullin' my leg!"

"Sorry, boys, but what I'm saying is as true as thorns on a mesquite tree and spines on a prickly pear cactus. I reached down in there and hauled that armadillo out of that hole and carried him back to the campfire. And all the while, he kept on singing that sad song.

"I figured he might be some kind of thirsty, bein' stuck down in that rock hole like he was, so I uncorked my canteen and poured a puddle in a tin plate. He didn't seem to even notice, or know where he was at, so I took a cup of that water and tossed it in his face — you know, like you would to wake up a feller who's passed out from too much tonsil varnish."

"Ha! Now I guess you're going to tell us that armadillo was drunk!"

"Drunk! Don't be silly — what kind of spirituous liquor could an armadillo find out in the desert? No, he wasn't drunk, but he was sure discombobulated. The shock of that splash of water brought him right to his senses. He kind of looks at me, looks around, and looks at me some more.

" '¿*Como se llama?*' he says to me — which kind of means 'who are you?' or 'what do they call you?' So I tells him my name. 'Muchath graciath, theñor RRRawhide RRRobinthon' he says to me, rolling them Rs and lisping them Ss as he does. 'You have freed me from a long imprisonment and you shall be rewarded.' I asked him what he was wagging his chin about — hold on a minute! Do armadillos have chins?"

"Oh, never mind! Tell the story!"

"Anyhow, he tells me he's a magic armadillo and a long, long time ago — we're talking centuries here — an old Aztec *bruja* imprisoned him in that hole on account of he went around doing good, and she was evil and wanted no more of his interference. Then he says that on account of I rescued him, and on account of he was magic, he would give me three wishes — anything I wanted, anything at all —"

"— Hold on there! If he was magic, why didn't he make a spell and get himself out of that hole?"

"Oh, he didn't have that kind of power," Rawhide Robinson said. "Said he couldn't use his gift to help himself, only other folks.

352

I asked that same thing myself, but that's the kind of magic that armadillo said he had."

Rawhide Robinson again paused to sip his coffee and collect his thoughts.

"Well?" an antsy soldier soon asked. "What did you wish for?"

"That armadillo, he said I had three wishes, mind you, and that I could wish for anything I wanted. 'You can wish for riches, señor. There is no limit to my power to reward you.' So, I thought it over for a time and said I wished I would always have a comfortable saddle to sit on, and good horses to cinch it to. 'It shall be so,' he said."

"What!? You could have anything in the world, and you wished for *that*?"

"It ain't such a strange thing to want," the cowboy said. "I've spent lots of hours and days and weeks and months and years horseback in my time, and any cowboy will tell you a good saddle is worth wishing for. And the way them horses of yours behaved this afternoon, well, it ought to be clear even to you army boys how valuable good horses can be.

"And I'll tell you right here and now, them wishes of mine came true. I ain't never been chafed or chapped, sore or swollen, irritated or inflamed by my saddle. And I have always

353

had the pleasure of good horses between my knees. Oh, some of them might bow their backs in the morning, but you want some spirit in a horse. So that armadillo did me right."

"Wait! What was your third wish?"

"Well, that armadillo reminded me I had one more wish. And he reminded me I could have anything I wanted. And he reminded me he could lavish me with wealth and riches, jewels and gems, silver and gold. I ain't never been the greedy sort, but I thought, what the heck, and I told that armadillo I wanted a thousand bucks."

"A thousand bucks! That's all! You could have had a million!"

"Like as I said, I ain't the greedy sort, and I figured a thousand bucks would keep me a good long time. Anyway, that armadillo gave me a funny look and said, 'A thousand bucks, señor? This is what you wish for?' I assured him a thousand bucks would be plenty. Then that armadillo sort of shrugged his shoulders — if armadillos have shoulders — and said, 'It shall be so . . .' as he just sort of faded away. And he was gone. Plumb disappeared, he did."

After a moment, one of the troopers, overcome with curiosity, asked what he did with the money.

"Money?" Rawhide Robinson said. "Well, that's where this story gets a mite strange. See, I was sleepin' like a calf with a belly full of mama's milk when along about dawn I was woke up by all this racket. I flung off my sougans, hitched up my britches, pulled on my boots and rubbed the night out of my eyes so's I could see what all the noise was about.

"I looks around, and darned if I wasn't surrounded by a whole herd of baaing, bleating sheep. Sagebrush maggots everywhere, there was! For a cowboy, that's about as insulting as it gets. Once I got over the shock of it, I started lookin' them sheep over and it dawned on me that every last stinkin' one of them hoofed locusts was a sheep of the male variety — a whole herd of rams, it was. Then I set to countin' them and you won't never guess how many of them woolies there was — there was one thousand of them — exactly one thousand male sheep. . . .

"A thousand bucks!"

CHAPTER THIRTY-FOUR

With assistance from the cavalry escort, the journey proved less eventful. Troopers rode out ahead of the caravan, warning others on the road of its approach, allowing teamsters and muleskinners and drivers of wagons and drays, buckboards and buggies, carriages and carts, horseback travelers and even those afoot to secure their means of conveyance and avoid — or at least prepare for — the possibility of pending panic and pandemonium.

The cavalry horses eventually became somewhat accustomed to the presence of the camels. But while rodeo-style uproar subsided, suspicion did not. Close calls were common, and skittishness and sidewise shying accompanied every equine encounter with a proximate dromedary. It was all the troopers could do to keep their seats in the saddle and their horses' hooves on the earth.

The upshot of it all was that the soldiers

were less accepting of the camels than even their jumpy mounts were. Various venomous attacks in the form of copious unkind words, profuse profanity, and recurrent cussing caused anxiety among the camel handlers. Major Wayne and Lieutenant Scott harangued the cavalry officer and Sergeant O'Donnell regularly, but to no avail. The enmity would not be eased, let alone eliminated.

Among the horsemen, only Rawhide Robinson — more horseman by far than any of the blue-clad troopers with yellow stripes down the sides of their trousers — accepted the presence of the camels. Beyond acceptance, the cowboy's appreciation of the bizarre beasts ever increased.

As the caravan approached San Antonio, the cowboy's excitement elevated. The city — whose population exceeded 20,000 souls — was familiar to Rawhide Robinson and as close to a hometown as the wandering cowboy could claim — although the amount of time spent in its environs was negligible when compared to his time on cattle trails. Many of the cattle drives on his *curriculum vitae* originated in the vicinity of San Antonio, as it had long been a center of the beef business. Much to his chagrin — and that of others with bovine proclivities —

San Antonio de Bexar now trafficked in considerable quantities of wool, shorn from imported herds of sheep in the nearby hill country.

The afternoon prior to the company's arrival in the city, Rawhide Robinson rounded up the camel crew and invited the commanders of the refractory cavalry troops to the confab.

"More than likely, these here camels will cause some excitement in San Antonio," he said.

"No doubt about it," offered the uneasy army lieutenant. "I am not confident in our ability to maintain order."

Sergeant Donald O'Donnell snorted. "Mark my words," he said — those words directed at Major Benjamin Wayne, "there will be hell to pay when these sand maggots of yours —"

"— Now hold on there, Sergeant," Rawhide Robinson said, interrupting the coming tirade. "The way I see it, we can turn this situation to our favor. Ensign Ian here —"

"— Lieutenant —"

"— is about as well-schooled and smooth as they come, despite his tender years. If we send him to town this evening to hobnob with the mayor, I suspect we can stir up a celebration of sorts. Why, when we was in Jamaica, that girl Hurry had folks lined up for a look at these camels. People here in San Antonio ain't so much different."

"Hmmmph!" O'Donnell said. "One look at them ugly animals will scare the pants off children, cause women to faint dead away, and make brave men cross the street. That's if the smell don't scare 'em away first. And there ain't no need to remind you eejits what the dogs and horses and mules will do — sir."

"Granted, we have had some difficulties," Major Wayne said. "Be that as it may, I believe Mister Robinson is on to something here. Lieutenant, would you be willing to engage in a diplomatic mission of sorts on our behalf?"

"Certainly, sir," said the energetic and ever accommodating young officer.

"Robinson, you go with him as you know the lay of the land here. And take Hurry with you, if you will. I believe the presence of a young lady — a child, really — will work to our benefit."

Rawhide Robinson smiled (as did the lieutenant). "That girl will jump at the chance. Once I tell her San Antonio women whip up the tastiest tamales in all the earth we won't be able to hold her back with a camel halter."

The camel ambassadors sneaked back into camp in the middle of the night so as not to wake their comrades, confident in the success of the mission. With municipal elections in the offing, the mayor of San Antonio saw the usefulness of an impromptu public spectacle — with himself at the head of the parade, of course. His network of supporters knocked on doors until long past bedtime, alerting business leaders and shopkeepers and civic officials to the event and eliciting their support.

Sunrise saw patriotic bunting retrieved from storage and draped from storefronts and balconies. A dusted-off, all-purpose "Welcome to San Antonio" banner stretched across the thoroughfare the caravan would plod along through the city. By the time most of the citizens of old Bexar came awake, an air of excitement was already in the air.

As the city prepared itself for the camels, the dromedary hostlers prepared the camels for the city. Currycombs and brushes cleared the animals of trail dust, the handlers straightened cinches, untangled halters and lead ropes, tidied up packsaddles, and otherwise prepared the camels for public display. Ornery Ibrahim even unpacked his exotic finery and polished himself and Tulu and his tack until all fairly sparkled.

After reveille, a disinclined Sergeant Donald O'Donnell supervised similar preparation of cavalry mounts, prodding his even-more-reluctant charges to do their duty. Orders, after all, are orders. "Boots and Saddles" sounded on the bugle and the buffed and beautified troopers mounted up and formed ranks to lead the way.

Rawhide Robinson, Major Benjamin Wayne, Lieutenant (formerly Ensign) Ian Scott, Happy Harry, and ornery Ibrahim lined out the caravan, climbed aboard their camels, signaled them to stand and fell in behind the mounted troopers. Hurry opted to walk behind the towering Tulu and beside Okyanus, bringing up the rear of the procession.

By the time they reached the city, word had spread and onlookers lined the road into town. Houston Street led the parade to Alamo Plaza, where every Texan in the cavalcade — or camelcade, if you will — tipped his hat to the shrine, and none with more panache than Rawhide Robinson. Some cheering from the crowds welcomed the caravan, but jeers and sneers were more the order of the day.

Giggles and guffaws greeted the dromedaries. As was the custom, dogs barked and chickens squawked and quit the country. Horses and mules tested their tethers, wanting nothing more than to run away from the freakish and fiendish animals causing the mess and muddle.

Fascinated children, however, ignored importunate parents, trotting along in the wake of the captivating camels, raising more dust than the dromedaries.

The camels did not care. They plodded across the bridge over the San Antonio River and along Commerce Street, paying scant attention to any of it. A pack of police officers held back the crowds as the parade passed under the "Welcome" banner into the Main Plaza, past San Fernando Cathedral and into the Military Plaza where doyen and hoi polloi alike awaited them. The mayor stood atop a cobbled-together podium, applauding the arrival of the procession. His attempts at speechifying, however, failed, lost among the raucous taunts and mockery, the riotous hoots and hectoring.

The troopers divided to take their places along the edge of the crowd to discourage curiosity seekers from getting too close to the camels. The soldiers' casual attitudes, mocking smiles, and insolent sneers revealed sensibilities similar to those of the citizenry.

The caravan halted, lined up across the center of the plaza. Rawhide Robinson and the other riders ordered their dromedaries to their knees and dismounted, and the remaining camels squatted like slow-motion dominoes as the handlers passed down the line signaling their repose.

The simple spectacle aroused the curiosity of the crowd and calm — of a festive kind — fell across the plaza like a fuzzy blanket. Major Wayne climbed atop the mayor's podium and offered up a short speech about the army's intentions for the ships of the desert under his command. His arms tired from repeatedly raising them to tamp down the jeers and raspberries, the scorn and catcalls. The man was, to put it mildly, desperate.

And desperate times call for desperate measures.

So he said, in his most commanding voice, "Let me introduce one of your own — a fellow Texan, a cowboy, and a convert to the cause of camels. Listen, if you will, ladies and gentlemen, to Rawhide Robinson!"

CHAPTER THIRTY-FIVE

Rawhide Robinson's teeth rattled when his lower jaw hit the ground, sending up a puff of Military Plaza dust. He reeled in his chin and reset his chops, struggling to catch his breath as he made his way to the podium.

He could not fathom, could not imagine, could not understand, Major Wayne's unexpected invitation to address the assemblage.

"M-M-M-Major!" was all he could manage to mouth upon meeting the military man on the platform.

"Robinson!" came the hushed but urgent reply. "Say something to these people!"

"Say what!? I don't know nothin' about public speaking!"

"They are not listening to me. Maybe they'll pay attention to you."

The cowboy swallowed a lump the size of a saddle horn that had somehow settled in his throat. "What am I supposed to say?"

"Tell them what you've learned about

camels. That should do the trick. Now, get over there and get to it!"

The crowd quieted when the cowboy sidled up to the lectern as if it were a bad-tempered bronc. He cleared his throat as he eyeballed the multitude lining the plaza.

He lifted his thirteen-gallon lid and wiped perspiration from his forehead with the swipe of a shirtsleeve, tucked back his forelock and reset the hat.

He cleared his throat.

He studied the toes of his boots as if inspiration resided there.

He cleared his throat.

He tugged at the lapels of his vest and hitched up his britches.

He cleared his throat.

"Folks," he finally squeaked.

He cleared his throat.

"My name is Rawhide Robinson. But my name ain't nothin' extra. An ordinary cowboy is what I am. But after punchin' cows all over Texas and beyond, and trailing more herds north than I can count on all my fingers and toes, and being horseback almost as long as I've been breathing, I reckon I've learned a thing or three about critters."

The crowd remained quiet, straining to hear Rawhide Robinson's words.

He cleared his throat.

"I ain't accustomed to speechifyin' so I hope you-all will cut me some slack. For months now, I've been a-babysittin' these here camels. I'll grant you that they are funny lookin' critters. Their necks is too long and wobbly. Their legs is too long and limber. They stink worse than a goat and darn near as bad as a sheep."

Scattered jeers arose in the crowd — apparently there were mutton conductors present, or perhaps wool merchants.

Rawhide Robinson raised a hand for quiet. He cleared his throat.

"They've got more hinges in their legs than all the saloon doors in San Antone. Then there's that hump they pack around on their backs. There ain't no doubt about it — these camels are as odd as a two-gun man at a tea party."

He waited for a smattering of applause to subside.

"All that aside, I'm here to tell you these camels have their finer points. Let me tell you-all a little story."

Rawhide Robinson removed his hat and held it reverently in front of his chest.

He cleared his throat.

"Whilst we plied the high seas on the way home from this recent camel excursion to far ports of call, of which I was a part, we encountered a terrible storm. Waves battered our boat — ship, I should say — so bad it near reduced the USS *Cordwood* to kindling. The wind ripped our sails to flinders and we floundered out there in the middle of the ocean, like bein' on a bucking bronc having lost your reins and blown your stirrups. There ain't nothin' you can do but pull leather and hope to ride it out."

The crowd, by now, was enthralled. Major Wayne, the erstwhile Ensign Ian, the girl Hurry, Happy Harry, and even the ornery Ibrahim (who could catch only the occasional word) were likewise riveted, hearing, for the first time, about an incident which must have included them but of which they had no memory; an event, in fact, that was as new to them as it was to the assembled citizens of San Antonio.

"Having no sails to catch the wind, nor no canvas to hang more, that ship and all us on board was at the mercy of the angry sea. Them camels," the cowboy chronicler continued as he pointed at the animals reposed on the plaza contentedly chewing their cuds, "these very ones right here before you, did not fear. They did not quaver. They did not panic at the hopelessness of our situation. No, my friends, these camels cowboyed

367

up and saved the day — or night, as it were."

Had they been seated, the crowd would have been on the edges of their seats with anticipation. The cowboy's camel-caretaker companions, meanwhile, were both confused and captivated.

"Here's what happened. Lacking any cloth or canvas to replace the ship's shredded sails, the camels shed their hair. Now, you folks may not know it, but back where these camels come from they are often shorn like sheep and their hair woven into fabric. And that's exactly what these shipboard camels accomplished, that fearsome storm notwithstanding.

"No one saw the whole thing, but I saw enough to draw some conclusions. Like as I said, the camels shed their hair, so each one was surrounded by a pile of fiber. Then each one proceeded to paw at the pile, rolling and twisting and spinning all that hair into wads then ropes then twines then threads, as slick as a spinster at a spinning wheel."

The revelation prompted heckles and hectoring, hoots and whistles from the skeptical crowd. The cowboy pressed on.

"Now, folks, I know it sounds unlikely — but I'm telling you what I seen, as sure as a fiddle tune'll make your feet fly. Once all that dromedary fur was spun into thread, them camels passed them threads up and down the line and back and forth, using the prehensile lips at the tip of their proboscis to push and pull it along, weaving up a warm, fuzzy, giant-size blanket-looking affair."

Again, the listeners expressed disbelief via various vocalizations.

Again, Rawhide Robinson the raconteur pressed on.

"Don't get me wrong — it wasn't fancy and the fact is it was right rough looking. And what them camels wove wasn't a blanket at all."

Rawhide Robinson looked around the plaza, basking in the attention of the audience. He reckoned that in all his years of spinning windies, this was far and away the largest assemblage of spectators he had ever had the pleasure of regaling.

As he watched and waited, his listeners, as he expected, became anxious and edgy awaiting the continuation of the tale. Once anticipation reached a fevered pitch, and encouragements to continue became cacophonous, he carried on.

"No, folks, what them beasts had whipped up was a sail! Like as I said, it wasn't pretty. And it certainly wouldn't pass muster should there be an inspection by an admiral or some other high-ranking naval officer. But it served its purpose. Them sailors on that ship hauled that sail aloft, lashed it to the yards and got their clew lines, bunt lines, halyard, and lifts all in order. When good ol' Captain Howard Clemmons saw the wind fill that sail, he grinned like a calf with a mouthful of mama. That sail wasn't perfect by any means, but it gave the captain enough control over the good ol' USS *Cordwood* that the ship rode out the storm."

Again, derision and disbelief flowed from the told toward the teller with all the force of an Atlantic gale. Rawhide Robinson raised his hand for quiet.

"Folks, you can see I'm a-standin' here in fine fettle. You can see Major Wayne and all the rest of us as was on that ship — including all these camels you can see here. Now, ain't that so?"

The crowd could not help but agree.

"So, you see — it's like I said. Otherwise, we'd have not survived that storm."

A rustle among the dignitaries behind Rawhide Robinson on the podium diverted attention. It was the mayor's wife, striding across the platform with a purpose, hiking her voluminous skirts with both hands.

"Mister Robinson," she said (in a voice that no doubt awakened those lazing about in the shade of the sacred walls of the Alamo, more than half a mile away). "I intend to challenge what you say!"

"How's that, ma'am?"

"I am not unfamiliar with the home arts. As a matter of fact, spinning and weaving and knitting and other such domestic crafts are among the interests that occupy my time. I shall test your contention concerning camel hair. Clip some of these curious creatures and afford me the fur, and I shall clean it, card it, spin it into yarn, and knit my husband the mayor a pair of socks! If, that is, your claim has any veracity whatsoever!"

Rawhide Robinson hemmed and hawed. He stuttered and stammered. He feared he had talked himself into a trap from which there was no escape.

He felt a tug on his sleeve. Hurry beckoned him to bend with a wagging finger. She whispered something pleasing into his ear. He stood tall, seated his thirteen-gallon hat atop his head with a firm tug, smiled at madam mayor and said, "As you wish. You go on along with this girl, Hurry, and she'll shear a camel for you."

"That I shall do!" she said with enthusiasm, then whispered to the cowboy, "But I shall not hurry — frankly, my feet are killing me from all this standing!"

Before Rawhide Robinson could correct her misapprehension concerning the girl and her moniker, Hurry spirited madam mayor away. (In the course of time the mayor's wife did, in fact, knit a pair of camel hair socks for Hizzoner, which she demanded he wear regularly despite his complaints concerning their comfort — or lack thereof.)

The calm and quiet crowd watched Hurry lead the mayor's wife down the line of camels, and eyed the beasts with even more curiosity than before. Then a heckler in the crowd hollered, "So what's the army gonna do with them camels, set 'em to knittin' uniforms?"

When the laughter subsided, Rawhide Robinson said, "No, sir — as Major Wayne told you-all, these camels will be used as pack animals."

"What's them skinny, spindly legged critters gonna pack, popcorn around a circus tent?"

Again, the jokester's jibe elicited laughter in the crowd. Rawhide Robinson surveyed the assemblage and saw, away off at the edge of the plaza, parked on Market Street, a mounted man with a leg wrapped around the horn of his Mexican saddle, taking in all the excitement. Tied head-to-tail behind were three mules, heads hanging, hips cocked, dozing in the warm sun.

"You there," Rawhide Robinson yelled. "You with the desert canaries!"

The packer perked up and acknowledged the cowboy with a wave.

"Ride on over here with them knobheads, if you will."

"Well, I won't," came the reply. "I ain't gettin' my mules no closer to them circus animals. They'll likely pitch a fit if'n I do."

"Aw, c'mon! These camels won't hurt a thing. And I'm willing to wager that any one of these critters can carry everything you got loaded on all three of them Arizona nightingales."

Never one to turn down a sure bet, the mule man led his pack train into the plaza and, as he predicted, the mules protested. They bellered and brayed, hung back on their halters, and one of them bucked — as much, that is, as its load would allow. As the audience tittered and tee-heed at the spectacle, the packer hauled the mules back into line, halted before the platform and looked up at Rawhide Robinson.

"The packs from all three mules? On one camel?"

"That's the deal."

"Which camel?"

"Well, sir, I reckon you can take your pick. All except Okyanus — that baby down yonder — or the big one we call Tulu. That wouldn't be fair neither way."

The mule man studied the herd and picked a likely looking prospect — a skinny, small-to-middling-size camel with a shaggy hump and lazy eyes. Happy Harry clucked and whistled and led it up, and Rawhide Robinson stepped off the podium to help him adjust the cinches. Harry signaled the camel to squat.

"What you got in them packs, anyway?" Rawhide Robinson asked.

"Canned goods, bound for Chihuahua. They're heavier'n they look. Them mules is packin' right around 200 pounds apiece give or take. You might'a jist bit off more'n you can chew, cowboy."

"Oh, horse apples!"

The crowd huddled closer as the men transferred the packs from the mules into the commodious panniers hanging from the camel's pack saddle. As they hustled and bustled, the camel chewed its cud, nodding off occasionally, and casting a backward glance now and then to see what his handlers were up to, although he did not seem to care overmuch.

"You sure 'bout this?" the packer said. "That load's likely to bust that beast's back."

On Happy Harry's signal, the camel awkwardly unfolded itself as camels do and stood, as if the 600-pound load on its back was no more an irritant than a fly. The camel spread its legs, ducked its head and gave it a shake, rattling the cans in the packs, slapping straps and flaps, and raising a right ruckus.

The crowd, having caught its collective breath after the tension of awaiting the test, burst into applause.

"Yeah, but can he walk with it?" said the mule man.

Happy Harry clucked and whistled and led the camel around the plaza, applause accompanying the trip like a wave through the spectators.

"Well, mister, I guess you lost that wager," Rawhide Robinson said.

"Looks as if. By the way, what'd we bet?"

Rawhide Robinson furrowed his forehead and kneaded his chin. "Airtights in them packs, you say?"

"That's right."

"Got any cans of peaches?"

"Yep."

"I'll take one."
"You got it."

CHAPTER THIRTY-SIX

Hurry hurled herself like a cannonball.

At full speed, her head wedged between the man's ankles. She grabbed his heels as her shoulders hit his shins. Her target toppled, his head hitting the hard Camp Verde earth, knocking him senseless. The girl leaped to her feet, fists clenched, and stood over the fallen muleteer. Cavalry troopers and packers gathered round, and Hurry spun slowly, challenging the threatening men with a piercing stare and cocked paws.

"Och!" Sergeant Donald O'Donnell said as he shoved men aside and stepped into the circle, joining the recumbent packer, the girl, and an unconcerned camel. "Faith n' begorrah! Why's this fella horizontal?"

"It's that Arab girl!" a mule man said. "She attacked him!"

The gathered men agreed with gripes and grouses, some going so far as to threaten the girl. The sergeant grabbed Hurry's arm and spun her around to face him.

"That so, girl?"

Hurry jerked her arm but could not free herself. A swift kick in the shin loosened her captor's grip and she jerked free.

"Why! You! Little!" —

Major Wayne interrupted the sergeant as he reached again and again for the darting girl. "Sergeant O'Donnell! Hold it right there!" He elbowed and shouldered his way through the crowd with Rawhide Robinson and Lieutenant Scott in his wake.

The newcomers surveyed the situation. Hurry sidled over to stand between the cowboy and the lieutenant. The man on the ground stirred, sat up, and shook his head until his lips rattled. "What happened?" he said, looking around with empty eyes.

"That's a good question," Major Wayne said.

O'Donnell stepped forward. "These men here say that girl there, she assaulted him. Sir."

A chorus of murmuring and mumbling seconded the motion.

"Is that right?" the major asked the still-sitting victim.

"Don't rightly know. Last thing I recollect was tryin' to teach that there camel some manners."

"Ha! He was beating the camel!" Hurry said. "I saw it!"

"Darn right I was! That ugly varmint wouldn't do one blamed thing I wanted him to!"

"Why should he? You mistreat him!"

The packer struggled to his feet and shook a forefinger in the girl's face. "*Me!?* Mistreat *him*!? That camel took to flingin' his head and slingin' stinkin' slobber all over me!"

"It is no wonder! Camels are — how do you say it? — sensitive. If you do not respect them, they will not cooperate. You cannot abuse a camel and expect him to work," Hurry said, now shaking her forefinger in his face.

He snatched her by the wrist.

Rawhide Robinson grabbed the man's ear and gave it a twist. "Unhand the girl," he said through gritted teeth. Lieutenant Scott took Hurry by the arm and drew her away from the man.

The cowboy said, "So, what Hurry says is so, is it? You been a-beatin' this here camel?"

The man nodded his head as much as his pinioned ear would allow.

The cowboy gave the appendage another tweak. "Sounds like it's you as needs to learn some manners," he said as he shoved the man's head aside.

With a vigorous rub of his embarrassed ear, the muleteer said, "I'm a mule man. I never signed on to handle no monsters."

"Need I remind you, mister, that you are in the employ of the United States Army as a packer. Whether with mules, horses, camels, or your own shoulders, your job is to move supplies where and when ordered," Major Wayne said. "If learning to work with these animals is not to your liking, you can draw your pay any time. Good luck finding future employment with the army if you do."

"But these camels won't do as they're told!"

Rawhide Robinson said, "Now listen you here, mulero. Not so long ago I never seen a camel myself. Like you, I thought it was a crazy notion to use these critters. But I learned better. This girl Hurry, here, is right. You've got to take a firm but gentle hand with the camels. You pay attention to what she teaches you —"

"— I ain't takin' no lessons from no slip of a girl like her!"

Major Wayne said, "Yes, you are. You will. Or you will be gone."

Rawhide Robinson said, "Like as I said, you pay attention to what Hurry teaches you — or Happy Harry, or Ibrahim, or

380

Ensign — Lieutenant — Ian, or me for that matter — and you'll learn a thing or three. And one of them things is that these camels will outwork them mules you're so all-fired fond of six ways to Sunday."

"Pshaw! I heard about your little trick in San Antonio. But we'll see what happens when them camels gits out on the trail. I'm bettin' mules'll walk those monstrosities' legs right off!"

Again, the assemblage of muleteers and their cohorts in army uniforms muttered concurrence.

"You'll find out soon enough," Major Wayne said. "In two days' time, an expedition will leave Camp Verde with a caravan of ten camels and a string of twenty mules and travel to Fort Stockton. There, we will outfit the pack animals to carry supplies and equipment to accompany a topographical and mapping excursion into the big bend region of the Rio Grande.

"You men choose your best mules and packers. Mister Robinson, Harry, Hurry, and Ibrahim will handle the camels under command of Lieutenant Scott. As it happens, many in the War Department in Washington remain skeptical of the suitability of camels. So, the topographical mission will serve as a test — a direct comparison of their capabilities vis-à-vis mules in harsh field conditions and difficult terrain."

Instead of grumbling, the major's announcement elicited applause and hurrahs.

Tragedy arrived the first day on the trail from Camp Verde to Fort Stockton. A rattlesnake launched itself out of the scrub to strike the leg of the camel Rawhide Robinson was riding. Upset while dozing in the shade of a pile of rocks beside the trail, the snake coiled up and rattled, putting the mules into a panic. As they brayed and bucked, jumped and jerked in fear, the camels plodded on, unaware of the danger. The rattler clung to the camel's leg by its fangs for a moment then dropped away. As it hit the ground, a bullet from Rawhide Robinson's revolver rendered it lifeless.

The caravan halted and deliberated what to do, there being no experience with snake-bit camels extant. The cowboy opened up his pocket knife and applied the accepted treatment, slicing across the fang marks, then making another cut to create an "X" so the flowing blood would flush out the poison.

A helpful mulero suggested shooting the camel. "A rattler bit a mule of mine on the muzzle one time and killed him dead," he said. "His nose holes swelled shut and he got to where he couldn't breathe no more. Might as well shoot the camel right now — save him the misery."

Rawhide Robinson considered the suggestion, knowing of similar situations with horses in the past. "Maybe so. I've seen that with horses bit on the nose. But I've seen horses bit on the leg that pulled through — leg swelled up and had a nasty sore that took a long time to heal, but they lived." He lifted his thirteen-gallon hat and scratched his head, then reset it with a purpose. "Nope. This camel acts like there ain't nothing happened. Let's douse that cut with whiskey, wrap a bandage around it and go on."

And so they did. Much to everyone's surprise, the camel showed no effects — ill or otherwise — from its encounter with the rattlesnake and plodded on toward Fort Stockton.

CHAPTER THIRTY-SEVEN

The usual hubbub ensued upon the caravan's arrival at Fort Stockton.

Cavalry horses bolted at the sight and smell of the camels. Sheep stampeded. Cattle decamped. Soldiers mocked and taunted, jested and jeered, teased and needled.

And, as usual, the camels chewed their cuds and paid little attention to the hullabaloo. The long days on the trail had not tired the camels or the mules. With water readily available, good grass along the way, light loads, and a layover at Camp Hudson, the trip to date offered little opportunity to test or compare the worth of the pack animals.

All that was about to change.

Lieutenant Scott, Rawhide Robinson, and Happy Harry huddled with the officers at Fort Stockton to plan the expedition. The land southward into the big bend of the Rio

Grande was unmapped and — to the United States Army, at least — largely unknown.

Likewise, the capabilities of the camels were untested, and no one, save those who handled the caravan, had any confidence in their ability to perform. The army officers questioned their ability to carry the kind of loads the handlers claimed. They doubted the dromedaries' capacity to withstand the rigors of rough country.

Lieutenant Scott did his utmost to reassure the officers, quoting facts and figures, statistics and history, accomplishments and achievements of the animals in their homelands. Rawhide Robinson related his experiences. Happy Harry offered up his impressive résumé and involvement with camel caravans. Hurry, lurking on the outskirts of every meeting, only laughed at the ill-informed and ignorant Americans.

And, of course, the muleros made every attempt to undermine the ability of the camels and voice their dissatisfaction at sharing the trail with animals God surely created as a joke on mankind. The presence of Hurry in the company also created a point of contention. But Lieutenant Scott had come to admire and respect the girl and was firm in his decision to include her. He further upset mule packers and cavalry troopers alike with his contention that her pluck and animal sense made her more valuable than any three of them.

Plans and preparations proceeded despite debate and disputation. The topographers required considerable equipment. Scant but sufficient rations for the men — the mapmakers, the cavalry escort, the packers — and one unwelcome girl — must be carried along as the availability of game and other provender was questionable. Camp equipment represented a considerable load. The assumption was that forage for the mules and camels would be adequate in the wild.

Water was the unanswered question. Where and when would they find it? Could they count on found water to be potable? How much must they carry? Could they carry that much? How?

Happy Harry worked with the Fort Stockton smithies to fashion iron hoops linked by a vertical bar to narrow shelf that would accommodate a twenty-gallon keg and hang from the packsaddles of his camels. He assured army skeptics that the camels could easily carry four kegs apiece, or two kegs each as part of a larger load.

The army officers wondered if the camels could actually carry such a load over the long haul — after all, each keg would weigh in at more than one hundred and sixty pounds. Happy Harry assured them it could be done. Hurry pointed out that were it not for thirsty mules needing two or more gallons of water a day, it would not be necessary to haul so much of the heavy liquid. She tweaked the mule men even more with the suggestion that the mules be required to carry their own water — a chore clearly beyond the long-eared hybrids' abilities for an extended period.

The journey into the West Texas desert proved every bit as trying as anticipated and, at times, even more so. Craggy trails, arduous elevations, declivitous canyons, capacious playas, sand and alkali, dust and brush all conspired against success.

As expected, adequate water proved a problem. People were frequently parched. Mules were often lop-eared from thirst. And while the camels tolerated the paucity of water with relative ease, they, too, at times suffered.

The end of one particularly dismal day found the expedition stranded on a broad alkali playa. The last water harvested was running low, and was so sulfurous and putrid it was hardly palatable. Canteens could barely raise a slosh. Most kegs were empty and supplies in the others skimpy.

The men were limited to a cup apiece, enough for a few swallows of acrid coffee boiled over flimsy flames from the final fragments of firewood found in the packs.

The situation was made worse when a hobbled mule, overwhelmed by thirst and unable to resist the allure of the water kegs, humped and hopped his way over to one and worked out the bung with his teeth. The dehydrated donkey offspring attempted to lap up what spilled water he could before it disappeared into the thirsty dirt, then rolled the barrel over with a nudge of his nose to dump more. Other mules, of course, smelled the spill and fought and jostled for a lick of the liquid and went at the other barrels.

By the time anyone among the two-legged thirsters was aware of the situation, it was too late. The water supply was thus further diminished, further depressing the disposition of the men.

"Aw, shucks, this ain't so bad," Rawhide Robinson said in an attempt to lighten the mood.

"Not so bad? What do you mean?" asked a topographer.

"You're saying it could be worse?" said a trooper.

"How could that be?" wondered a mulero.

"You mean to say you've seen straits more dire?" said Lieutenant Scott.

"Why, sure I have, Ensign Ian."

"It's lieutenant. I guess we had better hear about it."

"Well, there was this one time," Rawhide Robinson said, launching yet another tale of his extraordinary exploits, "that I was a line rider for this ranch out in the Arizona desert — 'Arizona' and 'desert' being redundant, as anyone familiar with that country can attest. It gets so hot on them long summer afternoons there ain't nothin' to be done but shade up somewhere and have a siesta."

"Hold on a minute, Mister Rawhide," Happy Harry said. "Is this the story of the magic armadillo I have heard before?"

"Oh, no! That was down south in the Territory. This was on a ranch up north and west of there. Anyway, this one day I was away out in all that emptiness looking for lonesome bovines when this jug-headed red roan-colored last-year's bronc I was riding tripped over a stone no bigger than a biscuit. He staggered and stumbled around some trying to regain his feet and in doing so bowed a tendon.

"Now, as any of you-all as has dealt with horses knows — even mules, come to that — a bowed tendon is serious business. His leg puffed up in a matter of minutes and it was clear we wasn't going anywhere anytime soon. We was miles from water, more miles from the line shack, and even more miles from the home ranch.

"I knowed that trying to walk out of there in the heat of the day was a fool's errand. So I settled in under what little shade that horse cast — there being nothing else upright anywhere in sight — to wait till the cool of night to see if I could lead him on home on the limp. Now, this was along about noontime and the day wasn't going to get anything but hotter. I hadn't but one little ol' canteen half full of water and I used that up rubbing down that horse's sore leg, trying to cool it off some to take down the swelling.

"Now, that would seem a silly thing to do to some, I suppose, but if a man's any kind of cowboy, he always looks out for his horse's well-being before he worries about his own. It's The Cowboy Way is what it is. See, when you make your living in the saddle —"

"Hush up with the philosophizin' and tell the story," an anxious audience member advised.

"Yeah! Get on with it!" urged another.

"Oh, hold your horses. It ain't like you

got anywhere else to be as of now." Rawhide Robinson sipped a tiny sip of his coffee before continuing — little more than a sniff, really, in an effort at conservation.

"Anyway, it got so hot that afternoon I could hear my brain bubblin' and boilin' under my hat. That horse sweated himself dry and I did the same. It was a hard job even to breathe, the air bein' so all-fired hot it scorched goin' in and still burned goin' back out.

"Late in the afternoon I noticed the buzzards showing up. I don't know how them carrion crunchers do it, but they somehow know what's on the menu before it even gives up the ghost. Must be a turkey vulture telegraph or some such thing in operation. So I sits there and watches them buzzards circle and circle and circle and circle around up in the sky. I swear I can feel their beady little eyes on me, and hear them smackin' their lips over the meal to come, that being me and my horse."

"Hold on a minute!" someone said. "Birds ain't got no lips!"

"It's a figure of speech!" Lieutenant Scott said. "Hush up and let him finish."

"Finished is about what I was. That sun didn't show no sign of goin' down and kept on burning and burning. I figured my goose was cooked —"

"Goose!? I thought they were buzzards!" someone interrupted.

"Figure of speech!" several said. "Shut up!"

Rawhide Robinson the raconteur resumed. "Then I noticed something strange. Soaring around up there in the sky was this giant buzzard. I swear, he was two, three, four times the size of them other turkey vultures. I ain't never seen nor heard of no bird that big. He must have been the boss buzzard, too, as him showing up cleared them other vultures right out of there."

"Bosh!" a cavalry trooper said. "There ain't no birds like that!"

"I'm telling you I seen it," Rawhide Robinson said. "Sure as I'm sitting here. That bird's wings spread wider than the antlers on any three side-by-side longhorn steers I ever seen. And I've seen lots of cattle in my time — but never a bird like that. By-the-bye, I found out later that particular breed of bird is called a condor. You can look it up."

"Nonsense!"

"Hold on a minute," Ensign — Lieutenant — "Encyclopedia" — Ian Scott advised. "He's right. The California condor is the largest flying land bird in the western hemisphere. It is indigenous to the western coastal mountains of the United States and Mexico and the northern desert mountains of the Arizona Territory. So, it is not impossible and, in fact, altogether likely, that Rawhide Robinson would encounter a specimen of *Gymnogyps californianus* in the locale in which his story is set and in the circumstances he describes."

It took a moment for "Encyclopedia" Ian's educational avian admonition to sink in. Once everyone absorbed the knowledge, Rawhide Robinson continued.

"So there I was, wasting away in the desert sun with that giant bird bearing down on me. He wasn't in any hurry — his patience was as wide as his wingspan. But as he got ever closer and closer I came to appreciate his size. He was even bigger than I thought. So I come up with an idea."

Again Rawhide Robinson paused to moisten his lips with the boiled bean brew in his tin cup.

And again, the audience voiced its impatience.

"What did you do?"

"What happened?"

"What are you waiting for?"

"Well, what I did was, I sneaked a reach up to the offside of my saddle — moving as little as possible, you see, so as not to look any more alive than necessary so that buzzard would keep coming — and unlatched my reata. I slow but sure built me a loop and sorted my coils. Then I waited. And I waited. And waited some more for the right time.

"It seemed to take forever, but the time did come.

"That bird came sweeping by on a slow, smooth glide. When he got to where he was almost overhead, I rose up from my squat and took my shot — tossed up an underhand loop and watched it slide over that buzzard's neck as slick as a wedding band on a blushing bride's ring finger.

"Right pronto-like, I jerked my slack, jumped aboard that jaded horse and took my dallies. That oversized turkey buzzard bogged down a bit when he hit the end of that rope, but then he took to beating them long wings of his like a woman beating a rug. He dragged us along in that desert dirt for a bit, but with a mighty flap he lifted us up into the air. We didn't get none too high, mind you, us being as heavy as we was. But we sure as shootin' flew.

"As we flew along behind that bird, I figured out how to rein that buzzard with my rope like it was a jerk line on a mule hitch. So, I set him on a course for the home ranch and sat back and enjoyed the ride. Don't know how that horse felt, but I near forgot I was thirsty as I lofted along on that pleasant flight.

"That there condor was wearin' out by the time we got to headquarters, so it wasn't nothing to haul back on that gutline and slow him down until me and that horse set down soft as you please in the yard. I unloosed my wraps and let that buzzard fly away with my lass rope, figuring he could use it to line a nest, if for nothing else. Besides which, I couldn't figure any way to get that loop off his throat anyway. And that's the way it was."

Again Rawhide Robinson sipped from his cup and observed the reaction of his audience. It appeared to be wide-eyed wonder all around, with the exception of Lieutenant Scott, Happy Harry, Ibrahim, and Hurry — all of whom had long since become accustomed to the ordinary cowboy's extraordinary escapades.

Chapter Thirty-Eight

A copse of scraggly cottonwoods signaled the presence of water, but the arroyo along which they grew was as dry as the bones in Ezekiel's valley. The need for water was extreme, so every member in the expedition took a turn on the business end of a short shovel or with any other implement able to scrape and scoop sand in an attempt to dig down to precious liquid.

The effort paid off, if only in pennies, when the sand moistened, saturated, and finally puddled water. Men, mules, horses, and camels visited the slow-to-fill trench in turn for refreshment. The men filled canteens and a few kegs from the paltry puddle before moving on. Hoping to find the source of the water that sometimes flowed in the channel, the expedition followed the arroyo upstream as it deepened into a ravine, then a canyon, then steep-sided gorge lined by barren mountains.

The treacherous trail took its toll — two mules lost their footing and tumbled down the slope but survived the fall and their handlers gathered the spilled packs and urged the animals back to the trail. One of Happy Harry's camels also took a topple but it, too, suffered no harm and the water kegs it carried stayed intact, thanks to Harry's iron rings.

Mules soon thought better of proceeding as the faint game trail reached a particularly perilous passage, and only whips and curses kept them moving, if only at a snail's pace. The camels, too, were uncomfortable but, instead of balking, dropped to their front knees and crawled along until reaching safe footing.

Near the head of the canyon, Rawhide Robinson espied a scruffy clump of scrub oak on the hillside above the trail.

"I reckon there'll be a spring there, or at least a seep," he said.

The cowboy and Lieutenant Scott scurried through the scree to reach the oak brush where it concealed a narrow defile in a cliff face.

Rawhide Robinson focused his auditory faculties and said, "Hear that?"

"I hear a drip. It must open into a cave, with pooled water."

"I do believe you're right, Ensign Ian —"

"— Lieutenant —"

"— only thing is, this here opening is so small there ain't none of us can get through."

"What about Miss Hurry?"

Rawhide Robinson examined the opening, looked downslope at the girl, studied the slit, and decided she might be able to snake her way through.

Lieutenant Scott had second thoughts. "It could be dangerous. Perhaps she will find a way in, but be unable to extricate herself. And who knows what she might find in there besides water? I cannot countenance the possibility of any harm coming to Miss Hurry."

Rawhide Robinson's eyes twinkled and he smiled. "Why, I do believe you're sweet on the girl."

The young officer only blushed in reply.

"You're right, though. It could be dangerous. We'll leave it up to her," the cowboy concluded.

Recognizing as well as everyone else in the expedition the ongoing need for water, Hurry was eager to give it a try. With a canteen dangling around her neck and a lantern in hand, she squeezed through the slot. She creeped and crawled only a few feet before the cave opened up. And there, shimmering in the torchlight at the back of the cabin-sized chamber, was a pool — more a puddle, really — of clear, cold water. She dipped a finger and the taste was sweet. The canteen glugged itself full when submerged, and Hurry nearly emptied it to satisfy a long-neglected thirst. She refilled the container and scooched back out to the sunlight.

It took hours for Hurry to fill canteen after canteen by lantern light and pass them out the opening where the men, in bucket-brigade fashion, passed them downslope to fill the kegs. The miniscule cave lake was up to the task, replenishing itself quickly despite the expedition's attempt to drain it. When every animal was refreshed, every man quenched, every keg and canteen sloshing a full load, Rawhide Robinson told Hurry to come on out.

Her reply echoed out the opening. "In a moment. There is one more thing I must do."

The cowboy and the lieutenant alternately furrowed their brows and arched their eyebrows, their curiosity piqued with the huffing and puffing, sliding and scuffing accompanying the girl's exit.

Hurry popped out of the hole, dusted

herself off, then reached back in and dragged out a dusty, musty rawhide parfleche. The men looked it over.

"Looks old," Rawhide Robinson said.

"Looks to be Spanish," Lieutenant Scott said. "At least that's what the style of cross carved into the hide suggests."

"What's inside?"

Hurry peeled back the flap and reached into the rawhide pouch. With some effort, she pulled out a shiny, sparkly, sizable ingot of gold. "There are three more," she said.

The treasure caused a kerfuffle among members of the expedition, each believing he deserved a share of the cash the cache would bring. The army officers relieved the cavalry troopers and topographers of any such notion, pointing out that they were agents of the United States Army and any claim they might proffer rightly belonged to the government. The mule packers, however, were under no such restriction and fairly salivated at the prospect of prosperity and argued vociferously among themselves over the division of the riches.

Rawhide Robinson took a different view.

"Pipe down!" he told the packers. "You-all ain't got no claim on that gold. Hurry found it, and it's a case of finders-keepers if ever there was one."

The packers, of course, protested.

Lieutenant Scott entered the fray. "Rawhide Robinson is right, I'm afraid. According to common law, in cases of abandoned property forsaken by a previous owner and verifiably antiquated and concealed for so long as to indicate the owner is probably dead or unknown, the finder of such abandoned property or treasure trove acquires the right to possess the property against the entire world."

"You mean we don't get nothin'!?"

"That Arab girl gets it all!?"

The learned lieutenant assured them it was so.

"We'll see about that!" said one packer, particularly passionate about presumed possession.

Rawhide Robinson drew his revolver from its holster and pointed it at the end of the mulero's nose. "You see that hole bored in the end of the barrel of this here pistol?"

The packer's eyes crossed as he looked certain death in its one eye. "Y-y-y-yes."

"You even hint at any kind of move against that girl or her gold, you'll find out what that little hole's for."

"Hmmmph!"

"And I don't mean maybe," the cowboy said as he ratcheted back the hammer.

"Now, uncross your eyes and get to work."

Work — hard work, on the part of man and beast — was what it took to top out at the crest of the canyon. But once over the summit, the way down the other side of the mountain range proved easier going. Now, the mapping mission faced only the long slog back to Fort Stockton. The cavalry mounts, bearing only their riders, had fared well on the journey, although insufficient forage showed in the ripple of their ribs.

Three of the mules, hip bones showing a sufficient hook to hang a hat on, had to be abandoned in the desert to find their own way home or fend for themselves in the wild. The others were so famished and footsore they could barely carry their weight, let alone a load, so their burden shifted to the ships of the desert.

Although in considerably better shape than the equines, the camels by no means escaped suffering. The rocky desert trails were hard on their padded hooves, slowing their progress. Many had aching backs; some even sported open sores. But they plodded on, their passengers and packs rocking along day after day.

When Fort Stockton appeared on the horizon, hurrahs and yahoos issued forth from the trail-weary travelers. Even the exhausted mules exhibited newfound energy for the home stretch. Hurry urged her camel into its rocking-and-rolling pacing gait, and her pack animals followed suit. That inspired Happy Harry, Ibrahim, Lieutenant Scott, and Rawhide Robinson to pick up the pace as well. The dromedaries hove to on the parade ground winded and gasping, but well ahead of the mules and horses who straggled into the fort for some time afterward.

It was obvious to all in attendance that the camels returned in better condition than the mules, some of which had not survived at all. The troopers and packers at the fort saw no need to celebrate the camel's accomplishment.

After a hot meal, a hot bath, and a short rest in the relative cool of the adobe officers' quarters, Lieutenant Ian Scott wrote up his report and delivered it to the telegrapher for transmission to Major Wayne at Camp Verde.

"The performance of the camels proved superior in every respect to that of the mules," he wrote. "While often exhausted, footsore, and galled from heavy loads, they out-performed their mule counterparts in terms of speed, docility, and handling. Each camel carried, on average, heavier packs than the mules by a factor of three. Without the camels, in fact, we could not have carried sufficient water to keep the mules alive. While man and beast alike suffered for want of water on many occasions, the camels showed no ill effects from the thirst. Their ability to forage more effectively and consume a wider range of plants contributed to their maintenance of flesh and conditioning as compared to the mules. Details are recorded in daily journal entries, which will be at your disposal upon our arrival at Camp Verde.

"In conclusion, I can only repeat that by any measure, the camels clearly demonstrated their superiority as pack animals. Their adoption as the primary vehicle for distributing supplies to remote outposts and performing other packing tasks should be encouraged and established with all deliberate speed."

CHAPTER THIRTY-NINE

After a couple of weeks of rest and relaxation to rejuvenate the camel caballeros and recruit the camels, the outfit hit the trail for Camp Verde. The remaining mules from the expedition were still in no condition to travel, so they and their packers stayed on.

The trip was uneventful, even enjoyable, and with little baggage, the caravan covered a leisurely twenty-five miles a day, making the trip in ten days. Rawhide Robinson, Happy Harry, Ibrahim, Hurry, and Lieutenant Scott relaxed in their swaying seats, laughing and swapping tales. Even the normally taciturn Ibrahim conversed from time to time, testing his limited English, but getting back to his beloved Tulu occupied most of his thoughts.

Hurry, too, was anxious to return to Camp Verde and excited to see how much Okyanus had grown in her absence. She and the young lieutenant spent considerable time at the tail end of the parade, riding side by side.

"I am concerned with Huri," Happy Harry confided to Rawhide Robinson one day. "She is spending too much time with the lieutenant. Such behavior is not proper for a young girl."

"Aw, shucks, Harry. I wouldn't worry none about Ensign — Lieutenant — Ian if I was you. He's as fine a fellow as ever forked a camel, in my estimation."

"This I believe. But with the wealth she now enjoys, I cannot help but wonder at his intentions. Besides, Huri is so young."

Rawhide Robinson laughed. "I don't guess you noticed it, but that young man had his eye on that girl long before she found that gold. It also seems to have escaped your attention that Hurry has grown right up into a young lady. She's still young, I'll grant you that, but she's no little girl anymore."

Happy Harry was unconvinced, but the cowboy's words were food for thought and he chewed them over as he rode, ruminating on his responsibilities to his niece and her future.

The caravan eased into Camp Verde with little ceremony — save the now-routine upsetting of mules and horses, the fright and fleeing of chickens and hogs, the shock and awe of people upon seeing such curious critters. As the crew unpacked and unsaddled the camels, a messenger from Major Benjamin Wayne came by requesting their presence in his office at first opportunity.

With all assembled, the major wasted no time. "Gentlemen — and Hurry — I have here correspondence from my superiors at the War Department in Washington: 'Major Benjamin Wayne, Commander, United States Army Camel Corps, et cetera, et cetera.

" 'We regret to inform you of our decision to disband the United States Army Camel Corps. Experiments investigating the suitability of utilizing the camel as a pack animal for purposes of supplying United States Army forts, camps, and outposts in the Southwestern deserts is determined to have been a failure. You are hereby ordered to cease and desist any further operations. Release the civilian handlers in your employ with reimbursement as seems equitable and dispose of the camels as you see fit, with an eye to recovering the costs of their acquisition and upkeep as much as possible, and remitting any funds so procured to the Director of Army Finance. These orders are effective upon receipt and we anticipate receiving notice of the carrying out thereof in due time. We are Your Obedient Servants, et cetera, et cetera.' "

Since the news knocked the earth off its axis and upset the normal course of time-keeping on the planet, there is no way to know how long the stunned silence lasted.

When Lieutenant Scott came to himself, he said, "I don't understand, sir. Our recent expedition proved beyond doubt the superiority of the camels over the mules."

"You are, of course, correct, Lieutenant. I forwarded your preliminary report to Washington but the only part of it they paid attention to were the words, '. . . often exhausted, footsore, and galled from heavy loads.' It seems the unfavorable reports they have received from the various cities along our route since landing at Indianola carried more weight. All filed complaints with the army demanding reimbursement for damages caused by frightened livestock. Only San Antonio failed to issue a negative report, and even it was less than enthusiastic. It seems the mayor found the camel-hair socks his wife knitted for him itchy and unpleasantly odorous.

"And, of course, it is no secret that the mule interests — both within the service and independent contractors — have been dead set against the use of camels from the outset. Their protests delayed funding for the project on several occasions, and their hostility to the idea has only intensified."

"Can we not appeal?" Lieutenant Scott asked. "Is there no recourse?"

"I'm afraid not. I have been in constant contact with army headquarters, the War Department, even members of Congress in an attempt to sway opinion. Between intransigence and reluctance to change, the deck is stacked against us. This was a gamble to start with, and I am afraid we lost — although there is no question the game was rigged."

Rawhide Robinson tipped back his thirteen-gallon hat and stood with arms akimbo. "Well, it was fun while it lasted. I reckon I'll go back to ridin' horseback and punchin' cows. Fact is, I've kind of missed it."

Happy Harry said, "What is to become of us?"

"I have arranged a generous severance for you and Ibrahim. Hurry, as well — from what I am told, she will not need it, but it is hers nonetheless. In addition to financial compensation, the government will arrange passage aboard a ship bound for the Mediterranean as well as any other conveyance required to return you to your homeland should you so desire. Robinson, you, too, are due a generous monetary severance."

"Why, thank you, Major. I suppose it will come in handy. I could use a new pair of boots."

The major managed a sad smile. "I assure you, you will have the resources to purchase much more than a pair of boots."

Lieutenant Scott snapped to attention and saluted the major. "Sir, it has been a pleasure serving with you. No doubt the navy will be issuing orders for my next assignment. Most likely as a ship's officer somewhere."

"Not so fast, Lieutenant. The War Department is launching a project to construct a thousand miles of wagon road across the desert from eastern New Mexico to the Colorado River on the Arizona-California border. They need an industrious and capable officer to oversee surveying and construction and I have recommended you for the job. It is yours if you want it."

"Thank you, sir. I appreciate your confidence. May I ask, sir, your intentions concerning the camels?"

"Truth is, I do not know. I am ordered to dispose of them but have yet to devise a plan to do so."

"If I accept the assignment to build the

road, I believe the camels would be ideal for the project. They have certainly proved their worth and I am confident their presence would hasten and simplify the work, sir."

"You are probably right. But there is no way the army would go along. They have made it abundantly clear they want the camels mustered out of the service."

The lieutenant looked stricken, but being a military man — albeit a young one — he knew the futility of bucking the brass.

"The camels are for sale, are they not?" Hurry said.

The major smiled. "Why, yes, young lady, they are."

"How many will you need for the job, Ian?"

The young officer wrinkled his brow and looked inward with his eyes as the abacus in his head worked. "I suppose fifteen head would be sufficient. But I do not have the wherewithal to purchase fifteen camels, even at bargain prices."

Hurry smiled. "But I do." She turned to the major. "I wish to purchase fifteen of your finest camels. I, of course, must be allowed my choice of the animals."

Major Wayne smiled. "I am sure that can be arranged."

CHAPTER FORTY

Hurry negotiated the purchase of fifteen of the army's camels and offered them to Lieutenant Ian Scott for use in building the wagon road with one stipulation — that she accompany him on the expedition. The desert road was built and the route serves travelers to this day. The budding romance between the two blossomed, and Ian resigned his commission upon completion of the mission and married the girl. Mister Ian and Missus Hurry continued on to California and established a ranch near Tejon.

Camels lived on the ranch as long as the couple lived, along with cattle, horses, and — heaven forbid — sheep. The ranch prospered under Ian's able management and the livestock they raised, improved by Hurry's husbandry, was in demand throughout the West. The Tejon ranch was a favored stopover and destination for travelers, where hospitality and a hot meal were always available.

Speaking of hot, tamales were always on the table at the ranch.

Hurry's uncle and guardian, Happy Harry, signed on to care for the camels on the wagon road project. He lived for years afterward near the road's terminus in south-western Arizona. With the gift of a few camels from Hurry, including the majestic Tulu, he operated a freighting business to area mines. Happy Harry married, became an American citizen and, in the best tradi-tion of his friend Rawhide Robinson, spun stories about his exploits — with emphasis on adventures with camels — to audiences large and small and far and wide.

The ever taciturn and often ornery Ibra-him took advantage of the government's of-fer of transport back to his homeland. Noth-ing is known of his subsequent history.

Major Benjamin Wayne continued his military career and was re-assigned to the Department of War in Washington, eventu-ally earning promotion to Quartermaster General of the United States Army. His ef-forts to reinstate the camel corps bore no fruit.

Our hero, Rawhide Robinson, saddled the horse acquired with his army pay, strapped silver spurs on the heels of his shiny new

Texas star boots, and rode off into the sunset whistling a happy tune to pursue further adventures of bravery and daring in the Wild West.

He never again rode a dromedary (although he would have, had opportunity and necessity presented itself, as he held the oddball animals in high esteem ever after).

414

POSTSCRIPT

What became of the rest of the camels?

The army found it difficult to dispose of the dromedaries upon dissolution of the camel corps. A few were acquired by showmen, angry muleros killed some out of spite, and the rest were allowed to wander away and fend for themselves in the desert southwest. Camel sightings were reported for decades afterward, including this excerpt from an account originating in the *Yuma Examiner* and reprinted on page two of the El Centro, California, *Imperial Valley Press,* on 19 June 1909:

WILD CAMELS IN DESERT
TRAVELERS FROM IMPERIAL VALLEY TO PHOENIX
ALLEGE THEY RAN ACROSS TWO OF THESE ANIMALS

Arrivals at Phoenix from the desert bring tidings of running into two camels between the Bonanza mine and Quartzite one day last week. They say that there is no question of this fact. They are engaged in the cattle business and were enroute to the range of the Wabash Company in Apache County and were returning from the Imperial Valley with horses.

When sighted, the camels were traveling in a southwesterly direction at a rapid rate, and as the weather was intensely warm no effort was made to run them down. It is their belief that the camels were making for the bottom lands of the Colorado River for water, the desert regions at this time being dry and water very scarce in the tanks that are usually well filled during the winter months and before the intense heat evaporates them.

The discovery of a remnant of this herd of these animals is an interesting incident. As to its reliability there is no room for doubt. A few years ago, a drove of five were reported to have been seen by two Los Angeles mining men in Mexico below Yuma, and in the vicinity of the Sierra Pinta range on United States soil others have been seen.

The existence of camels at this day is easily traced to animals imported by the government many years ago. They were assigned to perform transportation duties for the regular troops. It was finally determined to abandon them, and they were turned loose on the desert, and at intervals since remnants of the drove have been seen.

The camel was placed here originally because he is a desert animal and in the hope that his long endurance would combat the distances between water stations, as well as affording rapid communication with the troops on long marches. They were a failure due to their obstinacy in handling.

ABOUT THE AUTHOR

Author of the Western Writers of America Spur Award–winning novel *Rawhide Robinson Rides the Range* and Spur Finalist *Rawhide Robinson Rides the Tabby Trail,* **Rod Miller** also writes history, poetry, and magazine articles about the American West. The three-time Spur winner is also a recipient of writing awards from Westerners International, the Academy of Western Artists, and Western Fictioneers.

Born and raised in Utah, Miller lived for a time in Idaho and Nevada before returning home. He graduated from Utah State University, where he rode bucking horses for the intercollegiate rodeo team, and spent more than four decades as an award-winning advertising agency copywriter.

Learn more about the author at writer RodMiller.com and writerRodMiller .blogspot.com.

The employees of Thorndike Press hope you have enjoyed this Large Print book. All our Thorndike, Wheeler, and Kennebec Large Print titles are designed for easy reading, and all our books are made to last. Other Thorndike Press Large Print books are available at your library, through selected bookstores, or directly from us.

For information about titles, please call:
  (800) 223-1244

or visit our Web site at:
  http://gale.com/thorndike

To share your comments, please write:
  Publisher
  Thorndike Press
  10 Water St., Suite 310
  Waterville, ME 04901